Bernice Rubens won the Booker Prize for Fiction in 1970 for *The Elected Member*, her fourth novel. She was also short-listed for the same prize for *A Five Year Sentence* in 1978. her most recent novel is *Our Father*, also available in Abacus.

In addition to numerous novels, Bernice Rubens has written for the stage, television and films. Her novel *Madame Sousatzka* was filmed to widespread praise in 1989. She lives in North London.

Bernice Rubens

SPRING SONATA

A Fable

AN ABACUS BOOK

First published in Great Britain 1979 by
W. H. Allen & Co Ltd.
Published by Sphere Books Ltd 1981.
Reprinted in Abacus by Sphere Books Ltd 1986, 1989

Annotated music on page 122 reproduced from *Beethoven Sonaten Klavier Und Violine Band 1 Urtext*, with kind permission of G. Henle Verlag, Forstenrieder Alee 122, Postfach 710466, 8000 München 71, W. Germany

Reproduced, printed and bound in Great Britain by
Cox & Wyman Ltd, Reading

0 349 13024 8

Sphere Books Ltd
A Division of
Macdonald & Co (Publishers)
66/73 Shoe Lane, London EC4P 4AB

A member of Maxwell Pergamon Publishing Corporation plc

SPRING SONATA

Part 1

Prologue

My name is Brown. I am not in the book-writing business, a fact for which I make no apology. I am a simple, straightforward doctor, and that fact too I don't feel I have to account for. People have to do what they have to do. In the course of my work I come across much that is the stuff of fiction. Occasionally I suppose, a novelist might encounter an event that would fall with more logic and more interest into my province than into his. It's possible. Though I myself have never benefited professionally from any writer's peripheral discovery. Perhaps they keep their findings to themselves. As I propose to do with mine.

For if I were to tell a writer of my discovery, he would adorn it beyond anybody's belief. My story, just the straightforward truth of it, is extraordinary enough, and needs no novelist's imaginative leap. Besides, I have often fancied that, had I not studied medicine, I might well have turned my hand to fiction; my outrageous story has allowed me to indulge my fancy. It is the only book that I shall ever write, for such an unparalleled event will never occur in my life again.

I work in a general hospital in a large city. Like all hospitals operating under the National Health system it is grossly understaffed, and in a rush or an emergency a doctor has to turn his hand to anything. So it was that one day over Christmas of last year, I was called upon to perform an autopsy. Pathology is not an aspect of medicine that I particularly relish, but I took comfort in the fact that as soon as I'd finished, I would be off for a long week-end in the country.

I took the lift down to the mortuary and found the body

laid out on the slab. There was no assistant available so I had to work on my own. I did not feel comfortable. To be alone in the basement of a large building, with only a corpse for company, is a situation not conducive to comfort, and I resolved to hurry with the job as far as efficiency would allow. I put on a white rubber apron and laid the instruments to hand. Then I drew back the sheet.

It was the body of a woman. Youngish, I thought. I would have put her in her early thirties. Her youth unnerved me a little, but I set my jaw, drew on my gloves and started to work. I will not bother you with the details. They are technical and it is unlikely you would understand them. The single fact that concerns us here was a gigantic swelling between the thighs. It was, without doubt, a pregnancy, but of such vast proportions that it was unquestionably against nature. It had obviously deflated a little, as was evidenced by the widespread corrugation of the flesh on the lower abdomen. I had to take a few steps backwards to view the totality of its vast spread, and I began to think that this was an autopsy of sufficient scientific interest to merit the witness of certain specialists in the field. But for some reason I looked upon that corpse as my own property. It was sheer chance that had ordered me to its examination, but I believe that nothing in this life is accidental; that certain things are ordained in heaven, or whatever, to try us, and to enrich us in some fashion. That corpse had a personal message for me; of that I was certain. It fairly shrieked at me to investigate its secrets and to guard them with care.

I overcame my professional scruples by deciding to examine only the uterus, and then I would call for the participation of others and more exalted members of my profession. Deftly I incised the womb. At first glance I could see there was enough in that mysterious bowl to confound the world of medicine, and even, with little stretch of the imagination, to give the lie to divinity itself. I

4

trembled and stared at its contents, dumbfounded. Had anyone described them to me I would have laughed in utter disbelief, and possibly have pitied the teller for his unhinged hallucinations. So I shall forbear to tell you. In the course of my story it will all become clear, with medical evidence for backing, and my sanity will not be called into question. But amongst all those unnatural and alarming disorders, there is one item I must tell you of, for it is the very source of my story. You're going to find this hard to believe, but there it was, as my story will testify, in the middle of all that uncanny terrain, there lay a book. Yes, a note-book.

You are already scoffing. You think that this is a writer's desperate device to tell a story in which he himself has little confidence. So he must protest the truth of it with loud audacity. He makes the lie bigger so that it becomes credible. No matter. I have black and white evidence as to the truth of my story, so I need protest no further.

The book lay half-open against the uterus wall. Without touching it, I could see that it was a thick prescription pad, the kind we doctors use. I extracted it gingerly and gave it an astonished preliminary perusal. It looked like some sort of journal written in a large and childish hand. It was soaked in amniotic fluid and would need some careful drying out. As I held it, I noticed how my hands trembled, and for a moment I wished that I had a witness to prove that I was not hallucinating. After all, it's not every day that one drops into a morgue, splits an organ, and finds a manuscript within, and I clutched at the book as some concrete proof that I was not going mad. Then I put it gently into a polythene bag and hid it in the jacket pocket underneath my white coat. I now no longer minded sharing that corpse's findings with anybody, because whatever else it would yield, I knew I was guardian of its most precious secret. Besides, there was plenty else in that precious bowl to merit investigation, wonder, discussion, and downright incredulity.

I covered the corpse and went to summon senior members of my profession. Later that evening, a group of six of them gathered around the body, sighing, marvelling, and somewhat irritated by total disbelief, despite the startling evidence under their noses. What they found will become clear in my story and need not detain us here. I myself took a back seat in the proceedings, with the occasional prick of conscience that I was withholding vital evidence. But on the whole it did not trouble me, and I was anxious to get back to my quarters to investigate my find. It was early morning when the autopsy came to an end, and the corpse had yielded a body of information beyond medical comprehension. A decision was made for a further investigation and to invite as witnesses an eminent psychiatrist and even a dignitary of the Church. We were all enjoined to strict secrecy. The body on the slab was a threat to the very foundations of established medicine, and their separate eminences were not very happy. Their bewilderment somehow pleased me, partly because it is always pleasurable to sit on the side-lines and watch others' reputations at risk, but mainly because I knew that the key to all that body's mysteries was in my possession. And that gave me a very positive sense of power.

I returned to my hospital rooms at five in the morning. I had dismissed any thought of a week-end in the country, and I was too excited to sleep. I extracted the manuscript from its polythene bag and laid it carefully on my blotter. I intended to dry out each page separately before making any attempt to decipher its contents. It took me about two months to crispen each page. I had a friend at the local police station, and with his help I was able to gain information as to how to decipher ill-written or blurred manuscript, which is, after all, part and parcel of police detective-work. On some pretext, he would sneak me into the police laboratories where the latest decoding equipment was at hand, and after sundry visits, and many hours of work in the bright night-light of my study, the secrets of that wonderful journal were finally unravelled. The whole business had taken many months, but I regretted not a moment of it, for strange and incredible as my story was, I could not help but believe it. And believe it totally. In any case, I had to believe it, for it tallied in every detail with the subsequent findings of the extended autopsy.

I had problems with its presentation. I thought at first that I might publish it simply as it was, with a few editorial and explanatory footnotes. But that form presented certain difficulties, things the reader would have found obscure or unaccountable. For example, there are occasions in the journal when, in the middle of a highly tormented *cri de coeur* as to the misery of his condition, the writer suddenly inserts a recipe for rock-cakes. As follows: 'I shudder at the hostilities of my surroundings and find them inexplicable. Am I not, after all, an invited guest? Take three dessert-spoonfuls of sugar, a handful of raisins, a pound of sifted flour, and two eggs.' And so on. Perhaps all writers' note-books are dotted with these seeming irrelevancies. I don't know since, as I have already stated, I am not in the book-writing business. But I can't imagine how the writer ever thought he might put the recipe to a test, and perhaps it's just as well he didn't, for I have since checked on the ingredients supplied – my research has been very thorough – and found them deficient.

Or elsewhere the journal is dotted with what I can only assume are telephone numbers, though it would seem equally impossible that the writer could put them to any use. For example: 'Today I made some headway with the Kreutzer Sonata, though the double stopping is still a problem. Bob Welland 469 0098.'

There were also some numbers however, which, through digital insufficiency were obviously not meant for tele-phonic communication. I have heard that writers' manu-scripts are strewn with such numerical irrelevancies. The manuscripts of Scott Fitzgerald, I'm told, were littered with figures. Whether they referred to the number of words he had written that day, or were simply a summary of his dollar debts, I do not know. Possibly the latter, since he was known to be impecunious and grossly overdrawn. In the case of our present journal, it was possible that the writer was simply ticking off his days of gestation, rather as a prisoner etches away his sentence on the walls of his cell. Whatever. All I can say is that such indiscipline would never be tolerated in a doctor's note-book.

Elsewhere, interrupting the mainstream of the journal, are sundry bars of quavers and crotchets, each numbered from one to four, which, in the course of my research, I discovered pertained to a violinist's fingering. There was also a good deal of crossing out and rewriting which might well have irritated the reader and certainly held up the story line. Besides, from the writer's confined space, he could only guess at what was happening on the outside. His view, though highly imaginative, was conjectural, based solely on hearsay. It was limited too, as a first-person narrative must be, by the nature of geographical necessity. So I have opened it up, as it were. With all respect and humility, I have gathered together the details of this strange story, and have presented it, not as fiction, for it is far from that, but as a true-to-life novel. I have tried to execute my task in the manner, I hope, of the writer himself, had he more space, more time, and a typewriter. Its title, too, I think would have been the author's choice, had he ever envisaged publication.

I don't know if my readers are familiar with Beethoven's 'Spring Sonata' for violin and piano. It is a passionate dialogue between the two instruments, at times echoing and confirming, at others, raging in passionate argument, and every bar an overt declaration of love. It is undoubtedly my writer's story, whether in music or in words.

During the process of writing this book, I grew very

attached to the source of my inspiration. In the beginning, I simply referred to the writer as 'he'. Of his gender I was certain. That much was clear from the autopsy. As I progressed with the book, I came to look on him as a revered friend. Such intimacy calls for some means of identification. So I gave him the name of Buster. I don't know why. It just seemed to me to ring right and proper. It somehow exactly translated the deep affection I felt for him.

So here is Buster's story. Every word of it is true. For every event I have documented evidence. It sits on my bookshelf, carefully bound now in green Florentine leather. I have never let on to anybody about my secret find. If I had told the doctors, it would most certainly have dispelled many of their doubts, and, equally certainly, have created many more. Meanwhile, they are still deliberating, wondering, disbelieving, and raging in impotent argument. No matter. It gives them something to do. And in any case, even if they knew the truth of it all, I doubt whether they would have the courage to understand it.

So here is Buster's strange and desolate story, and let it be a lesson to us all.

Chapter 1

Mrs Phoebe Joseph was Buster's putative grandmother, though she was not aware of it at the time. Though in her sixty-third year, she had, as yet, hardly accommodated her role as mother, and she lay restless on her bed, trying to shut out thoughts of her two children. Sheila, her daughter, was downstairs, in temporary residence, until Mrs Joseph's convalescence was over. The other one, that son of hers, whose name clogged her heart but stuck in her throat, him she thought of only with rage, and when that rage subsided, its residual pain was unbearable. For it begged the terrible question: Was it all her mothering fault? So she sought refuge again in her anger, for her wrath was more manageable.

The vast ornamental head-board of her bed was upholstered in a quilted green damask. And on it were two amorphous and restless grease-stains. Nothing odd about that. Such marks, testimony to a long partnership, would possibly be found on most double head-boards anywhere. But what was so remarkable about the stains on this particular head-rest was their appalling separateness. The space between them was defined, as bare and as blank as a no-man's-land. The stain on the right had distinctly faded, and evidenced Mr Joseph's death or removal by at least three years. It would probably fade no more and remain for Mrs Joseph as a constant reminder that once upon a time she had not lain alone. She thought of that time rarely, and always with acute embarrassment. Despite her widowhood, she still kept closely to her side of the bed, and possibly even more to its edge, to avoid the restive nudging of ghosts. She looked at the untenanted space beside her and reddened. For thirty years Mr Joseph had slumbered and snored by her side. Yet even long habit had not inured her to the sheer *rudeness* of it all. She felt better now that she was alone. She knew that once she could inch herself into the centre of the bed, all shame would leave her, and that if she could, in a monumental act of courage, lie positively on *his* terrain, it would be as if her marriage had never happened at all.

She heard the front door-bell and Sheila's steps in the hall. In a few moments, the skinny Nurse Prior would unpack the dressings at the foot of the bed and ask how we are today. And Mrs Joseph would be tempted to ask Nurse Prior to raise her own skirts, and reveal the injury on *her* stomach, so that her stupid pluralising would be woundlessly clear. Nurse Prior had been coming to see Mrs Joseph every morning since she had been discharged from the hospital three weeks before. She'd had a hernia operation and the surgeon had botched it. There were two wounds on Mrs Joseph's stomach, the result of the surgeon's dyslectic reading of her X-ray. The needless one had healed happily. The stitches had melted of their own accord, leaving a reddish fishbone which undulated at ease along the folds of her navel area. The other opening was a different matter altogether. It was as if the surgeon, frustrated by his first fruitless attempt, had decided to punish her for his rank ineptitude, and had dug deep and hamfistedly into her innocent flesh. She'd left hospital with a gaping hole in her side, from which seeped a seemingly endless supply of pale yellow matter. She had asked questions, and so had her daughter, but both had faced a solid wall of fraternity cover-up. Nurse Prior, on seeing the wound on her first visit to Mrs Joseph's home, choked back her horror, for she too, though much lower down on the scale, felt herself in duty bound to the conspiracy. Mrs Joseph didn't like Nurse Prior very much and ascribed her improvement to the natural healing processes of time,

11

rather than to the Nurse's tender care. The hole was certainly closing over. Not that Nurse Prior ever commented on the state of affairs way down on Mrs Joseph's stomach. Every morning she ordered her patient to lie quite flat while the dressing was changed, so that Mrs Joseph could see nothing of her progress or otherwise. But she was able to gauge a little from the size of the dressing which each day covered a smaller area.

Nurse Prior patted the dressing, covered her patient with the duvet, and propped her head up on the pillows. She packed her little bag. 'Now be a good girl, Mrs Joseph,' Nurse Prior said, 'and I shall be in to see you tomorrow.'

God in heaven, Mrs Joseph thought, I'm sixty-two years old and she tells me to be a good girl. Yet Nurse Prior's bedside prattle did not displease her. In her heart, Mrs Joseph had always felt herself a little girl, and throughout her life had resented the trappings of womanhood that time and nature had saddled her with. Her own mother had felt the same resentment. Now she was lodged in an old-age home on the outskirts of the town, and was compensated with pink ribbons in her hair and constant cosseting. Of course the old woman would never admit to enjoying herself there. She insisted on an outcast role, partly because it gave her pleasure and partly because it was the generally accepted status of one who had been discarded. But even the knowledge of her mother's unadmitted enjoyment did nothing to assuage Mrs Joseph's guilt. For not to put too fine a point on it, it was Mrs Joseph herself, her only child, who had put her mother away. This same Mrs Joseph who now would view with horror the prospect of her own daughter doing likewise. As long as her late husband was alive she could blame him for it, for though he had not encouraged his old mother-in-law's disposal, he had done little to prevent it. Now that he was dead, she was careful not to blame him, but on the quiet she cursed him for leaving her to bear the guilt alone.

Just before her hernia operation, Mrs Joseph had visited her mother. She'd gone with the intention of exaggerating the gravity of her own condition so that she could offer her mother the slim chance of her offspring's demise, as some token of atonement for having put her away. But her mother disallowed the offer. A hernia was nothing, she'd said. She'd had one herself and she'd opened her house-coat to prove it with her scar.

Mrs Joseph was as unfamiliar with her mother's body as she was with her own, and with equally little appetite for viewing either. But she could not avoid an overall glance at her mother's exposure and what she saw hardly pleased her. The hernia scar was one of many, each testimony to the knife at some time or another. It was a body that had been to many wars. Hanging from the navel was the mottled rope of her own Caesarean birth, and traversing it like a gallows across the width of the pelvis was the abdication scar of a hysterectomy, the one scar cancelling the other, like a ledger account that had been closed. The eighty-two-year-old body was a battlefield of many deaths, of many scythings, a Flanders graveyard of all the old lady's rough expectations, of all her sad hopes, that had wilted as swiftly as plucked poppies. Mrs Joseph had turned away. She'd looked around her mother's room, with the pretty little bowls of primroses and the gay patchwork quilt on the bed, and she tried to believe that her mother could not be better off elsewhere. She had everything she wanted; a cuddly bear to hold her nightie, and pink ribbons in her hair. She herself had a lot more hair than her mother, enough to merit two plaits' worth of pink ribbon, and even an Alice band. But you had to be in an old-age home before you were entitled to such treats, and much as she coveted them, the price was too costly. Never, never, she assured herself; her daughter would never allow it. That's what Sheila always said. Over and over again. Sometimes Mrs Joseph wished she wouldn't keep going on about it, for the more Sheila protested her filial duty, the less her mother was convinced. Else she would have asked Sheila directly to tie a pink ribbon in her hair. Or she might have dared it herself. But such an action might hint at senility, and give Sheila cause for louder protestation. She tried to think of her daughter without fear.

She heard her whispering to Nurse Prior on the landing, and though she couldn't decipher the words, she knew what they were saying. 'How big is the hole today, Nurse?', and Nurse Prior, a woman of few words, would answer wordlessly. With her two hands, she would demonstrate the spread of the cavity. Though she didn't need two hands, Mrs Joseph thought. A span of fingers would have sufficed for accuracy. But Nurse Prior was given to exaggeration and pessimism.

'So in a few days it will be closed', Sheila probably said, relieved that soon she could return to her own home, leaving her mother able to fend for herself.

Mrs Joseph listened to their continued whispering, and rather resented their gossiping interference. It was, after all, *her* hole, and its vital statistics were none of their business. Only she knew how the hole felt. A hole was a pretty insubstantial notion in the first place, and you had to have it in you to understand the throb of its vacuum and the pull of its gravity. These feelings dictated its size to a millimetre, no matter how Nurse Prior gauged her hands.

Mrs Joseph peeked under the stomach dressing. The hole was indeed closing over and her daughter would leave her. She heard the front door slam. Nurse Prior was carrying her pessimism to another bedside. In a few moments, Sheila would come back into the bedroom and take her distant stand at the foot of the bed. She would rejoice in her mother's obvious recovery, and, assured that her parole was undeniably at hand, would offer to prolong her sentence to get her mother well and truly on her feet. And Mrs Joseph, in her turn, would decline her daughter's offer and declare that she didn't want to be treated as an invalid, and that the sooner she got up and fended for herself, the better. Why do people need people, Mrs Joseph thought, once the dialogue was so predictable? She knew her daughter so well, yet in the still small hours of Sheila's fitful nights, she knew her not at all. And they were fitful without doubt. They must be. Mrs Joseph could tell by Sheila's bitten nails which she spread so defiantly on the counter-pane. Mrs Joseph tried not to look at them. Sheila had bitten them throughout her child- and girlhood, then for some reason, possibly connected with that odd husband of hers, had suddenly stopped. But too late for elegance. The squat shape of her finger-tops was already defined by her long nail-biting years. Such a great effort, Mrs Joseph thought, for such a small pay-off. She forced herself to stare at them and to silently beg forgiveness for all those dollops of mustard and bitter aloes she had forced on her daughter's fingers throughout her childhood. Sheila suddenly folded her hands, and Mrs Joseph was glad, because the stubby fingers offended her. And the fingers weren't everything. There was a lot else wrong with Sheila, her mother recalled. Such a dreadful disappointment. All that money on piano lessons, all that promise, yet world-wide fame, and Mrs Joseph would have settled for nothing less, had eluded her. All she had managed was an arrangement with an indifferent violinist, and together they hawked their duos from one charity to another. Poor Sheila. Poor disappointing Sheila. Difficult girl, that one. Untouchable. And that fringe of hers. All her life, Sheila's black hair had shaded her eyelids, as if to protect herself from at least half of her sad reality. Mrs Joseph wanted to stretch over the bed and wipe the offending bangs off Sheila's face. Just to satisfy her curiosity as to what lay underneath. Did she *have* a forehead, her daughter? No, she didn't know her daughter very well, Mrs Joseph decided. Certainly not since her marriage. Between Sheila's sheets, she had never known her, never been able to accommodate that man who lay by her side. She simply could not balance Sheila with a marital bed. She saw her simply as her offspring, and even then only in principle. The flesh and the blood of Sheila totally bewildered her. Yet she had to acknowledge that she was a good daughter. For the past three weeks she had stayed at her mother's house, caring for her until Nurse Prior pronounced her well. Only occasionally during that time had she returned to her own home, and then only for a few hours. Bernard was away on business, she had said, so that her stay in her mother's house inconvenienced nobody. Mrs Joseph was not ungrateful, though she could not help questioning the measure of her daughter's marital bliss, since she seemed so willing to forgo it. Perhaps it was because she was childless. Sheila had been married for six years, and Mrs Joseph began to wonder if she would ever achieve the status of grandmother. Not that she craved such rank; she simply wanted Sheila to experience mother-hood. But more as punishment than pleasure. Was there something even more wrong with the girl? Or her husband, more likely? These were questions she would not ask.

'How's the piano getting on?' she said without asking. 'You haven't done much practice in these last few weeks. It's not as if there isn't a perfectly good piano downstairs.'

Sheila allowed a silence. She hoped that inside it, her mother might hear the echo of all her loveless words. Perhaps Mrs Joseph did hear. Whatever, she chose only to confirm it.

'All that promise,' she said. 'Such a disappointment.'

Sheila stared, as if looking at the terrible words. She wanted to reach out to her mother, to touch her, not with tenderness, but with assault. But the thought of any contact repelled her. For once she touched, flesh upon flesh, no matter what part, even an inoffensive eyelid, she would have faced a fact, and that acknowledgement would have required her to take some stand. It was easier to clench her

16

fists and take refuge in words. As long as she kept talking, she could skirt reality. Slowly she lashed every syllable with her tongue. 'You never let go, do you?' she said. 'You don't really care about me, except in so far as I can extend your ego, your pleasure, your vanity. You never cared. About either of us. That's why Robert . . .'

'I don't want to hear his name,' Mrs Joseph shouted.

'He's your son, for God's sake, but he's just not living the kind of life you mapped out for him, for your pleasure, for your gratification.'

'I'd like you to go back to your own house,' Mrs Joseph said firmly.

'I'll stay till you're better,' Sheila said coldly. She lit a cigarette, an act of rare defiance. Mrs Joseph opened her mouth with yet another reproof, but Sheila had left the room.

The next morning Sheila stayed in her mother's bedroom while Nurse Prior changed the dressing. She had never seen her mother's body, and much as the thought repelled her, she needed, for her own sake, to investigate the flesh and frame of all that bitterness, to face that body's threat, that perhaps she was heir to. So she stared at her nakedness, and tried to insinuate herself into the quicksands of her mother's skin. She felt the twin imprint of her mother's shrunken breasts on her own; she trod the descending flight of stomachs from nipple to thigh, skirting the dressing on the second bend. She marvelled at the mottled carpet of mother-of-pearl, and trembled on the uneasy landing of her groin. Somewhere in those dark regions, she had crouched almost thirty years ago, and her brother shortly afterwards. Tremblingly, she stretched out a hand and laid a stubby finger on her mother's thigh, and she waited for the clap of thunder.

The next morning Nurse Prior came with her dressings and the landing echoed with the question, 'How big is the hole?' Each day Nurse Prior's hands inched towards

17

encounter, until at the end of the week, they touched as if in prayer. Nurse Prior would not be coming again. Sheila was free.

'I think I ought to stay on a few more days,' she said, from the foot of her mother's bed. What she said was not merely a formality. She wanted to stay. She needed to stay to allay the bitterness between them. But Mrs Joseph was determined to give her no opportunity for remorse. 'Ridiculous,' she said, heaving herself out of bed. Suddenly she could no longer bear the sight of Sheila's stubby fingers or that terrible fringe. Her daughter must quickly take her head and hands away, else she would succumb to her nature which she knew to be unkind and faintly malicious.

'I'll do the shopping for you before I go,' Sheila said.

'I'll do that,' Mrs Joseph said.

'Then I'll run you a bath,' Sheila was desperate to be allowed one favour.

'I'll have one tonight before I go to bed.' Let her go home and cook in her guilt, Mrs Joseph thought. I'll not make it easy for her.

'As you wish,' Sheila said.

On her way back to her own home, Sheila wondered whether ever in her life she would be able to shuffle off her mother's stranglehold, to somehow come to terms with that grossly unmanageable root. But what worried her more was the possibility that she herself was no different, that in her mother's noose were many loopholes, and that she too, given the opportunity, could lasso with inherited accuracy. She had tried for many years to conceive a child; now she wondered whether her infertility was the decision of a greater wisdom that sanctioned her barrenness as a means of others' protection. She recalled her mother's terrible words. You're such a disappointment to me, Sheila. She said the words over and over again, writhing in their bitterness, affronted by their gross presumption. She hoped that by repetition they could be defused and rendered harmless. Yet as soon as she reached home, she went to the piano and began to practise with a punitive rage.

Which was exactly what Mrs Joseph expected her to be doing. It confirmed her maternal hold. Though she had to admit, there was little joy in it. Indeed there was little joy nowadays in anything. As she aged, she grew less accomplished in evasion. Possibly because she had more time on her hands, and idleness drove her to unmanageable thoughts, forcing her to face a past that had fostered such a joyless present. She must begin to think about her son, to understand where and how it had all gone wrong. She straightened the pillow behind her head, and now that nobody was looking and nobody could hear, she whispered his name aloud. Robert. Such an adult name. Always had been. Even in his swaddling clothes he had gurgled to Robert. Robbie, Bob, or any affectionate distortion she had always disallowed. Her son was a serious proposition, and she would not have it diminished by abbreviation. Had she been wrong? she wondered. She tried 'Robbie' on her tongue, and was surprised how it pleased her. When I see him again, I'll call him Robbie, she thought. It'll solve everything, she told herself. It had to.

She eased herself out of bed. She would take a bath, and potter about the house, occupying herself with domesticity, allowing herself no time for parental scrutiny. She had given a thought to Robert, and that was enough for one day. And she had actually lived with Sheila for three weeks. All in all, she reckoned that, for the moment, she had done her maternal duty.

Note from Brown, your simple, straightforward doctor. The reader may well wonder how I know about Mrs Joseph's headboard or hernia, or more accurately how Buster could have known, since it was long before his time. This time, I mean, and this place. It was simply that Mrs Joseph's story was divulged from Buster's hearsay later on in his journal, and I have used the novelist's licence to offend chronology for the

19

sake of clarity. I don't intend to footnote every time this happens, but while I'm at it, I might as well inform you that there will be further discrepancies in the manuscript. They are a writer's privileges — God knows there are few enough — and to question them is to cast doubt on Buster's authenticity, and that would be most offensive.

Chapter 2

It was the 22nd of September, 1977. A Thursday, and
sometime around ten o'clock in the morning a meeting took
place, a moment of encounter as fortuitous as when
Fortnum ran into Mason. Sheila Rosen's egg lay in her
womb, unaware of its auspicious state of ovulation, indifferent to any change, and quietly minding its own business,
when something ran into the back of it. One struggling
survivor of a billion Bernard Rosen seeds, who might
later have cause to judge that the struggle nought availeth,
one of these seeds affected a triumphant collision, and a
star, as they say, was born. In other words, Buster opened
his account.

Had the exact moment of conception been known, it
would have been open to various interpretations. Sheila
herself would have judged it as a straightforward moment
in late autumn, and a moment nicely timed, for it avoided a
carrying through a long hot summer. Sheila's brother,
Robert the unmentionable, hooked into I Ching, Yin and
Yang, macrobiotics and the stars, would note a Libra
conception, cusping Virgo by a hair's-breadth, with all the
exciting unpredictability of a Gemini birth-sign. Mrs
Joseph, grandmother-elect, would note only one auspicious
fact. And auspicious enough it was, for 22nd September of
that year marked the Day of Atonement, a day of a self-
induced orgy of suffering, a repenting of one's past sins, a
beating of breasts, and a strict unbreakable fast until
sunset. Which explains why Sheila and Bernard were lying
late-abed that morning delaying the hunger pangs that
would gnaw them throughout the day. Had Sheila known
of her condition, she could have been excused the fast by a

rabbinical dispensation, but at this moment, Buster was keeping a very low profile. So eventually she rose, dressed and accompanied Bernard to the synagogue. She took the empty seat next to her mother, who assured her, *sotto voce*, that she had been there since eight o'clock that morning. Sheila forbore to comment that since her mother had so much to atone for, she could do with the extra time. Instead she smiled, and glanced over the gallery to Bernard who sat below, and the empty seat beside him which had once belonged to her father. She hoped that during the course of the day Robert might show up, not for her sake, and certainly not for his, but for her mother's, who, rightly or wrongly, was grieving his pagan absence. Sometimes she hated Robert, and always on her mother's behalf, and this frightened her, for she knew that she too had to let Robert go his own way, as she had so often preached to her mother. She opened her prayer-book, and listened to the ringing voice of the cantor.

Buster listened too, and recognised the prayer and the fast it celebrated, for he had been in Jewish wombs before. And in a short interval between the cantor's suffering phrases, he donated to his little cell his very first words.

'Shit,' he said, 'what a day to arrive. Nothing to eat until sunset.'

He steeled his little self to a fast, though God knows he had little enough to atone for, unless there were some 'carried forwards' from his last account, and he resolved that once he was born, he would chalk up this day as payment for at least five fast days in the Jewish calendar. He intended to look after himself, to treat himself kindly, both in and out. He owed it to himself. This time round it was going to be very different.

He took stock of his surroundings. From his past experiences it was clear that this present lodging had never been leased before. It was always preferable to be second or third tenant. The previous occupiers, with their sojourn,

22

somehow made the place more homely. You didn't feel so bad about dirtying it up, because it was so obviously a place meant for habitation and comfort. This lodging, however, was immaculate, creaking with cleanliness, and shrieking hostility. It was a place in which you wiped your feet and minded your manners. Too bad, Buster thought. The very first tenant, and on Yom Kippur into the bargain. Not the most kindly of beginnings.

But Buster was not disheartened. Over his past lives, he had endured many setbacks, but withal had accumulated a good measure of optimism which he carried to each new dwelling-place. And he had a feeling that he was going to need every ounce of it here. But he felt well equipped. To start with, he was a genius. That he knew. His latest sojourn on earth had been short, but long enough to earn him a place amongst the greatest child prodigies of his time. Then on his way to a concert, he'd loosened his mother's hand, or it might have been the other way round, depending on whose synchronisity one has in mind. Whatever, a taxi had run over him, violin and all. But his memory and fingers were unscathed. Armed with these, and a flood of unfulfilled potential, for he was only eight when the cab mowed him down, he sought another refuge. A short stay in limbo had done nothing to blunt his powers, and he drummed his little fingers against the walls of his new home.

As a born musician, or, as the pedants would have it, as yet unborn, he was mindful of the acoustic properties of his new home. They pleased him with the accuracy of their reproduction, though he was somewhat irked by the off-key pitch of the cantor outside. One of life's small irritations, he conceded. He would have to put up with it. He settled himself down. There was no point in impatience. If he was to emerge whole and healthy, he must play his meek and humble part for around nine months. He would spend that time eavesdropping, and thereby assess the qualities or otherwise of his new family. He would evaluate his future needs for defence or attack. He would learn their cunning, decode their lies, spy out their weaponry. In short, he would arm himself for his début. He settled down to work out his strategy.

Whatever stirrings Sheila felt in her stomach, she ascribed to hunger pains. She looked sideways at her mother, whose face was buried deep in her prayer-book, buried there, not for piety, but for somewhere to put it, to hide her shame from the congregation who, surely, each one of them, must be murmuring about the late arrival and the outlandish appearance of her son. Sheila understood, and peeked over the balcony. She was glad to see Robert, glad for her mother's sake, that he cared enough to come to the synagogue in time for the mourning prayer for their father. But she was ashamed too, and not only on her mother's behalf. She had grudgingly to admit to herself that, no matter how wrong her reasons, his manner of dress embarrassed her. It was what he probably wore every day, and no doubt slept in as well, and hardly the habit for a crowded synagogue. His bushy beard might well have passed for orthodoxy, had not his long hair been tied back with a red ribbon. A flowered Indian shirt was half stuffed into a pair of frayed jeans. She was glad she could not see his feet, for she knew that they were black and bare.

She glanced sideways at her mother who had seemingly involuntarily begun to beat her breast. On whose behalf, Sheila wondered. On her twisted tormented own, or that of her son, who after all, however boldly, was only asserting his simple right to be his angry liberated self. But through all her understanding she could not help but dislike him a little. Dislike him for the grief he caused their mother, that stiff ungiving creature by her side, whom she didn't even love. She looked at her. Nothing made sense between them but their terrifying similarity.

Around her, and below, the children of the congregation

24

were sliding out of their seats, and with a small restraint, for decorum's sake, making for the exit doors and the freedom of the yard outside. *Kadish* time, the prayers for the dead, for lost parents and siblings, whom only grown-ups had the right to mourn. Sheila remembered how, as a child, she would thread her way through the pews, squeezing 'excuse-me's through the mourners who were preparing to remember their dead. She left her own mother to mourn her grandfather, and blessed his departed spirit for so licensing her freedom. Then into the synagogue yard with her friends, giggling softly, embarrassed by the smell of death they had left behind. Another's odour, rude, ripe and wrinkled, belonging to years that could never, even in time, concern them. In the yard they kept their voices low, so that God could hear the mourners' reverence, and give their dead His full attention, with no time or inclination to pay heed to the shenanigans of the quick in the yard. It was with this licence that she and Duncan Cowen had plighted their troth one *Kadish* time, and sworn to love each other until their own death licensed others. But the following year it was another troth in the synagogue yard, proof of the fickleness of *Kadish* loves. Sheila stood up to let a child pass through. The child smiled at her, her mouth choked with giggles, pent up for yard explosion. Sheila edged away, knowing her own rude smell.

She turned the pages to the *Kadish* prayer. Her father's death, three years before, had sealed her own mortality, and it pinned her to her pew, along with her brother downstairs, who had come solely for that purpose, to mourn a man who had, in his lifetime, been a total stranger. Now that he was dead, Robert was learning to know him, and perhaps even to love him, that man who had so hopelessly hidden his disappointments, relying always on his wife to voice them, which she never tired of doing, and would do so again once the mourning prayer was over, using his untimely death to chasten her children.

Poor woman, Sheila thought. How both her children disliked her so. Yet perhaps she was taking the rap for the simple and innocent reason that she had outlived their father.

Inside his new home, Buster listened. Somewhere, in some remote synagogue, he too was being mourned as a long-ago parent or a sibling, giving free rein to the children to take advantage of God's momentary concern with the dead. He was suddenly aware of his hunger. He had badly mismanaged this conception, and it augured poorly for the future. He comforted himself with scraps of foreknowledge, that, when evening came, he would be amply fed, overfed in fact, compensated for his atonement, though as yet, he had not sinned at all. He shifted himself into some comfort, and Sheila worried that the pangs of hunger were assailing her so soon. It was hardly noon. She wished she could slip out with the children and go home, not only to eat, but to avoid the acute embarrassment of her brother's presence. But there was no escape. She forced herself to look at him. His eyes were in the prayer-book. It's possible he had not even seen her, or his mother, nor even looked for them. He had come to the synagogue for one purpose, and when that was fulfilled, he would no doubt shuffle his black feet outside.

The *Kadish* came to an end. Duty had been done and seen to be done. In the yard, the watchful beadle called an end to freedom, and urged the children back to prayer. Inside, Robert Joseph closed his prayer-book, kissed it, as his father had done, and threaded his way through the aisle. He gave no glance to the gallery, and for that his mother was grateful.

'His poor father must be turning in his grave,' Mrs Joseph said.

'At least he came,' Sheila whispered. She was not altogether sure that her brother's presence was preferable to his absence, but for her own sake, she did not want to

26

align herself with her mother. She watched him hesitate at the exit doors, as if his business was unfinished. She hoped he would not return. Or perhaps he was standing there purely for the purpose of display. Heads turned to watch him, this outlandish invader from another faith, with his mumbo-jumbo of mantras and penitent's feet. Mercifully he turned and was gone, and the gallery whispered from pew to pew, and Mrs Joseph hid her face in her prayer-book, wondering what she'd done to deserve it all.

Sheila looked down and caught Bernard's eye. He smiled and shrugged his shoulders, expressing his understanding of their shame. But she did not want his understanding. What right had he to think it shameful? Her brother had simply chosen another way, and it was not the way of his father, to say nothing of his forefathers. In a way she admired the frightened stand her brother had taken. Frightened, because at first it had been so negative. He had simply removed himself from the battle. His mother had voiced her disappointment just once too bloody often, and just once too often his father had silently echoed her reproach. Robert had packed a rucksack, slung his guitar over his shoulder, and simply and silently walked away. Six months later he'd sent them a postcard. It came from a village in Sri Lanka. He had joined an Ashram, he'd written, and he was very happy. He wished them peace and understanding. There was no mention of any return, or of any address. Sheila thought it would have been better if he'd not written at all. It had taken the Josephs some time, and many oblique enquiries to discover the meaning of an Ashram, and slowly the magnitude of their son's defection became clear. Mr Joseph finally gave up all hope of Robert's take-over of his business, and promptly appointed Bernard, his new son-in-law, as heir-apparent to his textile firm. One way or another, the business, if not the name, would be kept in the family. Without doubt, his proud expectant heart was broken, but the major ingredient of his grief was the public humiliation. His friends never mentioned Robert's disappearance, as if they kindly understood that it was not a subject to be spoken of. And far from being grateful for their silence, Mr Joseph resented the shame that that silence implied, and he and his wife began to scratch around for some small advantage to be reaped from Robert's situation. They read about the purpose of an Ashram, and talked themselves into some kind of grudging approval. They were now ready to bring Robert's defection out into the open, and to feign some pride in the courage of a young boy who would investigate philosophy with such dedication. They praised Robert to their friends to the point of boredom. They prated that it was incumbent on any young man of adventurous spirit, to seek the ways of peace and understanding. Indeed, any young man who didn't, was tantamount to a cretin. So in sundry drawing-rooms they disseminated their desperate pride, and then they went home together to their separate rooms, and quietly wept. In another three months, another postcard arrived, this time from Liverpool. He was coming home for a short while, he wrote, before going off to Mexico. What new meshuggas of his were they now going to have to find a rationale for? But Mr Joseph saved himself the trouble for he succumbed to a massive heart-attack, and died a day before Robert's return.

When she saw her son filling the frame of the living-room door, his beard and hair of equal waist-length, his fingers and his toes a-jingle and a-jangle, Mrs Joseph wondered on which part of his face she could plant a welcoming kiss. A small area under his eyes was hair-free, but somehow she couldn't be bothered to take aim on such a limited target. Besides, the excitement of his promised return had, since her husband's death, curdled into anger, and all appetite for welcome had waned.

'Look what you did to him,' was all the gracious hospitality she could manage. 'I hope you're satisfied.'

28

Robert could never forgive her. He didn't make it to Mexico. He grew his own mushrooms in Earls Court. But every year, on the Day of Atonement, he'd salaam his way to the synagogue, and eavesdrop on his father's memory like an assassin. This was the role his mother had cast for him. Let her watch his annual performance. Let her cringe with her shame, and let her weep. It was the only way he could mourn his father.

Towards sunset, a dribble of women left the synagogue. With the rising of the first star, the fast could legitimately be broken, and the women were home-bound to prepare the feast to which their purged and cleansed menfolk were so richly entitled. Sheila was amongst them. Her mother stayed behind, bent on beating her breast to the bitter end. Bernard would bring her home and the three of them would break their fast together. Most of the evening they would studiously avoid talking about Robert, each sharing the hope and the fear that he might show up for a show-down. But he never had, and after supper, when the subject of food had outgrown all discussion, Mrs Joseph would refer to him, without name, and without hope, and with sheer undiluted anger. Then on a full and replete stomach, her real atonement would begin, and she would half wish for Robert's presence to ask forgiveness.

The three of them sat round the mahogany table, and slowly, and with infinite relish, the long fast was broken. Silently they ploughed through the four courses, each with their eyes on their plates, and keeping them there, even when the dish was under discussion. Once, during the fish course, the door-bell rang, and each one of them trembled and not one of them moved. The ringing persisted, and Bernard, knowing his kinless duty, rose. As he passed through the hall, he could see the sectional shadow of a bearded man through the mullioned glass of the front door. The possibility that the caller was Robert distinctly unnerved him. He did not know whether to accord him a great welcome, or simply to turn him away. There seemed to him to be no middle way. He hesitated towards the door. Perhaps if it was Robert, he would speak first, and give him some clue as to how he should continue. Encouraged by this possibility, Bernard opened the door wide.

The Jehovah's Witness put his foot inside, angling it between the base of the lintel and the doorstep. A living wedge. Immovable. He held out a copy of his mouthpiece, *The Tower*, displaying it squarely across his chest.

'Could I interest you . . .?' His voice was soft and compelling, intransigent as the foot that forbade closure. Bernard felt trapped. And angry.

'I'm Jewish,' he practically shouted. Had he not just spent a whole day proving it?

'And you've just broken your fast,' the man said. He'd obviously done his homework, and in doing so had invalidated Bernard's protest.

But Bernard pursued. It was the only weapon he had. 'We're not interested,' he said. 'We're all Jewish here.'

'But Christ our Lord was himself a Jew.'

The obvious comeback. Undealable with, for any response was bound to offend somebody. 'Excuse me,' Bernard said, 'but I must go now. We have company.' He attempted to close the door. The foot did not move. He watched its toes tapping beneath the leather. That foot had done the state some service. It was probably encased in cast-iron. 'I'm going to shut the door,' Bernard threatened.

The foot insinuated itself an inch further inside. If Bernard shut the door, it would now entail total amputation. For a moment he thought of leaving the man where he was, of just turning away and going back to the dining-room. But there were a pair of solid silver salvers on the hall table, and, Jehovah's Witness or not, there was speedier salvation in two if not thirty pieces of silver. He heard footsteps behind him.

'Who is it?' Sheila called.

He did not trust himself to look behind, in case the man took advantage and invited his two feet into the hall itself.

'It's a pedlar,' he shouted to the man's face.

'Peddling Jesus,' the man added. There were salesmen and salesmen.

Sheila reached Bernard's side. She took the doorknob firmly in her hand. 'We're not interested,' she said. 'Please go away.' She shut the door to the limit of his ankle, and between the crack, she shouted, 'Take your foot away, or I shall crush it.' She gave him a few moments to assess the sacrifice.

'I need it to march for Jesus,' he said, and slowly the foot withdrew. Sheila shut the door. The man did not move, and they stared at each other through the mullioned glass for a long while.

'Come on, let's leave him,' Bernard said. He was angry that Sheila had managed yet again to expose his weakness. It was becoming quite a habit with her. He wished to God she'd get pregnant and know her woman's place once and for all.

They went back to the dining-room. Mrs Joseph had convinced herself that the caller was Robert, and that the inordinate time they'd both spent at the front door was in an effort to send him away. She was both grateful and resentful. She wanted very much to see her son, but she didn't trust herself to welcome him. She would want him to come to her, and stand before her, and give her time to vent her ample spleen, to curse him, to loathe him, to kill him even, and then perhaps she could touch some hairless part of him with love.

Sheila served the coffee. Their eating was coming to an end. Their appetites could stretch no further. However imperative the need for postponement, Robert moved in from the side-lines, craving attention. Mrs Joseph plunged into the silence. 'I'm glad your poor father didn't live to see it,' she said, not realising that had the old man lived,

31

Robert wouldn't have been mourning him.

'At least he came,' Sheila said.

'You just wait till you have your own children,' Mrs Joseph mourned, 'then you'll understand.'

Buster cocked his little ear, pressing it to his listening-wall. And this is what he heard.

Sheila:	If I ever have any, I won't expect too much of them. That way I won't be disappointed.
Mrs Joseph:	Expect? Who expected? For a son to be a decent human being. That's an expectation?
Sheila:	He *is* a human being. What's indecent about him?
Mrs Joseph:	Like a Savile Row gentleman he looks.
Sheila:	What's the way he looks got to do with anything?
Mrs Joseph:	You're not ashamed to see him like he looked today? In front of all our friends?
Sheila:	That's it, isn't it? That's all that worried you.
Mrs Joseph:	You're no better than he is.
Sheila:	No. We're neither of us any good at all. What d'you expect for heaven's sake. All our lives, nothing but your reproach. Nothing but your ambition, your driving, grinding ambition, and nothing but your eternal disappointment.
	Pause.
Mrs Joseph:	I'm going home. I'm not here to be insulted. I haven't got enough grief. (*sobbing*)
Sheila:	I'm sorry, Mama. I didn't mean all that.
Bernard:	Here, let's all have a brandy.

Buster was disquieted. He wasn't in the least bit pleased with what he had heard. The conversation was, on all sides, punitive, and he could smell its threat through the uterus wall. He had been in such families before. In other

32

lifetimes. Perhaps he, too, had been such a parent. To be an offspring of such a greedy root could lead to small pleasure in life. To confront such enmity was to enter a losing battle. At best he could make his entrance into the world showing his white flag. Then perhaps they would leave him alone. But that would be hard for a child with so many cravings. His ears throbbed with the old melodies that had sung from his fingers. It would be impossible to stifle them. The thought crossed his mind that he might abort himself, instantly, before his mother even knew of his presence. But he knew that would be folly, for if he did not accept his given role, he would be doomed to repeat it, and perhaps next time the circumstances would be even less favourable. Besides, the brandy had made him light-headed. He knew it was not a moment to trust his own judgement. He recapped the conversation that had so unnerved him. The present source of destruction was, without doubt, his prospective grandmother, that is, in this place and in this time. No doubt the poor lady had had a similar mother, and that lady, likewise. Family patterns had a crippling habit of repeating themselves, and the old lady had been right when she had prophesied that her daughter, on assuming the role of mother, would change her tune. But what gnawed at him most was his putative father's silence. His only contribution to the highly charged exchange had been a suggestion of brandy. Buster's previous father had been the same, except that in his case and circumstances it had been a cup of tea. That had seemed to be the cure for everything. But such a suggestion in a crisis denoted an inherent weakness, and a weak father meant an aggressive mother. Had she not taken command of the situation at the front door with that so-called pedlar. It did not make her admirable so much as it diminished his poor father. Such weakness could only defend itself in bullying. He assessed the calibre of those three people who would no doubt play a major part in his future life. All he could pit against them was his musical talent. And that was a weapon possibly safer to withhold than to draw upon. His prospects depressed him profoundly. The only light on his future horizon shone possibly on the one they forbore to mention, his mother's brother, who had made some attempt to break the crippling chain. He hoped he'd show up some time, that he could hear his voice, and know that he might be his friend. He curled up in his sadness. He knew that he must try not to think too much. He must do his best to get his mind off his mind. He must spend his gestation period building up his physical strength, keeping his fingers in trim, and later on, when his space was larger, he could practise his bow-arm, and flex his right wrist. He hoped that his mother would soon go to the doctor, and be appraised of her condition, so that she would lay off the alcohol and give him some decent wholesome food. He tried not to think of his grandmother's reaction when she first would hear of his presence. She would gloat, of course, both with pleasure and with malice. For a moment he hoped that the old lady would have a good enough sense of timing to leave the stage before he made his entrance. But he knew that her sought-for demise would do nothing to alleviate the perils of his future kinship. Indeed it might confound them. His mother had enough guilt to mourn her own mother with the reverence of repetition. To ape the departed, to take over the values of the dead, was a cosy conscience-squaring way of coming to terms with them. Buster would not have welcomed that. All he could hope for was that his grandmother would quietly survive and keep her rotten priorities to herself. At least until he was old enough to cope with them.

He stretched the beginnings of his limbs and considered his first day. All in all, it had been eventful enough. His future family was not one to hide its feelings. Their lives, if nothing else, were public. He was going to be able to learn a great deal from their overt displays. Perhaps too much for his own good, he thought. He decided he would lie low for a while, and give himself time to revise his first lesson. It occurred to him that to be conceived on the most holy day of the Jewish calendar was probably the greatest single act of atonement that God could hope for. And if there were a God, which Buster doubted, that act itself would entail its own reward. Whether from God or from any other agency, he knew that in this life he was going to need all the help he could get. And for that he needed to pray. To whom was an irrelevancy. What mattered was an acknowledgement of a power outside one's own. Buster knew that the act of prayer was a ritual that called for trappings; the kneeling, the clasped hands. As yet he was too young for either. So in his little mind he prayed for hands to join, and for the wherewithal for genuflection. Until that time, he would glean from his eavesdropping the purpose of his prayer, some specifics that warranted supplication. So he curled up in his little cell, and offered up a simple plea for survival.

Chapter 3

Buster was woken by a prodding on the uterus wall. He yawned and looked about him. He felt refreshed as if he'd slept for a long while. The tapping continued and he wriggled a little in token of his presence. He heard a voice. 'Just lie back,' it was saying, 'and relax.' Buster was delighted. He was about to be acknowledged.

He listened for his mother's first words.

'Are you really sure?' she said, and he throbbed with the delight in her voice. It didn't matter what regrets came later, what anxieties, what second thoughts. Her first and primal feelings had been those of joyous welcome. If she could only hang on to them, they would see him through his first precarious years.

Sheila took a taxi home. She wasn't going to risk the jogging of public transport. She had been trying long enough to conceive a child, and she was going to make quite sure of carrying it safely to term. She was trembling with excitement. She wondered whether she should phone Bernard at his office, or wait until he came home to relish the reaction on his face. She knew it would make him happy, and for many reasons, some of which she did not want to question. She wanted very much to tell her mother. In a way it was she whom Sheila wanted to tell most of all. Perhaps this could be the sole attempt in her life that her mother could not reproach her for. She would telephone her as soon as she got home. But when she reached the house, she suddenly felt that she wanted to tell nobody. That for a while, she wanted to savour the good tidings on her own. She poured herself a glass of milk, and sat on the settee envisaging her future.

When Buster received the milk shower, he knew that he was being taken seriously. They always went for the milk bottle with some strange intuitive notion that it was good for you. Buster was not partial to milk whether it was good for him or not, and the prospect of some forty weeks of milk douches did not please him. Had he been able to eavesdrop on his mother's thoughts at that moment, they would have pleased him less.

Sheila was musing on her offspring's gender. She hoped without doubt that it would be a girl. Girls were more available to possession; they were, as it were, for keeps. They were more malleable too. They could be fashioned in one's own image. They could be dressed, careered, and finally married into one's own, perhaps unfulfilled hopes. One need never let them go, any more than one would lose hold on oneself. Yes, she thought, my daughter will grow up to do her mother credit. It did not occur to her that that very thought, in another's mind, had lamed her own childhood.

Buster heard her pick up the phone, and dial. His ear was so acutely trained that he could gauge the number from the timings between each digit – 431 5829, he reckoned, and smiled when he heard his mother question it on the line. But his smile faded when he cottoned on to the subscriber's name. His grandmother. He was appalled by his mother's priorities. Surely his father should have been the first to be told. He glued his ear to the wall, straining to hear his grandmother's reaction.

His mother played no games with the news. She gave it loud and clear, and he detected in her voice a note of triumph. He listened to the silence at the other end of the line. Then,

'So now I hope you'll give up smoking.'

Buster turned his ear away. He didn't want to hear any more. He wished he could be born right away, to come out unarmed and at their mercy, and face the already lost battle and get it over and done with, and hope for better luck next time. He was overwhelmed by an acute depression, and knew that he could only have caught it from his mother. He wondered whether, at any time during this womb's sojourn, there would ever be any catchable joy.

Sheila replaced the receiver. Never, never, never again, she thought. I'll never tell her anything ever again. Nothing, but nothing in the whole wide world would ever please her. She sat bristling with her mother's latest reproach, and, as if to spite her, she lit a cigarette. As she smoked, she calmed a little, and began to rehearse to herself how she would break the news to Bernard. The phone-bell interrupted her thoughts.

'Why didn't you tell me first?' Bernard's voice shook with hurt anger.

'Who told you?' she said, knowing the only possible informer. 'I wanted to wait until you got home,' she said limply. She listened to his pause. 'Well aren't you pleased?' she said timidly.

'Yes, of course. But . . .'

'But what?'

'I just don't like the way I've been told.'

'I'm sorry,' she said. Another pause. 'Shall we celebrate?' she asked. 'Go out to dinner, or something?'

'We'll see.'

'I've been trying for six bloody years,' she shouted at him.

He waited. Then very softly, with one of his rare shows of strength, he said, 'So have I.'

She put the phone down. She wished heartily that she could have the whole day over again. That she would go to the doctor, and go straightaway to Bernard's office, and give him three guesses as to the nature of her tidings. It would have been a game of love. The first guess, on the tip of his tongue, would have expressed his greatest wish, fatherhood, but he would have withheld it, and guessed

38

first at other possibilities. Her agent had arranged another concert tour. She'd come up with the big one on her premium bonds. He would have scratched away at all the remote likelihoods, and at the remoter impossibilities, tying his tongue on the miracle he wished for most. She would shake her head at all his suggestions, and silently keep him guessing. Then finally, he would risk it. 'You're pregnant,' he would say, and he would know it was true by the glow on her face. And he would politely disbelieve it, for miracles must not be taken for granted, and she would have proved it to him with the doctor's letter to the antenatal clinic, instructing their care. Slowly he would have allowed belief, and they would have planned a treat for themselves to celebrate their good fortune. Now all that was might-have-been. She tipped the long ash of her cigarette onto the white carpet. She ground it into the pile with her heel so that it left an ugly grey smudge across the virgin wool. The stain offended her, but she did nothing about it, for it would offend Bernard more, and for good measure she flicked the lit butt onto the smudge and let it burn itself out. She knew it was a pathetic act of self-assertion, and she ran to the kitchen for a wet cloth to repair the damage. But too late. The butt had burned a small and exact brown circle. She covered it with the leg of a chair. She was nervous of Bernard's homecoming. Perhaps he would ring again during the day and apologise for his lack of enthusiasm. Perhaps they could play it all over again as she had first intended.

She decided to put in a little practice before Clarissa came. She usually turned up about three o'clock, her lank greasy hair wandering aimlessly all over her face, her darned brown cardigan buttoned awry, and bursting from every split seam with enthusiasm. She would have a tale to tell of crowded buses, of long, endless queue-waiting, of the unfeelingness of people in general, and of all the things that were not as they used to be, all the sad bitterness of one who has nothing to offer but her availability. Then she would tuck her fiddle under her unyielding chin, and as she made her music, she would become a creature of gentle sensibility, so that she looked almost beautiful. Sometimes there were days when even the music could do little to dilute poor Clarissa's anger. She could play like a pig unparalleled. Sheila hoped that today, for the sake of her unborn child, she would be playing at her best. For her baby was going to be a musician. Of that she was sure. And if possible, a violinist, for although in that field the competition was keen enough, it was infinitely less keen than that in keyboard. Yes, he or she would be a great fiddler, and while she carried it, she and Clarissa would play it music. Indeed Clarissa would play at its birth, so that the child would be born into Mozart. She did not sicken herself with this thought, as she well might have, had it come from her own mother, for parental expectation is only a disease in others. She patted her stomach and sat at the piano. She would prepare for their rehearsal.

They had a concert in two months' time. A charity affair, it was true, but their agent had insisted on a fee. She was glad for Clarissa's sake. Poor Clarissa, Sheila thought, if only she could get married.

She took the set of Beethoven sonatas from the shelf, and opened them at 'The Spring'. She laid the violin part on the music stand beside her, open on the right page, so that Clarissa could start straight away. She would practise the opening of the first movement. The arpeggio accompaniment of the first few bars was deceptively simple, but a precise rhythm was essential to a flowing, unobtrusive obbligato, and as she played, she sang the violin melody.

Buster pricked up his little ears. He could hardly believe his luck. His mother played the piano, and from what she was playing there must be a violinist to hand. Perhaps his father. He hoped he had a good fiddle. He listened. Not bad, he thought, as the piano took up the melodic line. He was sorely tempted to hum the violin part, which he knew note for note, together with all the Beethoven sonatas in the cycle. But he did not trust his young vocal range, and Buster was nothing if not a perfectionist. So he sat back and listened. She was repeating certain bars, and he was satisfied with her diligence. His mother was a serious musician. He could happily look forward to a whole gestation of concert-going. What joy would be his if they would play the Mozart cycle too. The thought of succeeding to a piano and scores, and perhaps to a good fiddle too, was enough to offset his earlier fears and his disappointments in his putative kin. He was prepared to put up with a great deal as long as he was allowed to make music. He waited with impatience, praying for a violin to enter, and as he listened he relived his past music-making joys. 'My, my,' he chuckled to himself. Despite his ill-timed arrival, he really couldn't have chosen better.

He heard a door-bell ring, and the piano suddenly stopped. He hoped that whoever was calling had a violin-case in its hand.

Clarissa moaned her way into the hall. One bus after another had been full, and she'd had to stand all the way, the seats full of schoolchildren, and not one of them, not even a little boy, she spat, had offered her space. And as she complained, she took off her coat, without relinquishing her violin-case, transferring it from arm to arm as she de-sleeved. As always, she did not remove her hat. She seemed to need it for playing. Even at concerts, she wore a small jewelled skull-cap as if some head protection were a prerequisite for performance. She went straight into the living-room and sat by the stand. 'You want to practise the "Spring"?' she said.

'I'm having a baby.' Sheila hadn't intended to tell her, at least, not so soon, but in view of the recent responses to her news, she needed to tell somebody who, she was confident, would react with untrammelled pleasure. Clarissa put her violin down and threw her skinny arms around her friend. She buzzed with questions of when, how and why, and when Sheila told her the part she hoped she would play at the birth, Clarissa was beside herself with joy. 'I thought some Mozart,' Sheila said.

'Without piano?' Clarissa was doubtful. 'What about an unaccompanied Bach suite?'

'If you like,' Sheila said, suddenly realising that she would not be in on the act. 'I just want to give my baby a good start in life.'

Clarissa concentrated on her tuning. Then, putting her fiddle down, she said, 'Can you *make* somebody like music, d'you think?'

'What d'you mean?'

'Well supposing he's tone-deaf, or something. I mean, there are people who just don't respond to music. The baby might . . .'

'How could he possibly be tone-deaf? He's *mine*.' Suddenly Sheila had assessed its gender, as well as its potential. Perhaps her choice of its career had prompted its maleness too.

Clarissa heard her friend's anger, and tuned up furiously. She was anxious to get on with the practice. She had planted a seed of doubt, and such careless husbandry does little to nurture friendship. 'Shall we start with the first movement?' she said.

'If you like.' Sheila had lost heart. The joy she had experienced only a few hours before was slowly being eroded. Her mother's reaction to her news was as bitter as could be expected. She had no right to complain of that. She shouldn't have been in such a hurry to tell her. And it was not her fault that her mother had beat her to Bernard on the phone. And now Clarissa with her tone-deaf non-sense. It was the last that needled her most of all. and her irritation angered her. What did it indeed matter. for God's sake. if her child were as deaf to music as a post? Did it have to be anything, anything at all, except mercifully whole? Her anger no doubt sprouted from her unjust hopes. Only two months pregnant, and already the swift inheritance of her mother's expectations was painfully clear. She must fight it, she knew. She must at least try. She started to play, without even checking that Clarissa was ready, but Clarissa made no complaint, she caught up as best as she could.

Buster was not very impressed. But he made allowances for the tension that he sensed between the two players. He knew that in less fraught circumstances, they both could play a lot better. Their mistakes were not due to any lack of virtuosity, but simply to an absence of mood. His mother was cross, and quite unjustifiably, he thought. The violinist lady had made a simple, straightforward enough observation, and his mother had taken it as a personal affront. He was going to have trouble with his mother, he could see. It was just as well he *was* a musician. Else she would have found it hard to forgive him. He wondered who the violinist was. He decided that she could not be family. No family member would risk such an observation. Unless, of course, she was a childless in-law, who was prompted by malice. But he doubted it. There was a certain timidity about the lady, and he rather warmed to her tactless tenderness. He listened as they tackled the second movement. He was impatient to be out and give them some small advice on their phrasing. His fingers itched for playing and as he waited for the superb violin melody, his little ears began to water. He leaned back and listened as they played the movement through. He enjoyed it, although he knew that even without practice, he could play it so much better. He tried to remember when and where he had performed the 'Spring Sonata'. But the location and even his pianist were a blur. All he could recall was his own particular resonances, his own idiosyncratic phrasing, his own manoeuvred cunning, and it all added up to a sound that he longed once again to re-create. He was impatient to come to his term. He looked at the tiny span of his fingers. Hardly a minor second. He counselled himself to be patient. His erstwhile virtuosity would return as soon as his equipment was ready. He need not worry that he would have lost his touch. His time could be as valuably spent in theory as in practice. The snippets of information that he gleaned daily through his listening-post were grist to any artist's mill. The pain, the joy, the anger and bitterness that regularly filtered through the protective membrane, were as much prerequisites of a violinist's art as his bowing technique. He could only profit by patient eavesdropping.

His mother was establishing the theme of the final movement which the violin would take up in its turn. The players had certainly settled down, and he was able to concentrate for the first time on the tone of the instrument. Its quality was beyond question. Without doubt it was of special vintage. At first he thought it might be a Stradivarius. He himself had often played on one, and he quivered at its brilliant edgy tone. But its bottom register sang with an un-Strad like sonority, which belonged more to a Guarnierius. Could it perhaps be a great Guarnierius, even of the del Gesu vintage, which would account for its depth of tone? Whatever it was, it was without doubt a great fiddle, and he couldn't wait to get his little hands on it.

He wondered whether there was a concert in the offing. They were certainly a competent professional pair and the possibility that he would soon tread the concert-platform, albeit as a captive audience, gave him such a thrill of excitement that he could barely suppress a giggle, so he translated it into a great smile, that wrinkled over his wizened face, and he held it fixed until the end of the movement.

'I think with a little work on the Adagio, that's more or less ready,' Clarissa said. 'Are we the second half?'

'Yes,' Sheila said. 'There's a singer and a 'cellist before us.'

'How are the tickets?' Clarissa said. 'Have you heard anything?'

'They're practically sold out. So Mr Carney says.'

Buster listened enraptured. He'd be going to a concert after all. He was suddenly tired. He'd had feast enough for one session, and his listening-energy was quickly spent. As if to gratify him, he heard his mother voice her own fatigue, so he was free to fall asleep without fear of missing anything.

'They say the first three months are the hardest,' Sheila was saying, echoing her doctor's prognosis. 'It's a period of adjustment.'

Clarissa was full of understanding, though at the same time she was entertaining treacherous thoughts of finding another pianist. A musician had to be totally dedicated. Marriage was impediment enough, but motherhood was an insurmountable obstacle. She hoped that, in time, Sheila would recognise her priorities, and, on her own account, gracefully withdraw from their partnership. She started to pack her case. 'I'll start practising for the baby's début,' she said. 'I won't tell you what it will be. It'll be a surprise for both of you,' she laughed.

'You're a good friend,' Sheila said, and meant it, not as an absolute, but in strict comparison with the tokens of friendship she had experienced during the course of the day. It irked her that she should consider Clarissa such a friend, for it crystallised her own feelings of loneliness. For in truth, she did not particularly like Clarissa. She pitied her for her single state. She played the violin because there was nothing else in life for her to do. Whatever choices a poor spinster made, they were of necessity second best. Sheila was convinced of that, and her own marriage could become a miserable life-sentence without ever breaking that conviction. She thought of Bernard and wanted Clarissa to go in case he phoned with apologies, or returned with flowers, which, it occurred to her, he should do in any case, and the fact that he had not already done so, though he had been for almost two hours aware of his future fatherhood, marked him as callous, selfish, and downright unworthy of the pain she was about to endure on his behalf. Had Mrs Joseph known of her daughter's thoughts, she might have viewed her, for the first time in her life, without reproach.

Sheila's spiteful train of thought had unleashed a bilious fluid. Buster sniffed himself awake, recognising from past lives the sour odour of sacrifice. 'Ah,' he grunted to himself, 'Trouble.' He put his ear to the wall.

Clarissa was heading for the door. 'Next time, we'll work on the Kreutzer,' she was saying.

Sheila opened the front door. Clarissa's departures tended to be long-winded with door-step second thoughts, and post-practice post-mortems. She intended to cut her short, pleading fatigue, and would have done so forthwith, had not Clarissa's proposed exit been blocked by a large bunch of red roses, which Bernard, unseeing, thrust into her face, as an angry token of his antenatal duty. Then seeing his misplaced recipient, he tried to pass off his gaff with weary humour. 'Oh dear,' he said. 'I've really got the wrong number.'

Clarissa was deeply affronted, and her throat was too full of sobbing to make any attempt at a come-back. She took off in high dudgeon down the path, blessing her spinsterhood, and her virginity, and strictly in that order. Neither Bernard nor Sheila called after her, nor even watched her retreating figure, neither of them willing to take responsibility for her abrupt, offended departure.

'You're home early,' Sheila said. 'Is there any reason?'

He walked past her into the house, throwing the flowers onto the table. 'You'd better put them in water,' he said.

'Is that all you care about?' she said.

'They cost over £5. It seems a waste to let them die.' He could play that game too.

Sheila was distinctly aware of two choices. She could prolong the misunderstanding by silence. She could bottle her resentment, pickle it, preserve it, guard its fermentation, and then, at a suitable moment, pry the lid loose. It was a manoeuvre not without risk, for resentment could sour and curdle that core of real affection that had engendered it in the first place. On the other hand, she could come clean, apologise for her insensitivity, ask his forgiveness, and then share with him the anticipation of their parenthood. She knew very well which choice she should make, but something perverse in her forbade it. She would wait for him to make the first move.

Bernard, for his part, was equally aware of similar choices, but his pride silenced him. He was, after all, the offended party. Not only had she thought fit to break the news to her mother before advising him, but she had actually questioned his early return from the office, baiting him, though she knew his flowers and his return were gestures of his forgiveness. No. She could bloody well apologise. So each settled into their own self-justified silences. In silence she put the flowers in water, and in silence they ate their supper, and in silence they would have gone to bed, had not the evening been interrupted by the arrival of Mrs Joseph, intent on celebrating her new status.

Buster was greatly relieved when he heard the door-bell. The continued silence outside his wall was unnerving. The door-bell at least promised another presence, and even when he recognised its terrible voice, he decided that anything that would break his parents' silence was acceptable.

If Mrs Joseph was aware of the coldness of her reception, she was at pains to ignore it, and the continued silence between her daughter and son-in-law she attributed to the simple awe of future parenthood.

'Well it's happened at last,' she said, settling herself into an easy-chair and pinning her gaze on Bernard so that there was no doubt whom she had blamed for her daughter's prolonged infertility. 'It's a miracle, I suppose,' she added, as if nothing short of the supernatural would qualify Bernard as a father. 'Have you thought of any names?' She was trespassing already, and on a terrain that they had barely measured out for themselves. There was silence.

'What's the matter with you both?' she said. 'Are you struck dumb with the miracle?'

Somebody had to answer her, and both obliged at the same time. 'We haven't . . .' Bernard left the floor to Sheila. The intruder was, after all, her mother. 'We haven't discussed it yet,' Sheila said. 'Bernard's not talking to me.'

Buster shuddered at the treachery of the line-up. It did not worry him that he could feel no warmth towards his grandmother. In the fullness of time, she would be accommodated. She would either grow mellow with age, or death would overtake her. She was a problem not so much to be solved, as to be grown out of. But it was rather too early in the proceedings, he thought, to have conceived a dislike for his mother. Yet dislike it certainly was. She had enlisted her mother's support on the principle that in a battle any willing ally will do, irrespective of motive or morality. Buster felt very much on his father's side, and like a spy in an enemy camp, he glued his ear to his listening-post to pick up their strategy.

Mrs Joseph relished the line-up to such an extent that she could afford to be generous. 'Now is no time to quarrel,' she said, with a referee's authority. 'Such a joy you have in your lives. I thought at least you'd be drinking champagne.'

Buster heard the silence from over the hill. He begged his father to return fire.

'After all, it may never happen again,' Mrs Joseph warned. 'This one took long enough.'

Buster knew that his grandmother was staring at his father, diminishing his equipment both for battle and paternity.

'Pour us a drink, Bernard,' she was saying. 'At least you can do that.' Silence. Then a pop of a cork and a chink of glasses. Buster could have wept at his father's swift surrender. He listened as they drank his own health and toasted his future. But what future could there be for him in the rigid bosom of such weakness and such bullying? For the first time, and it was to be one of many, Buster entertained the idea that he would be better off if he never came out at all. He listened as they toasted his future fame, wealth and happiness, and he shivered at their order of preference.

'His health too,' his father added as an afterthought.

'Thanks buddy,' Buster whispered.

'It may be a girl,' his mother said.

'The first one's usually a boy,' Mrs Joseph pronounced with authority, adding 'usually', remembering her own contrary experience and not wanting it to be referred to.

'That reminds me. I must tell Robert,' Sheila said.

'Well I hope you keep him well away from the child,' Mrs Joseph said. 'Such an influence we can all do without.'

In his cell, Buster gave an amniotic toast to Robert, a possible avenue of friendship for his future. He did not want to listen any more. Yet it was difficult not to overhear their acrimony, as much in their silences as in their speech. He forced himself to listen. There was still hope that he could pick up some snippet of information, some hint of kindness perhaps, that would make his début worthwhile.

'Have you thought of names?' his grandmother hammered away, and it was quite clear that she had a list up her sleeve. Then, 'I think you ought to call him after your father.' This presumably to his mother, since his father in such matters was of no account. Buster noticed her phrasing. Not, 'I would be honoured if you were to call him after your father,' not, 'I think it would be a fine gesture, etc,' but 'I think you *ought*.' This was no doubt a family of 'shoulds', 'oughts', and 'musts', and each terrible monosyllable shuddered across the door of his cell like a triple lock.

49

'But we can't call him Abie,' Sheila said. 'And what if it's a girl?'

'I've thought of that,' Mrs Joseph said, 'and I've decided on Abigail.'

'Whose baby is it?' Bernard asked politely.

Bully for you, Dad, Buster thought, and predicted at the same time his mother's come-back.

'Don't talk to Mama like that,' she said, and his father, his weak, simpering, slack sire, actually apologised. Buster was fearful of hearing any more. He was aware that to eavesdrop on such malevolence was to build up for himself such a monumental depression that, in the course of his gestation, it would affect not only his health, but also, quite directly, his talent. He was, by many natures, a survivor, so he put his hands over his ears, and curled into his own dreams. As he dozed off, he picked up the echoes of names as if in a distant roll-call. Penelope, Sarah, John, Paul. Did his mother really suggest Yascha, after the greatest violinist of them all? Did she repeat it with the finality of absolute decision? And was his father's silence a token of his approval, or yet another unwillingness to do battle? Yascha, he heard, over and over again, and he tasted his mother's salivation. She was greedy, he thought, with a voracious appetite that could never be satisfied. Yascha, he heard again, and he hoped to God that he was only dreaming.

Note from Dr Brown. I think that it is pertinent at this stage to say a word or two about Buster's calligraphy. I myself have always been a firm believer in handwriting as a reliable indication of character, and no matter how young the signature, the traits of personality are visible from the beginning. I go further. Not only is one's script revealing of one's qualities or otherwise; its variations reflect the present stresses and strains that the writer is heir to. I have no better proof for this theory than the positive visual change which took place in Buster's handwriting during the course of his journal. In its beginnings, despite the infant awkward hand, there was joy and innocence in every pothook and hanger. Every comma was an act of delighted achievement; every stop, a song of glee. In those days, Buster was hopeful, and imbued with a consummate will to survive. Alas, things changed, evidenced by a graphic difference in Buster's script. From now on, the writing is slovenly and sometimes illegible – I'm not complaining. My work brings its own rewards. It was clear that our writer was going through a crisis. I shall not be referring again to Buster's calligraphy, and I confess to having taken the liberty of some personal interpretations of his journal, guided by the infallible signposts in the strokes of his pen.

Chapter 4

When Buster woke he had the impression he'd been
sleeping for a long while, and to confirm it, he spread out
his hands and gauged his present finger-span. A major
second. Progress. He must have been asleep for quite a
while. Yet he didn't feel rested. Some hangover of a niggled
memory lay heavy on his mind and he tried to remember
his last waking thought, and as he looked at his listening-
post, he had little difficulty in making the association. His
last session of eavesdropping had severely depressed him.
Hence he had slept so long and so deeply, as a cop-out. It
seemed to him too early in his life to abdicate, yet it was
also too late. He was growing, and to opt for a quietus now
could only endanger his mother's life, and, though at his
last listening-session he had found her so displeasing, he
did not wish her any harm. He tried to examine the nature
of his displeasure, and he had to conclude that he was a
little afraid of her. Her faults were evident enough in her
relationship with his father, and her uneasy alliance with
his grandmother only served to underline the weakness of
her position. He had a feeling that she was behaving
against her very nature, and that the front that she was
putting forward was for her mother's benefit, even if it
meant her husband's displeasure. His mother was indeed
sorely troubled, and with generosity of spirit he resolved to
give her the benefit of the doubt. He took up his listening
position. His parents were talking outside the wall. It must
be breakfast time, he thought, because his father was
asking if the paper had arrived.

'I think I just heard the letter-box,' Sheila said.

'I'll go,' Bernard said. 'You take it easy.' He was anxious

lest Sheila over-exert herself.

'I'm not an invalid,' she laughed. 'You mustn't let me get lazy.'

He stopped behind her chair and kissed her forehead. 'I'm prepared to spoil you for a little while,' he said. He fetched the newspaper, and propped it up against the marmalade. 'The railway men are threatening to strike again,' he said.

'We'll have to start thinking of schools,' Sheila said.

'They're coming out tonight if there's no settlement. Oh God,' he said, 'more delivery problems.'

'Bernard,' Sheila was patient. 'I think our baby's education is more important than your despatch difficulties.'

'What d'you mean, our baby's education?' Bernard said. It was a habit of hers to diminish his business problems and he made an effort not to raise his voice. 'There's surely plenty of time for that,' he said.

'Not if we want him to go to a decent public school,' she said.

He looked at her questioningly. He sincerely didn't know what she was getting at.

'You have to put his name down,' she said, 'years before he's ready to go.'

'But we don't even know his name,' Bernard said. 'In any case, it may be a girl.'

'Whatever it is, we must put its name down. The surname will be acceptable. I've made enquiries. Some people put their sons down for Eton and Harrow the day they get married.'

'Well you can forget about Eton and Harrow,' Bernard said, 'and for that matter, any public school. They all have Jewish quotas.'

'But why shouldn't we be part of that quota?'

'Because quotas of any kind, religious, race, nationality, are racial, and I don't want anything to do with them.' He was shouting now, and not caring any more. 'Our son or

53

daughter, whatever it is, will go to an ordinary state school, like I did.'

Sheila managed to resist the obvious comment. 'But surely we must try to make things better for them. Surely we have to give them the opportunities we didn't have.' She was trying to be reasonable.

'I don't see anything wrong with a state school,' Bernard persisted. 'Anyway, even without quotas, we could never afford a public school.'

'Supposing he's very bright? D'you want him to rot in a state school with forty kids to a class, and no discipline. We'll have to afford it,' Sheila was adamant. 'We'll just have to make sacrifices.'

Buster retched on the word. He found it deeply offensive. The notion of sacrifice was one of euphemistic blackmail. No more, no less. And here was his putative mother proposing it in the name of all her unjust expectations. And her own mother wasn't even there. Buster was very worried indeed.

'Why don't we wait until it's born,' Bernard was saying wearily. 'At least we'll know its sex.'

'I'm just trying to be far-sighted,' Sheila said.

Bernard put his hand on hers. 'Why do we have to make plans?' he said gently. 'Why can't we just let it grow up, just naturally, without any pushing from anybody?'

Right on, Buster thought with a great sigh of relief. At last his father had spoken, quietly and timidly it was true, but at least he'd shown some sense of priority. He would have his father on his side, and together they might be a match for the ladies.

'I'm putting him down anyway,' Sheila shouted, 'and one day you'll thank me for it.'

'As you wish dear,' Bernard said.

Buster hoped his father's response was a tactic, a recognition that this was no time for argument, that sooner or later she'd relinquish her activities on her child's behalf, and settle down to enjoy the simple fact of motherhood. This time, he gave his father the benefit of the doubt. He had to, or else face the prospect of a desolate future.

'What are you doing today?' Bernard said.

'I'm going with Mama to see Grandma.'

'Does she know about the baby?'

'Not yet. Mama thought we ought to visit her with the news.'

'Give her my love,' he said. 'We should take her out one day. We've been a bit neglectful. It's so long since I saw her, I don't think I'd recognise her.'

'She's not our responsibility,' Sheila said.

He let it pass. 'Drive carefully,' he said.

The old-age home was on the outskirts of the town, and was reached through a leafy lane which muffled the noises of the city into a continuous hum of silence.

'It's peaceful here,' Sheila said.

'That's what they want, old people,' Mrs Joseph said. 'I hope I shall be so lucky to end my days in such peace and quiet.'

Liar, Buster thought, having now cottoned on to where they were going. He himself in some past incarnation had ended his days in a so-called twilight home. The stubborn conviction of the authorities that all the old people wanted was peace and quiet was only matched by their arrogant assumption of twilight status. The old did not want peace and quiet. He knew that from experience. Peace and quiet only served to drive them into unmanageable dreams, and no one in authority had thought to profit by their management. For an old person's dreams were the last chance for sanity, a rich vein that could be mined with such gain. But is was easier and cheaper to label the dreamers as 'management problems', for all the bed-wetting that went with it, and to drug them into premature and blunting oblivion. Moreover, there was nothing twilight about old age. It was not a journey into darkness, save that into the shadows of

55

another womb. Ageing was as continuous as birthing. Buster wondered what poor victim they were about to call on.

'Mrs Singer?' Mrs Joseph asked the nurse at reception.

'Mrs Singer?' the woman echoed with some astonishment, as if it was inconceivable that that inmate had a visitor at last.

Her accusing tone was not lost on Mrs Joseph, who repeated the object of her visit with rude resolve. 'That's what I said,' she declared.

'Room 27, third floor,' the nurse said. 'The lift's down the corridor.'

In the lift Mrs Joseph gave Sheila a rare smile. Sheila knew it was a manoeuvre to enlist her aid. Her mother was nervous and she needed Sheila's support. Her visits to the old-age home were rare, and always uncomfortable, and the guilt that she thought would be assuaged by doing her duty was only augmented on the return journey home. This time she had come accompanied by the fruit of her mother's fruit, and with good news, that that seed too, had, in its turn, been fruitful. Mrs Joseph was blissfully unaware of the undertone of malice in her glad tidings.

Mrs Spengler sat outside room 27 like a sentry. She was said to be over a hundred. She was a woman racked and riddled with dreams that, on investigation, may possibly have unravelled the knots and tangled skeins of a threaded century. She felt their approach towards her door, and flicking her watering eyes, she offered her ever-tip-of-tongue words, in the hope that they might find some sanctuary.

'They took away Daddy's shop,' she told them.

'They shouldn't have done that,' Mrs Joseph said, cajoling her as if she were a child or a lunatic.

No, of course they shouldn't, Mrs Spengler knew very well. But why had they done it, and why had her father's pain and humiliation eaten through her own years, and wrought such devastation. She had to know why. She had to understand it, else she would be doomed to repeat it the next time round.

'Why?' she craved them, as they moved past her into the room. Would she ever know? Time was closing in on her in shattered stillness. Her 'why' would echo in her grave. Her life was the question, and the question, her life.

A doctor passed down the corridor, a stethoscope hanging around his neck. 'They took away Daddy's shop,' Mrs Spengler tried again.

'Poor Daddy,' the doctor said. 'They shouldn't have done that,' and he passed on his way, thinking how kind and understanding he was to old people.

Mrs Joseph manoeuvred Sheila into the room before her. Sheila's appearance was likely to provoke a warmer welcome than her own. Mrs Singer looked up from her crochet-work. 'I suppose your mother told you to come,' just about summed up the quality and size of her welcome, and when she saw her own daughter hovering in the wings like some fearful understudy, she included her too in her cold response. 'It's almost four months since you were here,' she said. 'I suppose you want something.'

Mrs Joseph laid the food parcel on the bed like a *metteur-en-scène*. Her gesture declared that on the contrary, it was they who had come laden with gifts. If her mother had a weakness at all, it was a weakness that she cared not to hide — a gargantuan appetite, and she was known to mellow if this was satisfied. You could buy her with a mere portion of chopped liver, and for a cheese pancake she would have changed her will in your favour. Mrs Singer was herself aware of her weakness and its easy exploitability. So she tried not to look at the sumptuous dishes that her daughter was laying out like a banquet on the bed, but her mouth already watered with the aroma. 'I marked it on my calendar,' she insisted. 'It's more than four months. Almost five.'

'I was in hospital,' Mrs Joseph said, though her oper-

57

ation and her convalescence could only account for a month of her neglect.

'I know,' Mrs Singer said, 'but it was only a hernia, and that's not serious. I had one myself,' and she made to open her house-coat for proof, but Mrs Joseph gently dissuaded her, not wishing to view that Flanders field again. Mrs Singer turned to her granddaughter. 'You're looking very pretty, Sheila,' she said, with the generosity that only grandmothers can afford. 'Are you married yet?' Very occasionally Mrs Singer would have a memory lapse, which was often followed by an astonishing act of recall.

'You came to my wedding,' Sheila said.

'Of course I did,' she said. 'You married Bernard, didn't you? It must be six years ago. In the summer. I wore a white silk frock.'

She was right in every detail, and it delighted her, for it warned any would-be deceivers that she was not to be taken for a ride on account of her great age. 'We had salmon for supper,' she went on, 'and raspberries. Are you still married?'

'Of course she is,' Mrs Joseph asserted.

'Well how should I know?' Mrs Singer complained 'Who writes to me? Who telephones? Who comes? Well, thank God, it can't go on much longer. Then you'll all of you be sorry.' It was out. It was her obligatory speech to every rare visitor. It was a conversation-stopper too, since her complaints could not be denied. It called for a change of subject.

'We've got some news for you,' Mrs Joseph said.

'So?'

'They took away Daddy's shop.' Mrs Spengler guided her walker into the room to claim her residential rights. She had it in mind to sit on the bed as some comfortable location in which to speculate on the unfairness of her father's dispossession. On closer inspection of her counterpane, she found it strewn with delicacies, and though she had never doubted her soundness of mind in any respect, she thought for a fearful moment that she was hallucinating. And daring to prove it, she stretched out her trembling hand to touch the splendid feast. Her gnarled fingers slithered over a pickled walnut. Whatever it was it was substance, and no raving dream. In her delight, she proved it yet again, and slipped it into her mouth where her three stubborn remaining teeth relished its disposal.

'That's mine,' Mrs Singer pouted. 'Leave it alone.'

'But it's on my bed,' Mrs Spengler said, claiming her territorial rights.

Sheila made to clear Mrs Spengler's decks and transfer the feast to her grandmother's counterpane. Mrs Spengler sniffed at the spoils with a hunter's zeal. Mrs Joseph sensed the possibility of a battle between the two old ladies, and she stood aside and welcomed it, since it might well, for the duration of the visit, take the heat off her own negligence. For a moment she wondered whose side she should be on. But Sheila forestalled any argument. 'There's enough for everybody,' she said.

'She never shares anything with me,' Mrs Singer sulked.

'No one brings me anything,' Mrs Spengler said, and with utter truth, for it was years since the poor shopkeeper's daughter had received a visit. She had certainly outlived her contemporaries, and even most of her younger relations. She had survived children and even grandchildren and always with a small sense of shame. Yet she knew there was some reason for her long sojourn. She simply could not depart this earth until she had fathomed the reasons for her father's dispossession. Even if she cared not to listen to the answer.

Sheila divided the gifts between them. Mrs Spengler accepted her share with little grace, and with an eye on her room-mate's portion to check that it was equal. She stored each dish in a cupboard beside the bed, and when it was loaded, she sat beside it, keeping guard. Her presence in the room inhibited further conversation, and Mrs Singer motioned to her kin to gather around her, for only a whispered exchange was now possible.

Mrs Spengler did not savour the line-up, but she kept her peace. She had little enough right to Mrs Singer's hand-out; she had even less to the affairs of her family. So she sulked a while, and then, to comfort herself, she sneaked another pickled walnut from her store.

'What news were you talking about?' Mrs Singer whispered.

'How would you like to be a great-grandmother?' Mrs Joseph said, coming straight to the point.

Sheila rather thought that it was her right to break the news, since it was she who was raising her grandmother's title in the hierarchy. Her mother was assuming proprietary rights on her baby and Sheila began to resent it. 'It's *my* news,' she said to her mother.

'Mine, yours, it's everybody's,' Mrs Joseph said, generalising the particular and thus diminishing it.

'Mazeltov,' Mrs Singer said, directing her congratulations exclusively at Sheila, and then with little confidence to Mrs Joseph, 'It should only bring you joy and happiness. Till the end of your days,' she added pointedly. 'When are you expecting?'

'Another six months,' Mrs Joseph said, as if she were the carrier.

'I should only live to see it.'

'You'll live,' Mrs Joseph said.

'And how would *you* know? How would you know whether I live or die?'

Mrs Joseph cowered. She could have been a child shrinking before her punishment. Sheila had never seen her mother afraid, and she was astonished and not unduly displeased to see her at the receiving end of parental reproach. There was something ridiculous in the whole role-reversal. And frightening too. For whatever it was that

60

throbbed in the name of relationship between herself and her mother was clearly a seed that had been sown in a former generation, and was thus genetically determined. She didn't want to be a mother like her mother, and possibly her mother had had the same wish, but as she listened to Mrs Singer's voice, she heard in both the sound and the matter an undeniable echo in her own mother's voice, with its grudging but irresistible acceptance. She was determined to give that echo no lodging, but had her own mother been likewise resolved, and even her grandmother too? And even before that, down a vast unending chain of determined women, who, one after another, without ever knowing why or how, broke their firm resolve.

'We've come to celebrate,' she said, trying to make peace between them. She reached for the shopping-bag, and took out a bottle of champagne which had not been included in Grandma's goodies. This was for them all to share, including Mrs Spengler, who was eyeing the bottle with salivating anticipation. There were no glasses to hand, except for a couple of plastic toothbrush mugs. Private drinking was discouraged in the home, and an ageing tippler was forced to drink from the bottle with all the stealth and concealment of a regular alcoholic. Sheila went down to reception leaving an uneasy silence behind her. She knew that during her absence that silence would not be broken. Each one of them, in their private undeceiving selves, felt at fault. Mrs Singer for her ingratitude, Mrs Joseph for her negligence, and Mrs Spengler for her greedy intrusion. A silence, respected for long enough, would obviate the need for any apology, and would finally absolve each one of them. So they sat there wordless, looking at the floor.

Sheila returned with four small glasses. The receptionist had been reluctant to part with them even after a full-blown explanation from Sheila as to their purpose. 'Please bring them back,' she had said. 'We need them for milk at bedtime.' She was intent on affirming the nature of her establishment where a glass of milk, like everything else, was respectable. Sheila checked that no one was walking the corridor, and she aimed the bottle towards the open door. But the bottle was warm from its journey, and its contents fairly flat so that the cork plopped unceremoniously onto the carpet. She poured, taking care to give each celebrant an equal share. It was the toast that broke the long silence. It was Mrs Singer who voiced it.

'Here's to my great-grandchild,' she said. And Mrs Joseph, who also had a new status to celebrate, echoed, 'Here's to my first grandchild.' And Sheila, who felt herself at least part responsible for making it possible at all, though this thought would not have been shared by her mother, raised her glass and drank to her first child.

'It should only bring you joy,' Mrs Singer said, and Mrs Spengler, who wanted to get in on the act, added her own contribution. She echoed Mrs Singer's words, though in a slightly modified form. Either the champagne had fuddled her thinking, or she quite suddenly had a flash of gentle wisdom. 'Yes,' she said, 'you should only give it joy.'

They finished the bottle, and it mellowed them all. Mrs Spengler dozed as she sat, rocking back and forth, till Sheila laid her squarely on the bed and secured the rail on each side. She had probably lain in such a cot as a child at the time when they'd taken away her father's shop, and stained her life indelibly for ever after. It was no doubt the cot that had evoked the dreams that had shipped her back to her sad childhood, and prompted her woeful recall. 'Why, Why?' she kept murmuring, her forehead creased with questioning, until she found her thumb and sucked herself asleep.

Mrs Spengler was now as good as absent, and the floor was free for unmuted family debate.

'Have you thought of a name?' Mrs Singer said, and without waiting for a reply, 'I should like you to call it after your grandfather,' she said.

62

Mrs Joseph bristled, and so did Sheila, but each on different accounts.

'Isaac,' Mrs Singer declared, with a hint that she was reminding herself as well as the others, for Grandpa Isaac had been dead for some twenty years, and the passing of time might well have blurred his identity.

'Supposing it's a girl?' Sheila gave the automatic response.

'First ones are always boys,' Mrs Singer said despite her own experience to the contrary.

'I thought Abraham, after her poor father,' Mrs Joseph put in.

'But my Isaac, God rest his soul, has been gone a lot longer. She'll have more children,' she prophesied, with the inference that Abie, whom she had never warmed to, could bloody well take his place in the queue. It didn't matter, Sheila thought. Let them argue it between themselves. Whatever she named the child, it would be neither Abraham nor Isaac, nor any of their female equivalents. In a modern and mildly racial society, they were punitive names, and faintly sacrificial, and though Sheila had nothing against sacrifice in the martyred nature of parents concerning their children, she did rather think that Abraham had gone a little too far with his son. No, she had something more prestigious in mind. A name that was already associated with wisdom and artistry. Such a baptism gave a child a better chance. Children often grew into their names and there was no harm in elevating their sights from the very beginning. She had a few names in mind, most of them associated with music, the pursuit she had chosen for her child, but she was keeping them to herself, for sometimes even she thought they were over-ambitious.

'You never had any respect for your poor father,' Mrs Singer was saying. Since she herself had had no respect for him, it was incumbent on someone else to do the honours. Likewise her mother had said the same to Sheila, and for the very same reasons. Perhaps she herself, in time, would admonish her own child to show some vicarious filial respect. She shuddered. Was there a race of men, weak, unobtrusive, fearful and colonised, who sat in corners of rooms waiting for their respectful due, unmerited and paid by proxy? 'I shall call it Yascha,' Sheila said suddenly, not because she meant it, but because she had to declare an extreme choice to let them know, once and for all, that neither Abraham nor Isaac were in the running.

'Yascha?' Mrs Singer said. 'That's a name?'

'A violinist's name,' Sheila said. 'He'll grow into it.'

'There's no telling her,' Mrs Joseph said to her mother.

'Unfeeling, that's what she is,' Mrs Singer said, and having found a common enemy, the two women made a temporary alignment.

Mrs Spengler stirred in her sleep. Sheila looked across at her cot. A single tear fell from the corner of her eye. And then another. Then the other eye watered, and very slowly, her face was awash with a gentle flow of sadness. Yet she herself was still, unresistant, as if she wished to drown in her grief.

'Poor soul,' Mrs Joseph said. 'Doesn't she have any visitors?' Then regretted the question, aware that she herself was such a rare caller. And Mrs Singer, not one to let any opportunity slip by, said, 'Who has visitors?'

Mrs Joseph let that one pass, and they sat in silence for a while. Then she tried again. 'So what's the news?' she said, then regretted it, since what news would a woman have who never went out, who never saw anybody, whom the world had almost entirely forgotten?

But Mrs Singer picked that one up too, with an almost literal translation of Mrs Joseph's thoughts.

'We might as well go then,' Mrs Joseph said. They had said what they had come to say and their continued presence seemed to be an irritant.

Mrs Singer was glad to see them making moves to go.

64

She was unused to company and ill-at-ease with the silences between them. 'Thank you for coming,' she said. 'And the champagne too.' Then to Sheila, 'Come again soon,' she said, and probably meant it at the time if only as a rebuke to her own daughter.

Suddenly Mrs Spengler sat bolt upright in her cot, and, feeling her wet face, wondered if she'd been crying, and why.

'Goodbye Mrs Spengler,' Sheila said. Silent leaves were taken all round. All over the twilight home, guilty rela.ives were sitting by silent beds and wishing there were some restriction on visiting hours. It took courage to get up and go when there was no end-of-hour bell, no one in authority to suggest you'd been there long enough. So you invented pressing business back home, and out of all her cobwebbed years, the inmate might wonder what in this life could be so urgent. What matter of import could not wait? Where was everybody so desperately running? For time must have a stop. Did none of them know that?

When Sheila and her mother had gone, Mrs Singer drew up a chair and sat beside Mrs Spengler's bed.

'They took away Daddy's shop,' she said, wiping away the tears with the sleeve of her cardigan. 'Why? I'm asking myself,' she said. 'Why, Mrs Singer, why?'

By comparison with her room-mate, Mrs Singer felt herself a child, and she took Mrs Spengler's hand. Then, because she understood, because for years she had lived day and night with the pain of Mrs Spengler's questioning, because she knew that it was real, after all those years, she found in her mind some kind of answer.

'I don't know why, Mrs Spengler,' she said. 'But it doesn't really matter any more. The only thing that matters is that it wasn't your fault.'

What she had said, she had meant perhaps only for comfort, but Mrs Spengler was wide-eyed at her so casual wisdom. She gripped Mrs Singer's hand, and dragged it slowly to her lips. If only somebody, anybody in the world, had said those same words to her a million griefs ago.

On the way back in the car, Buster took his ear from the listening-wall, and tried to take his mind off the revelations of the afternoon. He'd had a bellyful. All in all, they were a rotten lot. Root and branch. Only Mrs Spengler seemed to him to be half-way human, and she wasn't even kin. And in any case, she was unlikely to survive his début. So far, only his father might be suspected of a modicum of gentleness, but even he, only negatively. He was kind by omission. Nothing more positive than that. He wondered whether there were any aunts or uncles in the offing. He'd heard the name Robert crop up in one or two conversations, and always parenthesised in silence. They certainly didn't approve of Robert, and by that token Buster had high hopes of him. He tried not to feel too desolate. He still had six months to go. Anything could happen in that time. His mother might mellow with her condition, his father might find an assertive voice, and his grandmother might emigrate. Perhaps it was too much to hope for. He looked at his finger-span. An augmented second. Had he grown a whole semitone in only one day? This thought cheered him a little and reminded him of the purpose of his future. And he began to look forward, shutting out from his mind all impediment to that goal. To survive in order to make music. To know with absolute certainty that any single Schubert aria can finally surmount rage, that a Bach fugue could overcome the wildest injustice, and that in a Mozart quartet, even the most profound human grief would in time find reasoning, and be assuaged.

'I've been thinking,' Mrs Joseph was saying, 'I won't be upset if you don't call it Abie. Your father would understand. Your grandfather comes first. So call it Isaac. What's a name anyway? And it would give Grandma such pleasure.'

Buster made some genealogical calculations. If, in token

of Mrs Joseph's reasoning, he was to be named after his grandfather, then it would be his own child who would have to do its baptismal duty by the late unlamented Abie. The parents sin, and the children atone; the fathers eat sour grapes, and the children's teeth are set on edge. A vicarious assuagement of guilt. Atonement by proxy. Jesus, he marvelled to himself. What a family. He heard a crashing of gears. 'I'm not calling it after anyone,' his mother was shouting. 'Your dead are not my problem. It will be Yascha,' his mother was saying. 'I've made up my mind.'

Buster was not pleased. What had started out as a joke had now become something quite serious. Yascha, he said to himself, trying on the name for size. He swam in it like a sprat clothed in ocean. Grow as he might in virtuosity and technical skill, it was a name that would hang loose for ever. It belonged to a being divinely sired, and only arrogance could presume to inherit it. He prayed his mother might change her mind.

'Meshugga,' was his grandmother's verdict. 'I'm only glad your father isn't alive to hear it. What did I do, I ask myself, over and over again I ask it, what did I do to deserve it all?'

That night as Buster lay by his father's side, he felt the vast space and the silence between them. It was beginning to worry him. Almost every night since he had moved into his new quarters, he'd had an uneasy feeling of lying with his mother alone. Sometimes his father would mutter something about profits and turnover, and his mother would over-respond with feigned interest. Then he felt the silence more acute. He knew that all was not well between them, that even within their own privacy, their relationship was akin to a performance, and it occurred to him that the purpose of his conception had been to repair the broken threads between them. No role to thrust on a child, even inadvertently. 'If I can pull off the Japanese deal,' his father was saying, we should gross a hundred thousand next year.'

His mother did not respond. Instead she moved, increasing the space between.

'You tired?' his father said.

'Yes.'

'You're always tired.'

'The baby makes me tired.'

'He can't make you that tired. Every night.'

'Well it won't be much longer. It'll be different when it's born.'

'Are you sure?'

'It always is,' his mother said, and Buster wondered what the 'it' referred to and a sense of double responsibility overcame him, of a growing into Yascha, and a cementer of marriages and he wished that he could grow no more. He hid his hands behind his back. Any view of his finger-span would remind him of his approaching début, and there was little enough to look forward to. He heard his father stirring. 'Perhaps after it's born we can go on holiday together. A second honeymoon,' he said, with a painfully apologetic giggle.

Buster waited hopefully for his mother's reply, but there was only silence, except for a long inward sigh that only he could hear. His poor, hungry, needy father, whose whole hopes and expectations hinged on his yet unborn self. He wanted somehow to let his father know that his birth would alter nothing, that the space between could not be bridged by any third party, that his sad need to bleat on about his turnover and marginal profits would not evaporate, and that his silence could not be broken on anyone else's behalf, but only on his own. Buster recalled many of his former débuts. It was rare that one could be born totally into one's own right, and held throughout one's earthly sojourn in respected separateness. Rare indeed. It was certainly not to be his lot this time. He shut his eyes. Inside the womb, and

68

out, he knew sleep to be remedial, and that next morning, like any other, he would listen to music, and his fingers might itch again for début. And in every new day lay the chances of another aural encounter, that Robert perhaps, whose name stuck in all throats with righteous disapproval. Sometimes if you wished for something hard enough, it would come about, and little Buster went to sleep with the profligate's name on his tongue, and when he awoke, he heard it loud and clear outside his listening-wall.

Chapter 5

'Robert?' Sheila said, opening the front door.

He was standing with his back to her, as if afraid of turning around. She thought it must be Robert from the distinctive breadth and strength of his shoulders and the raven-black of his hair. Yet Robert's hair was almost waist length, draping a frayed denim jacket and jeans, while this head was close-cropped and not a hair of it touched the pin-striped suit that draped its broad shoulders. Moreover, there were highly polished shoes on its feet. But it had to be Robert if only because of the instinctive rush of pleasure she felt the moment she saw him.

He turned around. His face was shaven, drawn and pale. He wore a tie, inexpertly knotted, and an unaccustomed white shirt. He came towards her. He shuffled a little, a gait that was strangely at odds with his highly educated shoes.

'Robert, what's happened to you?' she said.

'Trouble.' He kissed her lightly and followed her into the living-room.

'Sit down,' she said. She was not worried. Her brother's appearance did not spell trouble. Far from it. It spoke of prosperity and conformity. He'd shaved his beard, cut off his hair, donned a suit. In other words, he'd done what his parents had for years been begging him to do. He'd pulled himself together. 'Would you like some coffee?' she said.

He looked at her, taking her in for the first time. 'You're pregnant,' he said.

She realised that she hadn't told him. 'Yes. Another five and a half months.'

He smiled. 'Well at least there's some good news around.'

70

'What's the matter?' she said, more as an automatic response to his statement, rather than an indication of concern. 'You look pretty good to me. I haven't seen you in a suit for years.'

'I had to wear it,' he said.

'Why?'

'Because I've got to go to court,'

She sat down. She tried to think of any reason for a court visit that didn't spell trouble. She didn't want to hear bad news. So she parried. 'Are you a witness or something?' she said. 'Has one of your friends been arrested?' Anything to keep him this side of the dock.

'Will you come with me?' he said.

Now she knew it was real. Only rarely in his life had he attempted to enlist her support, and then only as a child. As an adult he had known that she was on his side, but he had never sufficiently trusted her sympathy to ask her to translate it into concrete form. Now his need must have been desperate. She drew her chair towards him. At that moment she was prepared to deny all other allegiance. Her mother could take what stand she would, but if it wasn't in direct support of her son, then she would beat her breast to an empty wilderness. Bernard would moralise and pontificate, but if finally he did not come down on Robert's side, he too would forfeit her loyalty.

'What's happened?' she said.

'It's a drugs charge.'

Despite her former resolve, she felt her sympathies shaken. Those few people she knew who were marginally involved in the drug scene engendered her utter contempt. Pleasure had to be earned, and with damned hard work. To take short cuts to pleasure by puffing and snorting were to her an immoral cheat on life. The health hazards of drug-taking were of secondary importance to her, and were only introduced to reinforce the moral argument, and to this end they might be pronounced first, for concern for

71

another's health is in no way accusable. 'My God,' she said, 'are you an addict?' Then taking for granted his affirmative, she said, 'Don't you know you're killing yourself?'

He heard the grating echo of his mother's voice all down his skipping, slouching years. Any single thing that he did that was not for her pleasure or her approval was listed as self-destructive. He moved his chair a little distance. 'I've never taken anything. Not the hard stuff,' he said. 'I just sell it.'

Open road. A freeway for moral judgement, and Sheila proceeded at full speed. He half listened, not to her words, but to her strangled syllables of love and concern, that so embarrassed her that she had to distance them in a judge's delivery. It was a rehearsal for what he would later on endure in court from a total stranger. He waited for her to come to a halt. Then, 'Sheila,' he said, 'you're my sister.'

His reminder of their kin was a plea that whatever he had done, he was innocent, and given a little persuasion, Sheila would have confessed that in her heart she did not believe him guilty. Her little homily on morality was not her own speech, but one which she knew she delivered on behalf of her mother. It was her mother she had first thought of when Robert had broken his news, and the pain that it would cause her. No matter how wrong the reasons for her tears, nor how obscene her motivation, her pain would be real and burdensome. And it was on her behalf that she berated him, because she could not bear the load of her mother's sorrow. 'Why d'you have to keep doing it to her?' she said.

He said nothing, hoping that in the silence she would re-hear the utter silliness of her question. That she might understand that nobody could do anything to anybody else without a modicum of collusion. That it required two people to do almost anything in the world, except dying, that ultimate act of privacy.

'Does she have to know?' Sheila was saying.

'I'm likely to go down for three years. Two if I'm lucky.'

'We can say you've gone back to India.' Having so automatically settled the pretence that would nullify her mother's pain, she suddenly realised the truth that they were masking. Robert, her brother, behind bars. Two whole years or more, incarcerated, strait-jacketed in prison-black, his kaftans fraying, his beads unstrung, and his mantras silenced. She shivered.

'It'll be in the papers, I'm afraid,' he said. 'She's bound to read it.'

'Why?' she said, indignant. 'It's a common enough charge. The papers don't report them all.'

'I'm up with a prominent businessman. Someone in oil.'

'She'll never be able to hold up her head again.'

Robert was angry. He hadn't come to his sister for judgement. That he would receive in plenty later on in the court. 'Do you *really* believe what you're saying?' he said. 'Or are you just quoting *her*? If she really can't hold up her head again because of what this friend will say or that, then that's her problem and not my concern. She's far more likely to worry about a friend's opinion than to give a second's thought to my incarceration. So I don't give a shit,' he said. He made for the door.

'I'll come with you,' she said. 'I've just got to get my coat.'

Buster was glad of the diversion. He was always happy to hear new and perhaps exciting voices, especially when they belonged to those outside his immediate family with whom he was becoming increasingly disillusioned. Moreover he was anxious about Robert. He needed to know what was going to happen to him. He wanted to hear it loud and clear from the judge himself. He could no longer depend on his family's reportage. They lied, all of them, like eye-witnesses. They told only what they could afford to tell, sparing themselves as well as their listeners. He had a longing for the plain truth of things, the sure spelling-out of

73

unadorned facts that were in no way modulated by the teller's fears or wishful thinking.

Robert's car was not the smoothest of runners, and as they jogged along he heard the throb of his mother's hand against his listening-wall. He rather enjoyed the ride. At his early stage of development he was unable to exercise on his own account. Apart from his daily finger movements, his body was, as yet, physically untried. Robert's faulty springing acted as a rough, yet welcome massage to his young astonished limbs.

They jogged along for some time, and in silence. Or perhaps they were in conversation, but Buster could hear nothing through the din of the engine, which perhaps was just as well, for there was indeed some caustic sibling exchange which would not have pleased Buster at all. At length, they reached the court buildings. They were early. Sheila suggested a cup of coffee to kill time. But Robert wanted to stay outdoors. He wanted to avail himself of the crisp air, as if he knew that henceforth it would be strictly rationed. So he left her standing on the pavement while he crossed the road, and recrossed, dodging the morning traffic, skipping between the waiting cars, as if on a last bid for freedom. Sheila watched him and in her heart, she accepted that he would go to prison.

In the court-room, she sat in the visitor's gallery. She put her coat on the seat beside her, and her handbag on the other side, as if reserving them. She wanted no one in close proximity, lest they smell the kin on her. It was a magistrates' court, and the absence of a jury, and the general informality of the proceedings gave her heart. No serious punishment could be meted out in such an ambience. He would get a warning perhaps, and he'd promise to be a good boy, and then they could go back home and no one need ever know how they had spent their day. The bench at the front of the chamber was empty. Three chairs stood on one side. A full jug of water was on the table, together with three glasses. There was a readiness about the table, an air of expectancy in the court. Robert entered from a side-door with another man, presumably his lawyer, and they took their seats in the well of the court. They were followed by another pair, one of these a woman, so Sheila presumed that the man was Robert's partner-in-crime. They too took their seats, though at some distance from Robert and his adviser. They avoided each other's glance, as if whatever friendship had once existed between them was now plainly diluted and had possibly turned very sour. Sheila wondered whether they were to be heard separately. She hoped so. And that Robert would be the first, so that his story, honest or otherwise, would make the keener impression.

A door opened on the side of the court and a group of three people, all of them men, took their places at the central table. The chairman of the Bench took his seat without a glance at the manner or the matter of the business facing him. He motioned to the Clerk of the court, who handed him some papers, and there followed a discussion between the three Justices presumably on the matter of the case before them.

'Will PC Smythe take the stand,' the Clerk ordered, and the witness, note-book in hand, hatless, but still in his uniform, a keeper of law and order, mounted the stand and took the oath. He took it like his daily bread, which indeed it was, with no respect for taste or texture. It was a mere formality, a collection of vocabulary which he was obliged to reel off before his story, honest or otherwise, was allowed to be heard. And according to PC Smythe's story, and the notes that prompted it, he had accosted the accused Robert Joseph in Piccadilly Underground Station at seven o'clock on the evening of the 26th November. He was acting suspiciously. It was a phrase well thumbed in the lexicon of police phraseology, and it could cover anything.

'In what way?' the magistrate interrupted.

PC Smythe was not prepared for the question. He took it

as an affront. If in his opinion the accused was acting suspiciously, that was all there was to it. He didn't have to have a reason. He hesitated. Then out of the same lexicon, he scraped another chestnut. 'He was loitering with intent,' he said, and hoped as he said it that no one would ask him to specify the intention.

The magistrate nodded with the standard response.

'He was carrying what looked like a schoolboy's satchel,' PC Smythe went on, 'and I asked him to open it. He went red, and said, "It's none of your business," and he tried to get away. I caught him and took him to Savile Row Police Station to help us with our enquiries.' Another standard phrase, and usually a euphemism. When the police put out that a man was helping them with their enquiries, he is possibly having the shit beaten out of him for information. Sheila shivered at this possibility. Robert hadn't mentioned any man-handling. Probably because he thought it might have pointed to his guilt. She looked at his face for some clue. He looked angry and pale, and he stared at PC Smythe with a recollection of loathing. 'At the station,' the witness went on, 'the bag was opened in the presence of the accused. It was found to contain three blocks of brown substance, which on examination was proved to be cannabis. The accused was charged with possession and remanded in custody until the following morning. The magistrate granted him bail and he stands in his own surety of £1000.'

Where in God's name did he get that money? Sheila thought. Perhaps his co-accused, more affluent than he, had needed Robert's parole as well as his own to concoct some viable story.

'The accused's statement is in the hands of the court,' PC Smythe concluded, as if that was all that concerned him. He had done his duty in the name of law and order, no matter by what means, and it was now up to the Bench to see that Justice was done. He asked permission of the court

76

to leave the stand and go back on duty. The magistrate nodded and a sigh of relief came from the well of the court. No harm could now come to England. PC Smythe was back on his beat.

The magistrate took some time to peruse Robert's statement once more, then the Clerk of the court asked Robert to stand. Sheila found it hard to look in his direction. Her anger at his stupid behaviour was equalled only by the pain of seeing him accused. He got to his feet with difficulty, trembling, and as he stood, alone amongst all those seated around him, he looked totally guilty, a target for all their accusation. She raged with a terrible fear and anger, and Buster, sniffing her fury, turned himself over and held himself at bay. Sheila put her hand to her stomach, alarmed at the sudden frenetic movement within. She was suddenly frightened. Perhaps her continued presence in the court, and the effect it was having on her, was damaging to her health and the well-being of the child inside her. She rose quickly hoping that Robert would not see or misjudge her exit, and quietly she slipped out of the chamber.

She sat alone on a bench outside, her hand still cleaving to her belly, afraid to move it away lest it might disanchor her ward. She was trembling. She wanted to return to Robert's fray, so that her presence would give him some silent support. She tried not to think of the moment when he would catch sight of her untenanted seat and shiver at her betrayal. She hoped that that moment would not come in the middle of his fragile self-defence, when all he could plead was his regret and his stupidity. Perhaps such a plea might reduce his sentence. She was glad she didn't have to hear the rest of his story, or what part his partner had played in the deal. She would go back into the court solely to hear the verdict. She would need all her strength for that.

Buster was worried. From what he'd heard in the

court-room, his uncle had little chance of acquittal. He knew what a term of imprisonment would mean to his family. He already heard his grandmother's rhetorical scream as to what she had done to deserve it all. He already felt his mother's sorrow, and his father's marginal concern. But most of all, he felt sorry for himself. Of the few lights on his horizon, Robert was the brightest star, and to be born into a world of his absence held small promise of any joy. Perhaps he would delay his sortie, Buster thought, hang on a little until Robert's parole. If he should go to gaol, and it certainly looked more than probable, his future family would be even more fraught. Blaming each other and themselves for Robert's transgression, unsheathing their shame and humiliation in the only fight that ever seemed to matter to them. What other people would think. No, it was no battle-ground to set foot on unarmed, yet a butt for their scarring; innocent, yet a tangential target for their blame. He cursed his present dwelling-place, regretting his life even before its début. He felt his mother's hand withdraw from his listening-wall, and slowly he turned himself around again, assuming his eavesdropping position. His mother was still, and there was silence outside the wall. Some footsteps echoed on stone floors, and Buster assumed that the hearing had been too much for her. He was angry that she had absented herself from the proceedings. He needed to know of Robert's future, for it hinged so closely on his own. Suddenly his very sortie depended on Robert's acquittal. He needed to know. He needed to formulate his thinking. He willed her with all his throbbing heart to return to the fray.

He felt her movement and heard her steps on the stone floor. He heard a distant muffled sound of a man's voice, his hearing impeded by his mother's movement. Then she sat down, and the voice was distinct. It belonged to the chairman of the Bench and reflected his weary disgust at the whole business. 'In view of the seriousness of the offence with which Goldsmith is charged, he shall be committed for trial at the Old Bailey. Bail is opposed. We find the accused, Robert Joseph, guilty of trafficking. We sentence him to two years' imprisonment.'

Buster took his ear away from his listening-post. He had much thinking to do. If he acknowledged the natural time of his début, Robert would still have over a year to serve. He knew that the first year of a child's life would condition his entire future, and the absence of any pure love, untrammelled by need for feedback, could scar him for the rest of his days. It would stunt his talent, and ultimately his joy. From his avid eavesdropping he could discover no one else who might welcome him solely for himself, for his own person, whatever his potential. He crouched inside his cell and felt a gradual heating in his fluid bed. His mother was expressing some emotion for which words were inadequate. He shut his eyes tight and set to thinking.

A policeman took Robert's arm. He made no protest. He turned to look at Sheila, and his look beckoned her without pleading. She noticed how she hesitated before going towards him, before making that move that would fully, in the eyes of all the court, identify their kinship. Her hesitation displeased her, and to offset it, she rushed towards him. The policeman hovered at their side, and waited for their words. But they said nothing. They simply stared at each other. After a while, she took his hand. 'I'll come and see you,' she said, 'as often as they allow.'

'What about Mother?' he said.

Sheila shivered. 'I'll have to tell her, I suppose.'

'I don't want her visiting,' Robert shouted over his shoulder, as the policeman led him away. She watched him go, in that smart suit of his, with his respectable hair-cut, which had stood him in no stead at all. She had wanted to kiss him, a gesture that even he might have understood as love, but there had been a coldness about him which precluded touch. Suddenly she wanted to tell nobody about the events of the morning. Not even Bernard. She wanted to keep Robert's incarceration all to herself. She wanted to monopolise every visiting moment. He was hers, her secret, her cross perhaps, that she would bear gladly until his parole. But she knew that such events could not be secret. Robert had been right. Francis Goldsmith, his partner, was indeed a name in the city. The afternoon papers would salivate his downfall. She had to get to her mother before a well-meaning friend would appraise her of her son's latest folly.

Although she had a key to her mother's house, she never used it. She still harboured fantasies of finding her mother in some stranger's embrace, and she, unannounced, gaping in the doorway. The wish that some kind, undemanding innocent would take her mother over, and listen without murmur to her catalogue of complaints, who would take her away for all Jewish holidays, those terrible festivals of family disunion. Sheila daydreamed about it sometimes, of attending her mother's second wedding, so acutely sometimes, that it became a reality. So as she rang her mother's bell, she had to adjust her sights, and see her sitting alone, wondering who was calling and what terrible tidings attended her at the door.

'Oh it's you,' she said, straightening the smile that by rare nature had creased her face. 'And to what do I owe this honour?' Mrs Joseph could open fire even before the battle-field was agreed on.

Through his thinking, Buster heard her greeting. He knew that even a short eavesdrop on Mrs Joseph's monologue would encourage still further his début's delay. But he was aware that it was too easy in the space of one hour to come to a decision which would, after all, affect or defect his whole future. The temporary loss of Robert had depressed him, and he knew that he was in no mood to come to any conclusion. So he listened, though he knew that nothing would surprise him.

'I'm just making myself some coffee,' Mrs Joseph said. 'Would you like a cup?' It offered her a reason for delay, so Sheila accepted, following her mother into the kitchen. 'What are you doing up this way?' Mrs Joseph said. She could not imagine that her daughter would make the journey simply on her account.

'I've got some bad news,' Sheila said, easing into her story.

'Oh my God, who is it?' Mrs Joseph shouted. 'Is it Bernard?'

Buster was bewildered that she had volunteered his father for disaster. He wondered why, in her anxiety, she hadn't suggested someone of her own blood. Perhaps that was the very reason. She had chosen a distant target, a kinless quarry, with the fervent hope that it was not one of her own.

'It's Robert,' Sheila said. She saw her mother pale, her hand clutching the draining-board, her knuckles white with pain. It was a blinding vision of her wretched unmanageable love for her son, and Sheila put her arm on her shoulder. 'He's not dead,' she said quickly.

'He's hurt?' Mrs Joseph whispered. The tears were gathering.

'No. There's nothing wrong with him.'

'Then what in God's name is the bad news?'

'He's in prison.' She should have been relieved, Sheila thought. Having so painfully envisaged her son's death, and having it denied, should have been enough for her. For Robert to be simply alive should be enough. But nothing was ever enough for her mother. 'I knew he'd come to a bad end,' she shrilled.

Buster almost laughed aloud. His grandmother had not for one moment entertained the possibility that her son was innocent, that there had been some frame-up or perhaps a miscarriage of justice. She simply wasn't on his side. She had not even wanted to know the charge. Robert was her son, the no-good, the drop-out, he who had caused her so much heartache, he who had sent his father to an early grave, he was all of him rotten, that Robert, whose name only a short while ago had thrust her into the land of grief and sorrow.

'What will people say?' she said, as was monotonously expected of her. 'Oh my God, it will be in the papers. Oh the shame of it.'

Sheila hardened. 'Don't you want to know what he's in for?' she said. 'And does it occur to you, perhaps, that he wasn't guilty?'

'Of course he's guilty,' Mrs Joseph said, 'if they've sent him to prison.'

'I don't want any coffee,' Sheila said.

'I don't understand you. One minute you want coffee, and the next minute you change your mind. Who wants coffee anyhow?' she shouted turning off the gas under the kettle. 'Who can eat with such heart-break? Will it be in the papers?' she pleaded.

'Don't you want to know what he's inside for?'

'What does it matter?' Mrs Joseph said. 'He's in prison. My son the prisoner.'

'It does matter, for God's sake. He could have murdered someone.'

'Oh my God,' Mrs Joseph sat down. Sheila could see that the strain was real.

'Well he didn't,' she said. 'He's got two years for selling drugs.'

'What did I tell him? What did I tell you all?' Mrs Joseph was back in harness. 'That holiday in India, that Ashram rubbish, drugs, that's all it was. Your poor father said the same. Why d'you think your father had a heart-attack?'

'So Robert's a murderer after all.' Sheila could not resist the shoddy conclusion.

'I never said that,' Mrs Joseph shouted, wondering what

it was exactly that she had said, and how best she could extricate herself from the monstrous accusation she had levelled at her son. 'It's not true,' she said. 'You know I don't mean it, but it won't do *him* any harm to think so.'

'That's a terrible thing to say,' Sheila said.

'Well I wouldn't say it to his face,' she parried. 'Where is he?'

'They're taking him to Strangeways Prison in Manchester. For two years.'

'Manchester,' she echoed. 'For two years.'

'What does it matter where he is, if he's in prison all the time?' Sheila said.

'Can he have visitors?'

Sheila remembered Robert's parting words, making it quite clear that even in his sad isolation he would not welcome the rare visitor in the shape of his mother. Well he'll have to change his mind, she thought angrily. It's his mother. She's entitled to see her son. 'Once a month, to begin with,' she said.

'Will you come with me?'

Her mother's assumption that she would be his first visitor, and probably the only one who would ever want to go, did not offend her. She saw it as a reluctant gesture of affection. 'It's my duty to go,' her mother was saying, and Sheila forgave her because she knew that that wasn't what she meant at all.

'You love him very much, don't you?' Sheila said.

'He's my son.' Again the call to duty.

'But you love him. Say it, Mama. It'll help you to say it.'

Mrs Joseph took Sheila's hand and let the tears flow.

'Say it, Mama,' Sheila insisted, swallowing the lump in her throat.

'I'm his mother,' Mrs Joseph said.

A little closer.

'Say you love him.' Now it was almost an order.

'What are you doing to me?' Mrs Joseph sobbed. It was

as close as she would ever come to capitulation.

'I'll make you some coffee,' Sheila said.

'Will you come with me? I don't think I could manage it alone.'

Buster's ear was glued to his wall in wonderment. His poor grandmother actually had a heart after all. He could work on her with smiles and chuckles and all the blackmailing paraphernalia of infant cunning. She might even offset Robert's absence for a while. And now it was possible that they would go and see him. He willed it to happen.

'We'll go together at the end of the month,' Sheila said. 'I'll make the arrangements.'

Buster smiled. There was a silence outside the wall and in it he heard the unspoken declaration of a bond. They held the silence long enough to confirm and to license whatever hate, spleen or fury would forever be part of their daily converse.

Note from Dr Brown. I have elsewhere commented on the change in Buster's handwriting which accurately reflected the varying conditions of his life. His calligraphy was not the only clue. There were changes too in his style. When describing the straightforward events of his outside world, his style tends to be slipshod and languid. On the other hand, when he dwells philosophically in interior monologue, his manner of writing enters the realms of poetry. As the journal progresses, the latter idiom is more and more in evidence and it is testimony to his gradual withdrawal from the reality of his situation into the realms of fantasy and imagination. The section of his journal which deals with Robert's trial is especially rich in both styles. At times it is patently dull with a succession of prosaic facts; at others its phrasing soars like an aria. It occurred to me that had Buster not been so determined in the choice of music as a career, he might well have considered fiction. The style of the best writers, I am told, is a mixture of the perfect and the downright shoddy.

Chapter 6

Mrs Joseph had slept fitfully. In her dreams, the train doors were sealed at Manchester station. She cried out to be released, but everyone ignored her. Her own screams had woken her and she heartily wished she could sleep the day away. She wanted very much to see her son, but she was frightened. She was unsure of his reception. Perhaps he might even refuse to see her. For a moment she thought she would plead illness, and leave the journey to Sheila. But she wanted to see him desperately.

I shall be on my best behaviour, she decided. I shall not put a foot wrong. I shall call him Robbie, and perhaps he will forgive me. But she knew the folly of such a thought, that vocabulary, however tailored, does not heal; that silence is more remedial. And time. But Mrs Joseph had difficulty with silence. And she was too impatient to give time, time. She wanted immediate reconciliation, immediate oblivion of the past; she wanted to order forgiveness, and she expected that order to be obeyed. She hadn't meant it when she had welcomed him back from India with the cry of 'murderer'. He knew she hadn't meant it. He was simply using it to punish her for other reasons. And these she could not fathom. Or rather, she could not risk their understanding. She was going to Manchester to do her bounden maternal duty, her only luggage, her contraband undeclarable love.

As the train drew into Manchester station, Sheila began to panic. Robert was expecting her. She had written to the authorities to that respect. She had also applied and received a permit for her mother, and it was possible that Robert knew nothing of the extra visitor, and there was no doubt that he would extend her little welcome. All through the journey from London she had tried to prepare her mother for a possibly cool reception. But fixed in her mother's mind was the idea that she herself was the primary visitor and that Sheila had only come along for the ride. So it was difficult to discuss Robert's welcome on the basis of such a misguided premise. It had never occurred to Mrs Joseph that anybody else would volunteer to make the tedious journey to Manchester unless it was their duty. She felt the visit incumbent on her, though secretly she deeply longed and feared to see him. Which was why she had asked Sheila to accompany her, rather in the same manner as she had asked her support in her visit to the old-age home, a third party, to offset or postpone, and perhaps even nullify the guilts and accusations that such a visit promoted.

'I hope he'll be pleased to see us,' was all Sheila could say as they got off the train. 'I mean,' she added, with growing courage, and by way of preparation, 'you hardly ever saw him when he was free. He might think you've come to gloat on his imprisonment.'

'Don't you talk to me like that,' Mrs Joseph was angry. 'I don't want to have an argument with you. You think I haven't got enough heartache, just coming here?'

It was impossible to talk to her. In any case, she had little appetite for it. Nowadays she seemed to tire very quickly, and her body felt unwieldy and cumbersome. She would have been happier resting at home, but all she knew from Robert's single letter to date was that he was desperate for a visit, so desperate in fact, that he might even, she hoped, accept her companion.

Outside the station they queued for a taxi, and when their turn came, they both silently got inside.

'Where to?' the driver asked.

Mrs Joseph was not prepared to divulge their shameful destination, and she looked at Sheila. 'You tell him,' she said.

But Sheila had no shame, and her mother's reticence fed her directions to the driver with a sense almost of pride. 'Strangeways Prison,' she said, loud and clear.

The cabbie received the news with indifference and he flicked his meter-flag and was on his way. And now that Sheila knew there was no turning back, she panicked again, and Buster fluttered inside her as an echo of her own distress. Or so she thought. But in fact, Buster fluttered with anticipation. The prospect of hearing Robert once more, despite the calibre of the rest of the audience, excited him. The meeting might hold out for him some irrevocable reason to obey the natural order and to make his début on time. He hoped that Robert would provide some purpose to his future, that perhaps by some wild turn of fortune, he might actually come home with them in the train. He tried not to hope for too much. From his eavesdropping, he knew that this was only a visit, and from his finger-span he knew too that Robert had only spent a short while inside. But good behaviour would give him an early parole, and perhaps if he was as good as gold, he might even be waiting for him outside the delivery room. There must be someone in whose arms he could relax his limbs without fear of the damage in the embrace. He knew now that he would never lie easily in his father's arms; he already viewed him with too much pity. And his mother's embrace would strangle him, gentle as she might force it to be. He listened and heard the silence. Sometimes their silences were more acrimonious than their talk, and he sensed that this was one of them. He took his ear away from the wall and slept a little, lulled by the throb of the taxi engine. There would be time enough and matter enough to overhear, once they had moved in on their quarry.

The taxi drew up at the gates of the prison. Mrs Joseph was wary of getting out, in case anybody should see her, and she hid behind Sheila's ample bulk as she paid the cabbie off. They walked to the prison door, and Sheila rang the bell. Mrs Joseph looked around furtively. She wished they would open the door quickly and not leave the two of them standing there, available to all the stares of the sundry policemen who paced the yard. Such shame her son had brought upon her. 'Thank God your father's not alive,' she said to Sheila, as they waited in their full exposure.

A policeman opened a short wooden door, and they had to step over a rise to get inside. Sheila showed him their permit. He glanced at it and handed it over to an assistant. '406B' he said. 'Joseph's the name.'

Mrs Joseph tried to imagine that she was in a boarding-school and that she had come for Parents' Day, and once inside the vast assembly hall she would be greeted by an eager line of teachers, awaiting their turn to congratulate her on the brilliance of her son.

'406B,' the assistant said, having found the relevant file. 'A model prisoner.'

Mrs Joseph took heart, swelling with pride. They were saying lovely things about her boy, and it took her a little time to re-adjust to her present location.

They were told to go to the visitors' waiting-room, from where they would eventually be called. Mrs Joseph resented having to join others, even though they were of her present kind. Her image of herself was one of exclusivity, of something quite special. She felt totally superior to everybody else, without ever feeling the reverse inferiority which is usually endemic in that condition. 'Why can't we wait here?' she asked Sheila.

'We're in a prison,' Sheila said heartlessly, 'and we have to obey the rules.'

They went to the door marked 'Visitors'. Again Mrs Joseph refused the initiative and stood aside for Sheila to open it. Perhaps if the other visitors saw Sheila enter first, with her bulk shrieking her condition, they would show some deference, some respect, which respect would infect other matters they might be obliged to discuss. She followed Sheila inside.

A row of cheerful misery lined the wall, upright on a wooden bench. Most of the visitors were women, and they looked at Sheila with a mixture of contempt and pity. They shifted along the bench to accommodate her. Sheila sat down and though there was enough room, her mother remained standing, as if unwilling to accept classification. The woman next to Sheila eyed her neighbour's swelling, and said with infinite pity, "Is Dad's inside, is 'e?"

'No,' Sheila said quickly. 'It's my brother.'

'That'll be his uncle then,' another visitor offered her quick deduction. 'Uncle Nick,' she laughed. 'Run in the family, does it?'

'Does what?' Sheila said.

'The nick.'

'No. This is the first time.'

'There's always got to be a first time, dear. My first was twenty years ago. My old man it was then. He's still in and out. Then I've got two sons done their time. Three sons I've got, but one of them's always gone straight. I got a brother here too. Runs in the family, see.'

'Oh yes.' Sheila wanted to show some interest. She didn't want to be judged a snob.

'Know this place like the back of my hand,' the woman rambled on. 'In the old days they used to have armchairs. Then it got a bit crowded and they put the benches in. Used to give you a cup of tea too, sometimes. Nothing like that now. There's no service nowadays,' she lamented. 'Like a factory it is now. In, out. In, out.'

Mrs Joseph sat down, partly because standing was tiring, but mainly because she wanted to withdraw Sheila from the discussion, which threatened to engulf her. She and her daughter were not part of this regular rabble, and she wanted to make that quite clear.

'Make yourself comfortable dear,' another woman said,

as Mrs Joseph sat down. Then eyeing her Persian lamb coat, she said, making their equality totally clear, 'We're all the same in here, you know.'

The wind was suddenly taken out of Mrs Joseph's sails. She wished she'd worn her cloth coat, though she was convinced that, even in rags, her higher status would have been abundantly clear.

'You're 'is Mum, are you?' the woman said.

There was no point in denying it, and Mrs Joseph nodded.

'Don't upset yourself dear,' the mother of all prisoners said, stretching her hand over to touch Mrs Joseph's fur sleeve. 'You'll find they're cheery enough. You'll be surprised. It's not a bad life inside. My old man often says, when he's out, that he misses it. Misses the companionship, see. A man likes to be with his mates.'

The thought of her son actually making friends in this place appalled her.

'I don't think he'll make friends here,' Mrs Joseph said, in misguided support for her son. 'They're not his kind of people.'

There was a silence, then one of the visitors giggled and they all took it up into a roar of laughter.

'Nothing special about your son, dear,' one of them said. 'Once they're inside, they're all the same. Just numbers they are, see.'

Then a man at the end of the row, who so far had contributed nothing to the conversation, offered his explanation. 'They're all in the same boat, see, Missus. And so are we,' he added for good measure. 'The lot of us. It makes no difference whether you've got a fur coat or you haven't,' he was being cruelly specific, 'it makes no difference if you've got a fortune or not a penny, you're in the same boat as us because you've got someone inside. So don't you be getting any ideas.'

The other women were delighted that the Persian coat

had been put in its place, and especially delighted that it was a man who had done it. Thus their sisterhood had not been threatened. So delighted were they in fact, that they could afford to chide him a little for his lack of manliness.

'Don't go taking any notice of him,' one of them said. 'We're not all equal. Stands to reason. But in a place like this, we've all got one thing in common. Plain bloody misery.'

The other sisters nodded. Their member had maintained the impact, but had softened the blow.

There was a silence, always uneasy in a prison. It gives off an echo, without hint of population; it confirms the loneliness of those who have lost the habit of communication, yet ache for company.

'I don't know,' one of the women said after a while, 'it's not so bad. Gets you out a bit. And it means a lot to the poor buggers inside. See some of their own.'

Sheila wondered how much it would mean to Robert, and again she panicked at the thought of his response. She hoped that the waiting-period would go on, and perhaps curtail the official visiting hour.

The door opened and a large woman came in. She was dishevelled, her coat unbuttoned and one shoe-lace undone. It was as if she'd left a flurry of haste behind her. She was given a hero's welcome.

'Well if it isn't old Mabel,' one of the regulars said. 'Back again, old girl.'

'Can't keep away,' Mabel said, laughing.

'Who is it this time?'

'My baby,' she said. 'Donald. It's his first stretch. Like father, like son.' She planted her heavy bulk next to the Persian lamb. She stared at it in astonishment. 'Got to say it,' she said, 'you get a better class of person in the nick nowadays. Your first time, luv?'

Mrs Joseph resented the familiarity, and the automatic

assumption that she was and would continue to be part of their life-pattern.

'Yes,' she answered. 'We've never been in one of these places before.' She indicated Sheila at her side as sharing this new experience.

'Pity for her in her condition,' the newcomer said.

'It's her brother,' one of the other women explained.

'Oh yes,' Mabel said, settling herself in for a cosy chat. 'What's he in for then?'

Mrs Joseph was reminded of the time she was hospitalised. She lay in a Florence Nightingale ward, the rows of beds aligned on each side, presided over in the middle by a rota of nurses who varied from the strict to the lenient, and both kinds were ineffectual. But between them they maintained an air of formality in the ward, and you had to be lying in your bed at least a few days before you ventured to enquire of your neighbour what had brought her to circumstances similar to your own. Until then you had to establish some modicum of goodwill. You had to have given evidence of a measure of understanding and sympathy. But even when the ground was well prepared, you would never pose the question outright. You would skirt it with all manner of tangential enquiry, as to the present state of your neighbour's temperature or bowel movement. Then you would enquire about the projected length of her stay. There was much to be deduced from marginal investigation. And it was during the course of this method of enquiry that very often your neighbour would gladly volunteer the nature of her indisposition and propriety would have been satisfied.

But here there was no preamble, no loop-hole for apology before the beans were spilled. Excuses would have to come later, and, in such placing, would have little effect. Nevertheless, she would give it a try. She certainly couldn't trust Sheila to handle the situation with any kind of aplomb, and as her daughter was about to volunteer the information,

Mrs Joseph said, 'It wasn't his fault. He got into bad company.'

The women laughed.

'What did the bad company do then?' the fat woman said.

Mrs Joseph was not prepared to go any further, but she had no power to stop Sheila from satisfying their curiosity. Which she did, quietly, and with evident shame. 'Selling drugs,' she said. She was glad in that company that it wasn't rape. But from their contemptuous reaction, it was almost as offensive. They looked at each other, and shifted away, as if from contamination.

'That's terrible,' one of them said.

'Don't approve of that at all,' said another.

'What *do* you approve of?' Mrs Joseph was riled at their judgement.

'Most of our lot's in for breaking and entering. At least it's an honest trade, and it takes a lot of guts, too. But drugs. Turning poor innocent kids onto the stuff. It's criminal.'

'Sorry for your lad, I am,' the man visitor said. 'He'll be put into Coventry, with all those rape buggers, sure as I'm sitting here. Same sort of crime, really. Poor innocent defenceless kids.'

The ostracism that no doubt obtained in Robert's prison cell was surely and speedily transferred to the waiting-room. The women quite positively turned their backs on Sheila and Mrs Joseph, as if they carried a disease. It was not a good beginning. Whenever Sheila was in her mother's company, the blame for any embarrassment could be placed squarely on Mrs Joseph's door-step. This situation was different. Her mother had done nothing but turned an attentive ear to their discussion. The coat of course was a mistake. It roused immediate antagonism, and although most of the women in the room probably owned a fur coat paid for out of their husbands' pickings and which they wore every Saturday for going on the town, they had better sense than to flaunt their ill-gotten gains in a house of correction. She bridled at her mother's stupidity.

The other visitors continued their conversation. From what Sheila could hear, most of their talk centred around their families. They gave the impression of knowing each other very well. It was possible that they were bound together by their husbands' absences. They did not pity their men. They accepted imprisonment as part of the risk of a chosen trade, one in which the pay-off far outstripped the losses. At most, their men's temporary absences were a source of irritation. When the fuses blew, or the fire burnt low, it was good to have a man about the house. They talked about those willing handymen, always at your door if your man was gone. And they talked of them with contempt. The act of adultery was, in their eyes, the most heinous crime of all. Whatever moral judgement they had, it was concentrated on that one act of sinning, and not one of them would have tolerated it in the others.

Sheila looked at her mother, and for a moment shared her sense of outraged helplessness.

'I'm glad your father isn't alive,' Mrs Joseph said.

Sheila said nothing, but she thought that what her mother had said was very silly. Of course she wasn't glad that her father was dead. Incompatible as they were, she preferred even his company to her present lonely state. In any case, her father would have survived Robert's disgrace, as stoutly as her mother. Together they would have found a rationale to account for his downfall; they would have found others to blame, his school, his teacher, his friends, or society in general. But never once would they allow each other blame; together they would avoid confrontation, protecting each other's needling conscience. Such a pursuit was hard to follow alone, so why did her mother make such silly statements.

'Of course you're not glad,' Sheila said.

'Don't you start telling me how I'm supposed to be feeling,' Mrs Joseph whispered. She did not want an audience for her fury. Family disputes were private, and certainly were not to be overheard by this riff-raff, this mob of no account, whose men were regular criminals who spent half their time in prison. What was she doing in such company, she asked herself. She resolved never to come again, that Robert could do his time visitless, at least from her, and she couldn't imagine who else would want to trail all the way to Manchester. Sheila would be a mother soon, with better things to do. I hope he's grateful that we've come at all, she thought to herself.

The door opened and the warder told them to follow him. 'Don't all rush at once,' he said, holding back the mob of eager women, those without guilt, scruple or shame, their tongues bubbling with a month of news, snippets of information, gossip, questions, framed in their stubborn and tenacious loyalty. Sheila and her mother, not of their class or number, lagged behind, and brought up the rear of the column as they filed down the long corridor into the visiting-hall. Once inside, the doors clanged shut behind them, and they were directed to wooden benches facing a large grille.

'Oh my God,' Mrs Joseph said when she saw the bars, and realised for the first time that somewhere behind them was her son. Sheila put her hand on her arm. She was suddenly sorry for her, and she prayed that Robert would feign some kind of welcome.

There was a row of about thirty chairs, stretched at intervals behind the grille. Directly in front of each chair was another, with the grille between. Sheila realised that only one visitor was allowed at a time, and she was glad of it. She would try to go first and warn Robert of their mother's presence. They waited. Suddenly there was silence. The women at last held their tongues as if they were preparing for as much privacy as the public assembly-

95

hall would allow.

'Wiston,' one of the warders shouted. He entered from a door behind the grille, shepherding his prisoner towards a chair. Mrs Wiston made a dash from the bench and settled herself in front of the prisoner. Sheila watched her. The woman looked about her, shy with her isolation. She was obviously having difficulty in even greeting her man, since all eyes were on them both.

'Come on then,' Wiston's warder said from behind. 'You haven't got for ever.'

The audience tittered and gave Mrs Wiston some courage. She turned to look at her inaccessible target and clutched her fingers round the grille. Mr Wiston was seen to be whispering. It was clear that the Wistons had opened their joint account.

Another warder entered and called his prisoner's name, and a woman rose to claim her property. Thereafter the men arrived in quick succession. Sheila scanned their faces. But for differences in age, they all looked very similar. It was the uniform they wore, trousers of dull grey, and a fitted grey jacket that buttoned to the neck. Their hair-style, too, was of a common cut, razored short, as if after an epidemic of lice. Then suddenly the call of 'Joseph' was heard, and both women found difficulty in pinpointing the source of the sound. They scanned the line of prisoners entering through the side door, but none of them bore any resemblance to Robert. For a moment Mrs Joseph hoped there'd been some monumental mistake, that some other son of a poor Joseph had been a-peddling, and that her own special drop-out was minding his own business in Earls Court. Then she spotted one who sat alone, shadowed by his warder, both of them waiting, both of them hiding disappointment. She looked again, and by the prickings in her shrunken womb, she knew him. She said no word to Sheila and made straightway for the empty chair before him. Sheila stared at her as she rose, wondering where she was going. She watched her as she made for the empty chair. Then she looked at the opposing number. 406B, it said, stamped on his chest pocket as if he was a parcel for delivery. There was no other indication that he was her brother save that the number tallied with the one the receiving warder had issued at reception. She looked at his face. It was tense and angry. Then he spoke, possibly in response to something his mother had said, and though she could not decipher the words, she knew that what was coming out of his mouth was an articulated sneer. Her heart heaved as she saw him turn his back on her, as if, as far as he was concerned, the visit was over. The warder put his hand on Robert's shoulder, urging him to think again, while his mother turned and stared at Sheila, her face a mute appeal. Sheila got up, and as she approached the visitor's chair, she saw tears on her mother's face, and a rising hatred of Robert swelled inside her. Her mother got up and walked towards her. For once, words were failing her. She shrugged her shoulders and motioned Sheila to take her place. Sheila put her arm round her. It was such a rare gesture that it shocked them both. 'Don't worry,' Sheila said, 'it's an upsetting time.'

She watched her back to the wooden bench, where she sat alone, like a wallflower, wishing to God that she'd never come.

Sheila moved into the attack, for attack it was going to be, for all her compassion on his behalf had drained out of her, and had rechannelled itself towards her mother. He felt her there, and without even looking at her, he snarled, 'Why in God's name did you bring her?'

She waited for his full face. 'She's your mother,' she said. It was a fatuous thing to say, she knew, yet that was exactly what she meant, that within that status, she was entitled to some feedback, some pleasure even, yes, even some gratitude that she had made the journey to tell him in whatever way she had, that she loved him and feared for his welfare.

97

Robert looked at her. 'Is that what all mothers are made of?' he said with disdain. 'D'you know her first words to me?'

She stared at the hardness in him.

'She came all the way to Manchester to say to me, what have I done to deserve this. As if it were she behind bars.' He paused. 'I haven't waited a whole month just to listen to that crap,' he said.

'She's worried,' Sheila said. 'She's anxious, and she wouldn't bloody well care about you at all, if she didn't love you.'

'I don't want to see her again,' he said quietly.

At her side, Mrs Wiston was regaling her spouse with the recent antics of their children. Wiston was laughing. There was no envy, no bitterness in his face, just the sheer joy of sharing. The occasional incarceration was part and parcel of his trade, and they both accepted it without question. On the other side of Sheila, an older woman sat listening as her son listed their daily menus. He dwelt long on the Sunday bill of fare, salivating each item. 'You don't sound in a hurry to get home,' his mother joked.

He twiddled his little finger through the grille. 'They don't make a Yorkshire pudding like you do, Mum.'

Sheila looked along the line. Between some of the grille partitions there were silences, but there was no sense of either partner scratching in panic for dialogue. These were silences that they shared often enough by their own firesides: it was a simple transference of home from home. She looked back at Robert and wondered why their family was so abnormal.

'Have you made any friends here?' she said. She was prepared to forget the visit's poor beginning, and time was passing. It would be another month before he would be entitled to another visit. And then she realised that her pregnancy would be too advanced for her to see him again, and she wondered whom she could send for his comfort.

'One or two,' he was saying. He too had decided to ignore their first non-words.

'What are they like?'

'One's a carpenter,' Robert said. 'The other's unemployed.'

'What are they in for?'

'Same as me,' he said. 'That's why we stick together. No one else talks to us. That's the only reason we're friends.'

She looked at his drawn and desolate face. Theirs was a friendship he obviously found faintly resistible.

'What are you going to do, when you come out?' she said. Pehaps she shouldn't have asked. That kind of question belonged to her mother. The assumption that one had to do something of value, something of note, that one had to *be* somebody was a sanguine expectation that had dogged them both throughout their childhood, and it was hardly the time and certainly not the place to raise its ghost again. And that's exactly how Robert saw it.

'You talk like her,' he said. He had as much difficulty with her name, as she with his. They were so alike, Sheila thought, so stubborn, so frightened, so proud, and finally so untouchable.

'One thing I have decided,' he said 'I'm going away. I don't know where. But I want to rid myself of the whole family.'

'But you'll be an uncle soon,' Sheila said. She wanted to cry. She needed Robert, and not only for unclehood. She thought of Bernard and the growing distance between them. She needed a brother either as a bridge or a defence. In those roles her mother had proved less than adequate. 'Don't you want to see your nephew,' she said. She tried to give light to her voice, but instead it broke with her effort.

'It may be a niece,' he joked, embarrassed by her concern. 'I'll send it a postcard from foreign parts,' he said. 'That way I can start it on stamp collecting.'

Sheila felt sick inside, but it was Buster's own sickening

that hurt her. He'd heard Robert's decision and it sounded irrevocable. His future now looked very black indeed. It was now no longer a question of delaying his début but of cancelling it altogether. He had much to think about. He did not need to listen any more. Robert would not be persuaded to change his mind. He looked at his left hand and stretched it to its limit. What a pity, he thought. With the stretch between the fingers and the fine arch of the palm, it was tailor-made for double-stopping.

'When is it due?' Robert said.

'In another four months or so.'

'I'll still be here,' he said. 'Will you let me know what it is?'

'I'll bring it to see you,' she said.

'No,' he said quickly. 'This isn't a place for a child.'

'But it'll only be a baby.'

'One can wreak havoc from the beginning,' he said, and if Buster had still had his ear to the wall, he would sadly have seconded Robert's opinion.

Sheila looked at the clock. There was another half hour to be disposed of. 'Would you speak to Mama again?' she said. 'Please.'

'I've nothing to say to her, and I'm not sitting here for her eternal reproach.'

'Please see her,' Sheila begged. She didn't wait for his response. It was mean, she knew, to take advantage of his captive position, but she couldn't face the journey home unable to deal with her own anger and her pity. She went back to the wooden bench.

'So?' Mrs Joseph said, 'he's also had enough of you too.' She was back in harness, unbreakable, and Sheila was glad of it as her pity ebbed.

'Go and talk to him,' she said.

'What is there to say?'

'Just *be* with him,' Sheila said, though she knew that her mother had no skills in that art.

Mrs Joseph's pride prompted refusal, but at the same time she sickened for some acknowledgement from her son of the love that she tried with all her heart, and utterly failed, to show.

'Please Mama,' Sheila begged. She didn't know why she was so eager an arbiter. Neither of them wished to be with the other, yet each would regret the opportunity they had shunned. Mrs Joseph rose warily from the wooden bench. Like any professional wallflower she was equally afraid of two events. One, that she wouldn't be asked to dance, and two, that she would. She could accommodate neither proposition. Sheila watched her reluctant approach to the grille. She made to follow her, but Robert's warder caught her movement and shook his head, then he bent his mouth towards Robert's ear. Perhaps he was encouraging him to receive his mother with some semblance of grace. Robert shrugged and turned his face towards the grille. He just looked at her, and she presumably at him. But it was no mutually accepted silence between them. Each was waiting for the other to take the offensive and it was Robert who opened fire. Sheila saw her mother's shoulders shiver with the wounding, too hurt to reply, and Robert stared at her, wounded too by the pain she wrought in him. Then he put his fingers through the grille and tried to touch the lamb on her, that sacrificial outer skin of hers that his father, in his own sacrificial turn, had grafted on her. She saw his movement, and to facilitate it she moved her arm towards him, so that he could clutch at the curled fur, and for both of them it would pass for communication.

'Are they giving you enough to eat?' she said. She placed herself firmly on home ground. She needed harbour after her unwitting and painful excursion into her not-so-buried feelings.

He smiled. 'It's not Cordon Bleu,' he said, 'but it's adequate.'

'You eat it all up, do you?' she said, dragging him back

into his high chair, securing her own ground.

'Yes Mama, I eat it all up.'

'You know that if you behave yourself in these places, they let you out quicker.'

He chuckled, playing the baby she needed.

'Now you be a good boy, now, won't you,' she said. She was almost happy inside herself. Behind that grille, he could have been her little Robbie in his play-pen. She leaned forward as if to divulge a confidence, and Robert's warder did likewise. 'You know Bernard,' she said.

'Of course I know Bernard,' though he realised he didn't know Bernard at all, but as a cipher who had eased his sister's departure from home.

'He tells me the business is expanding. He needs help. He admires you a lot.'

Robert knew what was coming, the cunning device of her preamble, and he prayed that here of all places, she might leave him in peace.

But she laboured. 'I'm thinking, when you come out of here,' she said, 'you should take over the business. Then your poor father would rest in peace.'

Robert rose. He'd had enough. She'd broken the spell that for a moment was so finally and joyfully woven between them. 'I don't want to talk about it,' he said. He nodded to his warder, who, with his hand on his shoulder, led him away.

The clock showed ten minutes of visiting time to run; Mrs Joseph stared at it. She couldn't understand his abrupt departure. Had she said something wrong? It had all seemed so well between them. Perhaps he was too overcome by their sudden affection. She clung to that solution, else she would have to face herself as cause of the disruption. All I asked him, she said to herself, was to go into the business. Is that so terrible?

Sheila looked at the row of men behind the grille and saw the yawning gap of Robert along the line. She was sorry he had left before the appointed time, but she was glad too that it was all over, that they could each go home to their own separate torments, each finding comfort in a love that was only negotiable in absence. She took her mother's arm.

'What happened?' she said.

'Should *I* know? All of a sudden he's had enough.'

Sheila knew better than to enquire about their conversation. 'It was too much of a strain for him, I suppose,' she said.

'That's exactly what I thought,' Mrs Joseph said, glad of an ally in her self-delusion. 'Next time perhaps, he'll relax a bit.'

'Next time, you'll have to come alone,' Sheila said. 'I'll be too near my time.'

'What about Bernard?' she said. 'Wouldn't he want to go?'

'They've never been very close,' Sheila said.

'Well they should be,' Mrs Joseph asserted. 'What are families for, after all?'

Occasionally it was convenient to leave the kinship door open.

As the train shunted out of Manchester station, Buster awoke. He knew by the sound of the engines that the visit was over, and that they were on their way home. When he'd just fallen off to sleep, he knew that he had made an important decision, and his nerve was in no way less resolute when he awoke. He knew his decision was the right one, yet he regretted that it had to be taken. Out of long habit, he leant his ear to the listening-wall, and this is what he heard.

Sheila (niggling):	What did you say to him that he went away so suddenly?
Mrs Joseph (innocent):	Me? What should I say? We were talking nicely. About the food. About what they gave him to eat.

Sheila (angry):	Yes, but what else?
Mrs Joseph:	Why are you shouting at me? All of a sudden, it's my fault.
Sheila:	You must have said something to upset him.
Mrs Joseph:	All I said was he should come into the business when he comes out. (*Quickly*) Together with Bernard of course.
Sheila:	So that's why he got up and left. Why can't you just let him go? Once and for all.
Mrs Joseph:	When have I interfered with him? He wanted to sell drugs. Did I stop him? Look here, you Mrs Know-every-thing, when your baby is born, you'll sing a different tune. You'll want him to do what you want him to do. Already you've got him a violin. Already you've got him a teacher. Already his name is down for the best schools. But for you, Mrs Know-everything, that's not interfering.

Buster heard the terrible silence outside the wall, broken only by the metronomic rhythms of the train. In vain, he waited for his mother's denial, or some statement from her that all her plans for him were mere fantasy. But not a word. Her silence in the face of her mother's accusations was a recognition of a common subcutaneous sisterhood. Between his grandmother and mother was a difference only in age.

Buster took his ear away. If he had needed a last straw to confirm his decision, his mother's silence had neatly provided it. For months now he had glued his ear to the listening-wall and winced at their crippling presumptions, their offensive trust, hoping all the time that between their outrageous syllables he could sniff a semblance of love. But there was nothing but their unbearable expectation. If he could fulfil that, then and only then, would he be entitled to loving. That message, over the months, had been increasingly clear. No. He was not going out to all that, to be colonised, to be blackmailed, expected of, disappointed in, reproved for. He was going to stay exactly where he was. He was aware that perhaps he was making gynaecological history. He wondered whether anyone had ever done it before. It occurred to him that there was some undeniable logic in such an action, that possibly many infants, eavesdropping on their presumptive families, might well have decided that they were better off where they were, no matter what hell that might turn out to be. And how would one ever know, he wondered, how many of those children had in fact refused performance, and were slotted into the catalogues of still and aborted births. Perhaps, he thought, there was indeed no such thing as a still-birth, or involuntary abortion. That every day, all over the world, in millions of breeding-places, little people listened-in, and concluded that they didn't fancy what they'd heard. Not one bit. And they turned away and hid themselves, praying for better luck next time. And that was what he was about to do. He would hide behind the curtained tubes of his little cell, and refuse deliverance. If he emerged into the raucous market-place of such a family, with all its manoeuvring, its cunning, its bargaining, he would stand no chance. By staying where he was, there was perhaps a remote possibility that he could survive and even defeat them from within. He viewed his little cell, and shivered with the first experience of loneliness, that only a foetus can know. He had to conclude that it would take as much courage to stay in his cell as to leave it behind.

Note from Dr Brown. Who knows at what exact moment little Buster made his momentous decision? For my part, I believe it came later, possibly during the process of labour, when he was faced with the fact that he could not put off his decision any longer. He had wavered so often and for so long between coming out or staying where he was, that only this factor would have catapulted him into making a choice. But in the business of birthing one has better things to do with one's time than keep up a journal. I myself have attended many deliveries, and the sheer process of labour is a full-time occupation for both mother and child. Again I have used the writer's licence to offend chronology.

There is one more comment that in my capacity as a doctor I feel I must make at this stage. Buster's vain hope that he might 'defeat them from within' – this from the actual text of his journal – must have sprung from a certain desperation, for there is no logic in it. A foetus that, for whatever reason, doesn't emerge, is doomed to natural abortion, so that no battle could have started, let alone be waged. Or so I thought. As it turned out, I was wrong, and I have no hesitation in admitting it. The borders of medicine are not necessarily scientific. Only a bigoted member of my profession would insist on that security. But I am prepared to allow for another kind of frontier to medicine, that which fringes on the supernatural, or whatever word one may choose to use to cover our lack of understanding. The subsequent contents of Buster's journal were a warning to any man of medicine, or indeed of any other field, that he should forever keep an open mind. Buster *did* survive, but at a cost, as subsequent events will show.

Chapter 7

Buster woke up in the middle of the night. His little cell vibrated with a womb-quake. He looked at his finger-span. An augmented fourth. His time had come, or, as he had decided, his non-time. Ripeness is all.

In her double bed, Sheila called out to Bernard, who had once more laid himself down in the study, but more for comfort than pride. Sheila felt an unaccustomed twinge of pain in the region of her back, and she knew she had come to term. 'It's started,' she said, as Bernard opened the door. 'Ring Clarissa.'

'You're not serious,' Bernard said. Surely that whole business of Clarissa playing at the birth had been a joke.

'Do as I say,' Sheila ordered him.

Meekly he went to the telephone. It was three o'clock in the morning. 'D'you know the time?' he said, before he risked dialling.

'It doesn't matter. She's expecting my call.'

'You're crazy,' he said, under his breath, and he dialled Clarissa's number. She was indeed waiting, for she answered immediately in a perky voice.

'Shall I go straight to the clinic?' she said.

'I suppose so,' Bernard answered, 'if that's what you've arranged.'

'I'll see you there, then,' she said. 'Oh I'm so excited.' She put the phone down. There was no question of it, he thought. Both women were round the bend.

'I'll get the car out,' he said. 'D'you need any help?' He watched her as she manoeuvred the bulk of her around the bed, and then she stopped, transfixed in fear.

'What's the matter?' he said.

107

'I'm frightened, Bernard.'

Buster put his hands over his ears. Now was no time for wavering. He wasn't going to change his mind, conned by pity or false compassion. But he daren't risk listening. Though his resolve was firm, he was, after all, only human. He would eavesdrop no more, at least until after the abortive delivery. And perhaps never again, he thought. He was not sure that he could survive in his cell after his mother's term had passed. He knew of no precedent. But his will to survive was so keen, his appetite so sharp, that it must prolong his life, even perhaps till the end of hers. Then he would eavesdrop again, and hope for a better harmony. He decided to try and sleep, and so conserve his strength.

'It'll be all right,' Bernard said feebly. He ventured to put his arms around her. For a moment, as she stood there, panicked and pale, the thought crossed his mind that he might lose her. He held her as close as her condition would allow, hoping she could not smell his own fear. 'Just think,' he said, 'by tomorrow, I'll be a father.' As he heard the word, he accepted for the first time that there would be a change in his status. It was now no longer a dream, a piece of make-believe. Very soon he must assume paternity. For the first time too, he realised that he would change, but in which way he could not specify. Still, the prospect of any change excited him. He didn't know why, but already, while only on the brink of fatherhood, he felt a sense of power. Perhaps it was because his seed had proved fruitful. He hoped it was just that, and only that, for any other reason might have been suspect. 'I'll get the car,' he said again. He could hardly wait for his baby to arrive.

Clarissa was already at the hospital. They were shown into a small private room with the standard bowl of flowers provided by the clinic just for starters. Bernard and Clarissa waited outside the room, while the doctor examined Sheila. 'It'll be a little while yet,' he said, when he emerged. 'Probably not till morning. I advise you both to go home and get some sleep.'

'I have to stay,' Clarissa said. 'I'm going to play the baby into the world.' She didn't know about Bernard, but it was clear she considered her own presence as essential.

'You mean you're going to play as the baby is born?' the doctor said. He was smiling a little.

'That's right,' she said. 'He will be born to music.'

'I rather look forward to that,' the doctor said. 'Music while you work.' He left, and for a while Bernard and Clarissa sat by Sheila's bed. Occasionally she twitched with the pain. Bernard was nervous. He felt *de trop*, and he began to resent Clarissa's presence.

'I think you'd better phone Mama,' Sheila said.

'Can't we wait till the baby's born? Must everybody be in on the act,' he said, staring at Clarissa.

'I think she ought to know.'

'D'you want her here?'

'No, but she'd resent it if she were deprived of worrying time.'

Bernard laughed, though Sheila hadn't meant it as a joke. 'She's entitled,' Sheila said with utter seriousness. 'She's my mother.'

Buster wasn't listening. He'd given up on that pastime. In any case, it was now difficult to eavesdrop. His listening-post was shifting, and his cell was like a little barque, buffeted by storms at sea. He kept as still as he could, gathering his strength for what he knew might be his last stand.

The telephone by Sheila's bedside was equipped only for incoming calls, and Bernard was dispatched to the nearest call-box to warn Mrs Joseph of her imminent change of status. He went down the corridor, passed by the call-box at reception, and out into the street. He had no intention of calling his mother-in-law. It was enough to have Clarissa at the bedside. Sheila was disseminating to all and sundry an event which surely should have been private. Yet even he, in a way, did not want any part of it. He would have to see the concrete fact of the baby, to hold it in his arms perhaps, before he could accept the notion of fatherhood. He would not go back to the clinic, he decided. He would let the women get on with it. And in the morning, he would put on his best suit and introduce himself to what Sheila would assert was his child. Was it his, he wondered? The thought frightened him. He couldn't imagine an adulterous wife. Sheila was far too puritan, too unadventurous to put herself at such a risk. Yet it had been so long before she had managed to conceive, and often, without words, she had suspected his sterility. He'd had all the tests and all proved positive. Yet the fact remained that it had taken them over six years. Had she managed to overcome her righteous scruples, and sought a planting elsewhere? It alarmed him that he was beset by such thoughts. It would only take a little more persuasion to convince himself that he had been cuckold. Is that why she wanted her mother there, and Clarissa, a united front against his doubts and uncertainties? He had a sudden urge to run away, to run to a distant land, as Robert had done, but unlike Robert, never to return. He debated to himself for a while as to the manner of the life he would be leaving behind. The business was prospering. He lived in a large comfortable house, he had a circle of friends, he lived with a woman who was catalogued as a wife, that is, she cooked for him, she ironed his shirts, and she kept his house in order, and occasionally, at least in the old days, she would let him share her bed. Was there supposed to be more to a wife than that? he wondered. Then there would be a child, with no substantial proof that it was his. But whosoever had sired it, it would be there, and would need to be accommodated. It would be the recipient of the best education, the best teachers, the best instruments, the greatest of all expectations. And Bernard really wanted none of it. Yet he was too weak to make any protest. It would be easier for him to put himself at an inaccessible distance, and now, at this very moment, without giving himself the chance of viewing his possible offspring. But first he would have a drink to cheer him on his journey. He was not a drinking man, but he felt that such a monumental decision had to be celebrated in some way. A hearty drink would also confirm it and preclude any reversal of his plans. Besides he needed men's company. He needed to enter their camp. He needed to tell them of the enemy's position and the nature of their weaponry. He went straight to the nearest pub, and with his elbow on the bar like a time-honoured drinker, he gave a whispered and timid order for a shandy.

'I wonder what's happened to him,' Sheila said. 'There must be a telephone in the clinic. He should be back by now. In a way,' she confided to Clarissa, 'I don't mind if he stays away till morning. Somehow men are out of place here.' She twinged again with the pain, and she grasped tightly at Clarissa's hand until the spasm had run its course.

'Would you like me to start playing?' Clarissa said. 'Perhaps when he hears the music, he'll be still, and give you no pain. And he'll be eager to come out to see where the sound is coming from,' Clarissa giggled. She was embarrassing herself with her lack of personal experience and wild conjecture. But she was eager to start playing. She was never good at making conversation, especially if the onus was solely on herself, as it was in this confined room with only one thing to think about, and no expression to put it into words. Besides, she had to confess to herself that she slightly resented Sheila's condition. There were enough children in the world to feed, she thought, without adding to their number. Sheila could have adopted one of hundreds if she'd wanted one that badly.

'What are you going to play?' Sheila asked.

'I've brought the three Bach Partitas,' she said. 'They'll

keep us going for a little while. And they bear repetition,' she giggled, 'if we should go on for longer.' Already she felt herself part of the parturition and she couldn't imagine how any birth could take place without the participation of an active celebrant. She took her fiddle out of its case, rosined the bow, and tuned from the pitch of her portable metronome. 'Are you ready?' she said.

Sheila gripped the metal bars behind her head. She was having another spasm. Sheila waited for it to pass. 'They're coming very often,' she said. 'I'm sure the baby's ready.'

'You should ring for a nurse,' Clarissa said nervously.

'You do it,' Sheila said. She didn't want to take the responsibility of a false alarm. 'You go and get one,' she added, realising that no nurse would know who had put her finger on the bell.

Clarissa put down her violin and did what she was told. In a short while she came back with a nurse who asked Sheila how often the pains were coming. Sheila did not scruple to exaggerate. 'All the time,' she said.

'That's not possible,' the nurse said. 'Have you got a watch?'

Sheila nodded, tearful that her small lie had been uncovered.

'For the next half hour, I want you to time the pains,' the nurse said. 'Nothing is likely to happen until the morning.'

'That's what everyone keeps saying,' Sheila said. 'But I can feel it. I know it's coming.'

'That's how it always feels,' the nurse said, from long vicarious experience. 'Now you just relax and sit and talk to your friend.' She looked across at Clarissa, nervous of the violin in her hand. It called for some kind of comment, but it was such a bizarre article to find by a birthing bedside, that she could think of nothing to say. She smiled shyly and left the room.

As soon as she had gone, and before Sheila could start complaining again, Clarissa started her recital. She opened with Bach's 'Air on the G string'. She was obviously saving the partitas for the grand opening. Sheila listened. The sound was soothing, and she closed her eyes and tried to drink the melody into her womb. Inside her, Buster heard a muffled echo. It sounded vaguely like the Bach 'Air', that infallible encore he used to give after each recital. But his cell was no longer stereophonic. The quality of the sound was uneven, and at times, inaudible. This change of acoustic quality did not worry him. He knew that it was only temporary, and that once his cell had accepted the fact that there was no hope of turfing him out, that it was saddled with a permanent tenancy, it would give up all efforts of eviction and reassume its former home comforts. He saw how his listening-wall vibrated, and swirled into waves the fluid it contained, and he knew from past experience and with vivid recall that his expected arrival was now imminent. He offered up a silent prayer for deliverance, his own deliverance that is, and not to be confused with the deliverance they were expecting outside his cell. The sound of the violin cut out suddenly, and he heard a triple echo of his mother's screams. He flattened himself against the uterus wall, 'This is it, kiddoes,' he shouted. 'Sink or swim.'

Clarissa rang for the nurse, but she was already on her way, alerted by the sound of Sheila's screams. 'Now what's this all about?' she said, as if there were any question as to the matter of the disturbance.

'What the hell d'you think it is?' Sheila said, her anger fed by her pain. 'It's coming, and I bloody well ought to know.'

The nurse hesitated, but decided against argument. 'I'll fetch the doctor,' she said. 'We'll get you into the labour ward.'

Clarissa packed her violin. She was excited. And nervous too. Never before had she had such an audience. And she respected it. Its ear was clean, untainted by a single ugly

113

sound, innocent of manoeuvre, pristine, fresh, and totally available. No artist of whatever medium could ask for more.

The nurse returned, directing a trolley shunted by two male orderlies. Gently they shifted Sheila from her bed and wheeled her on the stretcher down the corridor. Clarissa followed.

'You can't come into the labour ward,' the nurse said, shouting back at her.

'It's all been arranged,' Sheila managed to say. 'My doctor knows all about it.'

The nurse was convinced that she had an hysterical patient on her hands, and made a mental note to warn the doctor who was in charge of the delivery.

The labour ward, as they called it, was no bigger than Sheila's private room, but it contained no bed. From the trolley Sheila could see pieces of equipment along the wall. A large sink, a weighing balance, and what looked like an oxygen cylinder with nozzle attached. They aligned her trolley with the cylinder. The nurse unhooked the nose-piece and instructed Sheila in its use. 'When you feel the pain coming,' she said, 'put this over your nose, and breathe deeply. Just relax, and breathe deeply and you won't feel the pain.'

Sheila grabbed the nozzle.

'Only when the pain is coming on,' the nurse warned her, and with little sympathy.

'It *is* on,' Sheila managed to mumble as she clamped the nozzle on her nose. 'It doesn't help,' she said after a few intakes.

'Give it a chance,' the nurse said, by now at the end of her patience.

Sheila tried again, and slowly the pain subsided. The nurse watched her and saw her relief. Then she took the tube away. 'Only when it hurts,' she said, 'or it won't work when you're really in pain.'

Sheila shivered. Was it really going to get any worse? The intervals between the pains were so relieving that they induced a sense of euphoria, and in one of those intervals she asked Clarissa to play. And Clarissa gladly complied, tucking the violin under her chin, and after a formal retuning, she started on the first Bach Partita.

The nurse looked at her in astonishment.

'It's for my baby,' Sheila explained. 'I want it born to music.'

'Well now I've seen everything,' the nurse said, and she went to fetch the doctor.

Clarissa went on playing.

'It's beautiful,' Sheila said between the phrases. 'You're a good friend, Clarissa.' It was during one of her euphoric intervals between the pains, and she felt at peace with the world, and full of generosity of spirit. She wondered what had happened to Bernard, and whether her mother was on her way. She really didn't want either of them by her bedside. What was happening was solely between her and her baby, and Clarissa's presence was so unobtrusive that she looked upon her as a superb invisible sound.

The doctor and the nurse waited in the doorway as Clarissa gave her all. The doctor smiled, but whether from an appreciation of the music or from a benign tolerance of human foibles was not clear. Until he reached the trolley.

'D'you like music?' Sheila said.

'I can take it or leave it myself,' he said. 'Still, it's your baby and you can have it any way you like. Now let's have a look at you. Up with your knees,' he said. The doctor fumbled below, while the nurse stood in attendance. The pains came again and Sheila reached for the nozzle. She felt their nether fumblings.

'If you say it's coming,' the doctor raised his head to speak to her, 'then it probably is. You're certainly in a late stage of labour. There's no doubt about that. But as yet there's no evidence of any arrival.' He patted her shoulder.

115

'Don't worry,' he said. 'He's just taking his time. Probably a boy. They're always lazy. Now you just lie back and listen to the music.'

Clarissa had not stopped playing during the examination. The baby might come out at any moment, and she didn't want to be caught napping. The doctor took the nurse aside. 'Ask Dr Harris to come, would you. You'll find him in the canteen.'

The nurse went off. She knew there was something radically wrong. The patient was in labour. Without any doubt. And in an advanced stage. But there was no sign of a baby. The pains were coming at intervals which merited at least some small appearance in the birth-canal, the top of a head, or a leg if it were a breech. But the canal was empty.

Dr Harris resented the interruption of his tea-break, and reluctantly he followed the nurse to the labour ward. He hesitated at the sight of Clarissa, then shrugged his shoulders and went to the trolley. He was obviously as indifferent to music as his partner. But the fortissimo passage that Clarissa was playing at that moment irritated him, and he turned to her. 'Turn it down a bit, will you,' he said, and then went into nether conference with his partner.

Sheila tried to hear what they were saying, but the pains were on her again, and she grabbed the nozzle and concentrated on her breathing. Clarissa played on manfully, her fortissimo swelling.

'Let's get going on the pushing,' Dr Harris shouted above the noise. The nurse bent down over Sheila. 'When the next pain comes,' she said, 'push hard. Until we tell you to stop. And push again when we give you the signal.' She had to yell out the instructions, for Clarissa was completely carried away. She was playing her heart out, much louder than the score indicated, because she wanted to make sure that the baby would hear her every note. And every note is a good one, she thought. She knew she had never played better.

The doctor prised Sheila's knees well apart. And the pains came again.

'Push,' the nurse shouted.

Sheila did, with all her strength.

'You're not pushing,' the nurse said.

'I am. I can't push any harder.' Sheila had begun to cry. The pains were excruciating. Clarissa watched her warily, and felt her need for a soothing and pianissimo melody. She stopped playing, muted her violin and went into an adagio. Sheila nodded weakly in her direction. She was mindful of the change, and she was grateful.

'That's better,' Dr Harris said, referring to the decibel rate, and certainly to nothing else, for things down under were very much the same. It puzzled him. He'd been delivering babies for over ten years, and he'd never seen a case like this one.

The pains came again.

'Push,' the nurse shouted. 'Push hard.'

'I'm pushing as hard as I can.'

'D'you know what I mean by pushing?' she threatened Sheila with a whisper. Things didn't go wrong in her department, and she wasn't going to tolerate a saboteur in her ward after the reputation she'd managed to maintain as chief labour sister. 'Pretend you're constipated,' she said. 'And push.'

'That's what I'm doing,' Sheila said tearfully, 'but something seems to be pulling inside me.'

She was right, though none of her attendants would have believed it. Inside her, Buster had pinned himself to the wall, and each time his mother pushed, he drew himself back as if from a sudden rush of air that threatened to suck him forth into the unknown. As his mother pushed forward, he pulled back. In the intervals of her pushing, he chuckled to himself, wondering how those important people in authority, the experts, would eventually solve the dilemma. Soon he heard the muffled echo of their solution.

117

'There's an obvious blockage here,' an expert voice said. 'We must do a Caesar.'

The nurse was gleeful. She regarded a Caesarean section as unnatural, as punitive almost, and it was about time this hysterical patient of hers got her come-uppance. She happily informed Sheila what she could expect, and the doctors tempered her glee with assurances that all would be well, that they would give her an anaesthetic, and that the birth would be painless.

'We're moving,' the doctor said to Clarissa. As he watched her repack her violin, he suddenly felt sorry for her. 'We're going to the theatre,' he said, tapping her shoulder. Meekly, she strapped down her case and followed them. She caught up with the trolley and walked alongside it. In transit, Sheila had another spasm of pain, with nothing at hand to relieve it. She held on to Clarissa's arm, squeezing it until it hurt. Clarissa understood. 'It'll all be over soon,' she said.

In the theatre, the anaesthetist was waiting. The doctors went to wash up, and left instructions for Clarissa to be masked. She submitted herself to their veiling, and giggled when one of the nurses made the point that it was just as well she didn't play the trumpet.

The doctors were now ready. And so was Clarissa. She'd been saving the Chaconne of the D minor Partita for the child's actual début, and it was now certain and visible when that would be. The anaesthetist placed the nozzle over Sheila's mouth and as she succumbed, Clarissa drew out her long and beautiful bow on the first chords.

Dr Harris made a swift examination of the swollen abdomen, and decided on a vertical incision. He held his scalpel at the ready, and at a sign from the anaesthetist, he made a deft and skilful cut. From the look on his face it was clear that what he had expected to see had not materialised, and he looked at his partner with some consternation.

'Manual?' his partner said, though he did not offer it as a

118

suggestion, for Dr Harris was eminent in his field, and didn't need any advice from a novice such as he. He said it rather as a confirmation of what Dr Harris must surely be thinking. And that great man nodded his head. He regretted now that his incision had not been lateral. It would have given him more room to manoeuvre. Only once before in his long experience had he had to resort to manual investigation. It had been a tricky job, with the mother's life at stake, but he had managed to save her, and the baby too, though the latter was severely handicapped by oxygen deprivation.

He put his hand gently into the abdomen. Buster saw it coming, and he dodged. With every frustrated movement of the rubber fingers, he dodged again. He was enjoying himself. It was like a game of hide-and-seek that he remembered playing with his father in his last existence. Underneath the stairs was his favourite hiding-place, and his father always pretended that he couldn't find him. He watched as the rubber fingers groped along the empty uterus wall. Then the fingers spread, encompassing the whole of his cell. Buster laid himself flat underneath the arched rubber palm, and prayed that he would not be detected. Then the hand shrugged and withdrew. Buster let out a small cheer.

The cavity was yawning, and Buster crawled to the hole. From the opening he had a bird's-eye and -ear's view of the proceedings outside his little cell. The light dazzled him a little, but after a few moments he grew acclimatised and this is what he saw and heard.

Clarissa was playing the Chaconne with such a beauty of tone, he could have wept. Dr Harris cut her off mid-phrase. 'You can wrap that up now,' he said with the unprovoked harshness of one who was looking for someone, anyone, to blame. 'Bloody silly idea in the first place.'

'What's wrong?' the other doctor said.

'There's nothing there,' Dr Harris said with finality.

119

'Nothing at all. Never was. A phantom pregnancy is what I opened her up for. Not our department, gentlemen. More in the field of psychiatry.'

Clarissa went over to the stretcher, put down her fiddle and bow and sadly stroked her friend's arm. 'Poor Sheila,' she said.

'O.K., let's sew her up,' the efficient Dr Harris said. 'Incredible, all the symptoms, every single one, and nothing to show for it. Poor devil. Out of the way now,' he said to Clarissa, pushing her aside. He turned round for his sewing-up equipment, and in the split second that all backs were turned, Buster, without forethought, stretched out his little arm, and whipped the fiddle into his little cell. Another arm-stretch captured the bow, and another, a prescription pad with pencil attached, simply because it was there. Then he settled back against the uterus wall, watching the gathering darkness as the slit of his cell was closed, and then he realised what he had done. He heard Clarissa shouting beyond the wall. 'But I put it here. I know I did.'

'You couldn't have,' Dr Harris said. 'It's not there, and no one could have taken it.'

'Perhaps one of the orderlies put it away,' a nurse said. 'They'll be in the annexe.'

'She's all yours,' Dr Harris said after a while. 'Take her to the recovery room.'

'And then?'

'Then she gets dressed and goes home. I'll refer her to psychiatry. Then it's out of my hands.'

It was silent then, save for the squeak of the trolley wheels as it trundled down the corridor. Buster was suddenly very tired from his long exertions, and almost immediately he fell asleep, the fiddle across his lap. When he awoke, he heard his father's bewildered voice. Bernard had come back after all, and in a questionable state of sobriety. The final shandy he had ordered had done little to

120

confirm his resolve to pack his bags and depart, and he had asked for another, and another. Somewhere along the order-line, the barman misheard his tipple, and shandy gave way to brandy without Bernard knowing or caring. At some time in the early morning he remembered that the time had surely come for fatherhood, and he arrived at the clinic, his arms open for embrace. The doctor dodged the alcoholic fumes on his breath and told him. 'I don't believe it,' was all he could say, over and over again. Then he laid his unshaven cheek on Sheila's arm and sobbed. She looked at him with utter contempt, then, turning to Clarissa, she said. 'Take me home.'

Buster held the fiddle on his lap, and stared at it in wonderment. Now he really had something to live for. Slowly he tucked it under his chin, and a sudden and total recall of his former life flooded him. He had never, in any of his lives, felt so deliriously happy. He held the bow, but refrained from laying it on the strings. He had worked so hard at avoiding detection, he wasn't going to risk it now. He would bide his time. Much could be achieved by silent practice. There would come a moment, and he would lie in wait for it, that, by all the stars and music of the spheres, would be propitious for his début, and he needn't even make a sortie to do it. He would sing his songs from within. He trembled with his joy.

Note from Dr Brown. All that I have written to date has been fashioned from data given in Buster's journal. And naturally, up to this time, it has all been retrospective. It was in the moments after his birth-refusal, as he sat in the gathering shadows of his cell, that he placed the pen between his thumb and first finger, embarking on that very first step to creativity, and he penned his first entry. I ask the reader to bear in mind that this introduction was my first taste of Buster's 'weltan-schauung', so that he will understand my immediate fascination with his story. I give it you here in full.

'Today is my non-birthday. I have caused panic; I have caused sorrow. I pray for forgiveness. I solemnly conceived

myself on the Day of Atonement, and it is that notion of
expiation that will henceforth guide me. I look to my future.
Without pride, without assumption, without arrogance. I will
practise every day, silently, and with prompting from no one. I
consider myself highly blessed. I shall play in no one's image
but my own. I am obliged to no one's expectation, to no one's
reproof, to nobody's praise. I am my own true and total self.
The choice I have made, with such pain and such wavering, is
a choice of sole-ness, lone-ness, and at-one-ment, all this, in a
self-imposed exile, the embrace of true creativity.'

This, Buster's very first entry, concludes with a music
quotation. He was obviously eager to test his musical memory.
My research gave its source as the opening of Beethoven's
Sonata for violin and piano in F major, the work from which
this book takes its title. I am told by reliable music copyists
that the clarity of Buster's notation is remarkable in one so
young.

Part 2

Chapter 8

Note from Brown, your simple straightforward doctor. Are you still with me, dear reader, or have I overstrained your credulity? Bear with me. Buster's story, as I have said elsewhere, was an unparalleled event. But every single detail of it was proven. I myself am regarded by my colleagues as a sceptical fellow, yet, in Buster's case, all my doubts were confounded. I ask for your patience. Take my word for it, you will be rewarded.

For the next three years, Buster's journal is spasmodic. The reader may wonder how I am able to gauge a period of passing time, since Buster had no notion of calendar. I have simply taken my cue from the growth measurement of Buster himself. That is, his finger-span, and his growth in technique. From the spasmodic entries in his journal, it is clear that he reached an octave's span. Moreover, he himself refers to an improved double-stopping and staccato bowing, both techniques dependent on long practice. I have researched into the methods of other violinists who have assured me that two years of diligent practice is a minimum to perfect a technique of staccato bowing for instance, and there was no doubt as to Buster's diligence. But his practice was silent, so clearly he needed a little longer than the two years my research indicated. So I have reckoned three years, as an approximate non-writing period. Though I must repeat that there were entries, and highly charged ones at that, but there were long silences between them. Though Buster wrote little during this time, it was nevertheless a highly creative period, as subsequent events will prove.

Those events which were to misshape Buster's future were taking place outside his listening-wall with bustling activity. For to be in the business of fantasy is to be in full-time occupation, and it was in the name of fantasy that Bernard and the rest of the family viewed Sheila's stubborn and continuing condition. With a deep and abiding faith, Sheila

125

believed that a child was growing inside her, a child unready to make its sortie. In its own time it would emerge and repay her patience tenfold. After her abortive delivery, she was referred to a psychiatrist. When Buster heard that word, first from the doctor's mouth, and then echoed in shameful whispers by Bernard and Sheila's mother, his full-grown heart faltered. Out of the dark memories of his former lives, the word echoed with an obscene vibration. He could not pinpoint any specific event attached to the obscenity, but he recalled it in general as an anti-life pursuit. The phrase 'licensed killer' flickered dimly through his mind, and he feared for his mother's welfare. Out of reach, sight and hearing, he begged her to resist the doctors' referral, but she, wearied by their persistence, and the constant nagging of her own family, was brought, feebly protesting, to the couch.

'Tell me about your baby,' the psychiatrist said.

You silly bugger, Buster thought, sniffing the man's pretence. He was an I'm-on-your-side doctor, an I-don't-believe-what-the-others-say-either doctor, a tell-me-all-about-it doctor.

'There's nothing to say,' his mother said softly. 'It's mine. It's inside me.'

Take it from there brother, Buster whispered, and let's see how far you can go. Not very far, according to the silence outside the wall. The tell-me-all-about-it doctor rarely had the patience to sit and be told. It was a ruse to get on the patient's side, to finally force her to admit her folly, to satisfy the shrink's desperate need to prove that the mad are wrong.

'You say that it's inside you,' he said patiently.

'Yes. And it's true,' his mother said.

Buster heard a sudden strength in her voice, a brave reaffirmation of her condition, as if, dwelling in another dimension, she had gained the courage to contradict one who had not travelled there.

'It's mine, and it's inside me,' she said again.

The doctor shifted in his chair. He was fast losing the little patience he had. This stubborn woman with her stupid fantasies needed to be taught a lesson. 'There are ways of proving it,' he said. His voice was gentle, covering the threat in his words, masking their punitive intent.

'What ways?' his mother said.

'You could have an X-ray.'

Sheila put a protective hand on Buster's listening-wall. He strained to hear her response.

'I won't have an X-ray,' she said. 'I know about X-rays. They would damage my baby.'

Buster smiled, waiting for the psychiatrist's next move.

'They would damage your baby, would they,' he said, echoing the tone of her voice and injecting every syllable with his contempt. And then, in almost the same breath, 'Tell me about your mother,' he said.

Sheila rose from her chair, signalling that the interview was at an end, and nothing could be gained from further questioning.

'My condition has nothing to do with my mother,' she said. 'I'm pregnant.'

'Thirteen months pregnant,' he reminded her.

'My baby is not ready to come out. It will come in its own good time.'

'I would like to see you again nevertheless,' the doctor said.

'There's no point,' Sheila told him. 'I'll let you know when the child is born.'

He took her gallantly to the door, sweeping the space around him with his hands, as if the vocabulary of her fantasies had polluted his air.

'You will make gynaecological history, Mrs Rosen,' he said.

Sheila made no reply, and her silence was a token of her own confidence, and of her utter contempt for his painful trivialisation.

Buster was saddened by the tempo of her gait, and for a moment he wondered about his future, and whether perhaps he had cause to re-evaluate his decision to stay where he was. Over the last few months, since he had concealed himself behind the arras of his mother's chamber, his heart had often been moved by pity for her condition. She had grown gentle and kind, aloof almost, with the sure and certain knowledge of her strange motherhood, and Buster might well have welcomed her embrace. But his father, on the other hand, had grown gross with disappointment, and his anger and impatience at his wife's stubborn insistence grew daily more acute. That man, who, in his putative-father days, the legal ones, was gentle abdication personified, the appeaser, the peace-at-any-price maker, had now turned with impotent fury into a monster. Denied his rightful parental status, hoodwinked by his lunatic spouse, who, growing fatter and uglier each day, shamed him before his business associates and a dwindling circle of friends. He couldn't understand his misfortune. It simply wasn't fair. Had he not been a good husband? Had he not been patient enough with his wife's irritating fantasy? But enough was enough. She had to go to the hospital and have an X-ray, and have her silly illusions shattered once and for all. Then she could go on a strict diet, and in a year or so she would look normal. That was all that mattered to him. Her look. Her presentation. Whatever erosion might rot her soul as a result of such mean unveiling did not concern him. The soul did not *show,* however warped or assaulted. He wanted an outward image of her that would not shame him, one that would not arouse in him those terrible questionings, those desperate challenges that throbbed from her swollen belly as it nudged and nagged him to confrontation. For what, after all, had happened to his seed? Where did it go? What terrible detour had it followed in preference to the known and natural route?

What availed the struggle, what mattered the victory over millions of protesting claimants, if only to settle in some aborted cranny from whence to sour the mind and spirit. Often Bernard looked at his body to try to discover perhaps a cloven footprint, some evidence that a devil had entered his loins. His appetite, so long unsatisfied, often drove him to other women, but once in their embrace, fear froze him, and a hateful mistrust of his sly seed drove him back to the monumental pillow of his thwarted fruit. Sometimes he hated her, with a hatred that was aggravated by his helplessness. Sometimes he entertained the idea of a divorce, but his involvement in his father-in-law's business was complicated enough to override the change in his affections. He felt himself caught in a snare, and in a lethargy that was too indifferent to investigate the nature of the trap.

He sat in his car outside the doctor's consulting-rooms. He had wanted to take her to the doctor himself. But Sheila had refused his company. It was a visit that she was quite capable of handling on her own, and she gave the impression that she would give it short shrift, and that he would not have to wait a long time. Through the driving-mirror, he could see her coming towards the car, her gait slow, her girth vast and peaceful. As he looked at her, her body swollen with its larded illusion, he prayed that she would explode. He saw himself bend down to pick up the pieces of her, without sorrow, without pity, without remorse; just a simple mopping-up operation after the storm.

He got out of the car to help her inside. 'What did he say?' he practically shouted at her, as she folded her girth into the seat. She waited until he was seated beside her.

'He said what you all say,' she said. 'There's nothing inside my body. It's all in my head.' She smiled, untouchable.

'Well he's right, isn't he,' Bernard hissed between his teeth. 'You bloody well know he's right.' He simmered his way home, and when he got to their gate, he stopped the car and made no move to help her out. He hung on to the steering-wheel, his head drooping between his arms.

'Oh, Sheila,' he said, 'what's to become of us?'

Buster heard his plea, and for a moment he was tempted to reveal himself. But he must beware of pity. It was an emotion that would curdle soon enough, and if it ever prompted his sortie, he would be left, with only his foolish appearance, stranded on a dry, hostile shore. He put his fingers over his ears.

'Wait,' Sheila said. 'You must be patient. You must believe in me. And you must believe in the "in" of me.'

Bernard shrugged. My wife's round the bend, he thought. Even her language is bananas. Wearily he stepped out of the car, and helped her out of the other side. Next time, I'll put her in the boot, he thought, where the baggage that she had become ought to be. 'I asked your mother for lunch,' he said, as he propelled her girth up the drive. They were closing in on her, she knew. Since her non-confinement, Bernard had allied himself squarely with Mrs Joseph, and together they did battle with the unrepentant source of their shame. Mrs Joseph's tactics were crude and unadorned. A simple and chilling scream that ordered her daughter to stop all this madness and to pull herself together. As her screams grew louder, Sheila withdrew into silence, and Bernard floundered in the echoes in between, bewildered, ashamed, and willing his wife's explosion.

'You'll have to entertain her yourself,' Sheila said. 'I'm tired and I'm going to bed.'

'You're bloody well not going to bed,' he shouted. 'You're not going to get out of it as easily as that. You're going to sit down, and you're going to listen to us once and for all. If you don't,' he shouted, 'I shall have you certified.'

Buster heard the word. It shrieked under his mother's protecting hand, perforating through the wall's membrane, undulating through the amniotic fluid, and piercing his

130

inner ear with such pain that his eyes watered, and with horror he tasted his first tear. I'm too young to cry, he thought, too young to begin the sterile accumulation of suffering. Whatever happens, he thought, and no matter how old in years I may grow, I must always in this life be too young to make up a parcel of pain. The cult of suffering, he knew, was a brake on anyone's growth. It had encumbered him often enough in past appearances. He wiped away his tears in disgust. The word 'certified' was his father's word, *his* problem, *his* threat, *his* paltry defence. Let him deal with it.

Slowly Sheila took off her coat and made her way up the stairs.

'Where are you going?' Bernard said.

'To bed.'

'What about lunch?'

'I'm not hungry.'

'*You're* not hungry. What about me?'

'There's food in the fridge.'

'What about your mother?'

'There's enough for both of you.' Sheila colluded in their alignment. She could afford to, for it did not threaten her. Bernard had become for her a stranger. Sometimes she wondered what he was doing in her house. And the same too of her mother, who was now such a frequent visitor. Occasionally, her mother would stay over and leave her clothes behind in the guest-room wardrobe. It was possible that, very slowly, she was moving in. But Sheila was not disturbed even by that possibility. Her entire world was peopled by herself and her child, whom she could feel growing slowly inside her, biding its time. She was prepared to nurture it until it was ready. Meanwhile she went ahead with her preparations.

There was a dressing-room adjoining her bedroom, and this she had turned into a nursery. The small chest of drawers was already full of baby-clothes, and her constant knitting added to its bulk. She embroidered wall hangings with illustrations of fairy-tales, she made fancy lamps and woolly toys. The crib she had draped in organdie and lace, and often she would sit alone in the room and rock the empty cradle. She understood that to an outsider's eye, she must appear to be deranged, but the proof of her seed was inside her, moving in its growth. She didn't care that no one believed her. She didn't even relish a sense of triumph when the baby would be born. Neither did she urge it to hurry. If, while inside her, he grew out of the crib, she was happily prepared to replace it with a cot that would accommodate him. She realised that never in her life had she been so serene, so at peace with herself. Her playing had improved too, not only technically, which was to be expected, since she was practising more than ever before, but it had achieved a new musical dimension which she felt had something to do with the fertility of her condition. She didn't concertise any more; her appearance would have embarrassed an audience. But she and Clarissa were working daily on the Beethoven and Mozart sonata cycles. For Clarissa the sudden disappearance of her violin was still a mystery, and Sheila thought, and so did Clarissa, that one of the orderlies had smuggled it out of the hospital, and had probably sold it. There was nothing Clarissa could do about it. She'd been to the police and told them her story, which they relegated to fantasy, patting her arm, and telling her to go home and rest. She could find no nurse or doctor who would bear witness to the theft. It seemed that everybody who took part in that disastrous theatre event had conspired together to claim that it had never taken place at all. Clarissa was now playing on her second instrument, one that she had always kept as a stand-by. She was content not to be concertising, for it gave her an opportunity to run the fiddle in, as it were, and every day its tone improved. It no longer occurred to her to find another pianist to further her career. Her loyalty to

Sheila was absolute, not only as a partner, but as a waiting mother, for she was as convinced as Sheila herself that the baby would arrive in its own time.

Mrs Joseph was on her angry way. She sat on the bus, steaming. She was irritated by the slowness of the journey. She couldn't wait to get to her daughter's house and lay her hands on her. Her constant anger at Sheila's madness had that morning been fed by a letter she had received from her mother. The receipt of the letter was disturbing enough to her conscience without even looking at its contents. She had sat at the breakfast table, mulling over the envelope, delaying its opening. She had not been to see her mother since Sheila had accompanied her to bring the good news. 'Good news,' Mrs Joseph muttered bitterly to herself. 'With such good news, who needs the bad?' She had not even phoned her mother, and had now left it so long that it had become more and more difficult to make contact. Her mother had never before made a move to get in touch, so the contents of her letter must be urgent indeed. Well, at least she's not dead, Mrs Joseph thought, and with the butter knife, she slit the envelope open. The writing was spidery but legible. The spaces between the words were minute, as if she had written it all in one angry breath. 'Dear Phoebe,' it said, followed by a space, the intake of breath for the tirade to follow. 'Have I a daughter, I ask myself? Have I a granddaughter? Have I perhaps a great-grandchild? Who, you are asking, is this letter from. You have, believe me, a mother. Not well. Who knows for how much longer? You remember the woman you called Mama you put away many years ago? I tell you, you should know it, she's still there. All right, so you don't come to see me. My part. I should live to worry about that. You, I don't care about. You daughter, she also doesn't come, also her I don't care about. But a great-grandchild. Four months old it is already. Not so stupid I am I can't count. Have I seen him? Has anyone told me? A boy perhaps he is? A girl? Twins even? Perhaps you should tell. You shouldn't come. Don't put yourself out. Just a postcard. What it is. Boy, girl, and the name. That's all. Also the weight I'm interested in. Just a postcard. You shouldn't trouble anything else.'

The letter was not signed. The old lady had clearly not known how to identify herself. The signature 'Mama' would have begged a million questions, and in Mrs Singer's mind, the answer to every one of them was negative. Mrs Joseph read the letter over and over again, her anger mounting. 'It's all that girl's fault,' she spluttered. 'Wait till I lay my hands on her.'

She dressed quickly and simmered her way on the bus, the letter sweating its wrath inside her handbag.

'She's sleeping,' Bernard said as he opened the door.

'I'll give her sleeping,' she said, brushing past him and up the stairs. Bernard made no move to stop her. He was delighted whenever she went into the attack. They were a small army, his mother-in-law and himself, but their bullying, their cowardice, and their sheer fury was sublime. He heard her crashing into Sheila's bedroom.

'Sleeping in the middle of the day,' she scoffed. 'You're not ill.' She sat heavily on the bed. 'I want to talk to you.'

Sheila sat up. 'Why can't you leave me alone?' she said.

'I'm not touching you,' Mrs Joseph said. 'You've landed me in a lot of trouble.'

'What trouble?'

She pulled the letter out of her handbag. 'Read it,' she ordered. 'See what you've done to me.' She waited, panting, while Sheila read.

'Why is this my fault?' Sheila said softly when she'd finished reading.

'It's *my* fault?' Mrs Joseph said. 'Who runs around telling everybody she's having a baby? Who goes to see your grandmother and gets her all excited? Who brings such shame on the family?'

'I'll go and see Grandma next week.' Sheila said. 'She'll understand.'

'You'll do nothing of the sort my girl. You'll not go to the home to shame me, shame me in front of all those people, with your madness. It's *you* should be in a home, and I don't mean old age.'

'Well, you seem to be an expert at putting people away,' Sheila said quietly. 'Why don't you do it?'

Then Mrs Joseph slapped her. Hard across her face.

'Poor Mama,' Sheila said.

Mrs Joseph left the room. She was totally deflated, and for the first time in her life she acknowledged that she did not like herself at all. She went down to the sitting-room and picked up the phone. Slowly she dialled the home. 'Can I speak to Mrs Singer, please?' She waited, trying not to think of what she would say. 'It's her daughter,' she said. She started to cry. 'Mama?' she whimpered when Mrs Singer reached the phone. She suddenly wanted to be with her, in her little room, in that shared unprivacy of age, reeking with the cobwebbed smells of years. She wanted to be in her arms, she wanted her comfort, her forgiveness. 'Mama?' she said. 'It's me.'

Mrs Singer was not going to pave any way. 'So who's me?' she said, as if there were any other offspring.

'Phoebe.'

'So what do you want? All of a sudden you telephone. After a year, you suddenly remember you have a mother. You want something?'

Mrs Joseph could not control her sobbing, and from Mrs Singer's stern end, it was unmistakable. 'Oh my God, what's happened, Phoebe. Tell Mama what's happened.'

'The baby died.' Mrs Joseph didn't mean to say it, but her mother's unexpected melted response seemed to require some devastating cause.

'When? When?'

'It never lived,' Mrs Joseph said. 'It was still-born.' That

135

way Mrs Joseph felt less like a murderer. In any case, there was no body, so why should she make a production of it.

'So she'll have another one.' Mrs Singer said, who found difficulty in accepting death when there'd been no breath at all. 'I should live to see it,' she said. She was obviously disappointed.

'Can I come to see you this afternoon?'

'By me you're always welcome. Will Sheila come?'

'Not this time. She's not feeling well. A bit depressed.'

'She'll get over it.' Mrs Singer said with the assurance of her eighty-three years. What was offensive about human nature, she knew, was that it *did* endure, over and over again.

'I'll come as soon as I can,' Mrs Joseph said.

'I'm here. Don't rush yourself. Where should I go? And Phoebe, you should give my love to Sheila. Tell her I also had a still-born. She'll get over it.' Mrs Singer put the phone down. Mrs Joseph held the dead line in her hand. Her mother's sudden titbit had astonished her. She wondered at the truth of it. Perhaps it was her mother's invention, as a gesture of sympathy towards Sheila. But it could be true. If it were, had it preceded her own birth, and was she a compensation? Or had it succeeded her and closed the door for ever. Either way, she had been deprived of a sibling, some other pair of shoulders to bear the brunt of kinship. Some other hand to cast the sire aside, some sharer now of guilt and culpability. She resented her solitary status, and began to pride herself that she at least had provided two to bear her sorrow. The thought of Robert pained her. Since her first visit she had not been back to the prison. Bernard had made the reluctant journey and had reported that all was as well as could be expected. Robert had told Bernard that all his future visiting hours were pre-booked by friends, and she didn't know whether or not to believe him. To think of him at all was too painful and when she did, it was to hope that he was sleeping.

Bernard was setting lunch in the dining-room. Through the open partition she could see his angry hands as they dispersed the cutlery chaotically over the table. He looked up for a moment and caught her stare. 'One day, she'll burst,' he shouted.

'What are we going to do?'

'We'll have to put her away,' he said.

Mrs Joseph got up. 'Never.' she shouted. 'A daughter of mine? Put away? Over my dead body.' Mrs Joseph, the time-honoured expert in disposal, was about to draw the line.

'D'you have any other suggestion?' Bernard said.

Mrs Joseph went into the dining-room. 'Perhaps we should all pretend that she really is carrying a baby. Then she won't think it's so funny any more. She's only doing it out of spite. If we all join in, there won't be any point in it any more.'

'I've tried that,' Bernard said. 'Last week, I even built a toy-cupboard in the nursery. She's bought twenty-three teddy-bears. I had to put them somewhere. But it makes no difference.'

'Has she seen the doctor again?'

'He says the same as he always says. She has to have treatment, long-term treatment. She just refuses to co-operate. She says there's nothing the matter with her. And she's not mad enough to commit. Unless I do it, with the doctor's help. But I have to give permission. That's the law.'

'But you wouldn't do it Bernard.' Mrs Joseph was afraid. 'You wouldn't put her away. Think of the shame.' Mrs Joseph was back in harness.

'Bugger the shame,' Bernard shouted. He couldn't be bothered to discuss it with her. 'Sit down,' he said. 'We might as well have some lunch.'

She wasn't hungry, but she knew that she would need some sustenance for her afternoon visit. 'I'm going to see my

137

mother this afternoon,' she said.

Bernard was forking a piece of meat, and he held it mid-air. 'That's an idea,' he said. 'She always liked Grandma. Maybe Grandma could talk to her.'

'I'm not taking her out there.'

'We could bring Grandma back here.'

Mrs Joseph wondered how she could reconvert the lie she had told. One minute the baby had been born dead, and the next, it hadn't been born at all. For a moment she thought she might confide all to her mother, tell her the whole sorry story, weep her heart out to her, and ask for her help. But the price for such sympathy would be costly, so costly in fact, that it might even mean her departure from the old-age home, and a claim on her daughter's bed to die in. Such an eventuality did not please Mrs Joseph. She would rather keep her pain to herself.

'Bernard,' she said patiently, 'my mother's an old woman. Her life has not been easy. Why burden her now at the end of her days?'

His mother-in-law's unaccustomed concern for the old woman did not fool Bernard. He knew that she simply wasn't going to run the risk of having the old woman return to her family on a one-way ticket. 'I don't know what I'm going to do,' he said.

'What about that Clarissa woman? Can't she talk to her?'

'She's as mad as Sheila. She's also waiting for the baby.'

'Then you have to do it yourself. And you have to do it gently.'

That's good, coming from you, Bernard thought.

'You've got to do it with love,' she went on.

Even better. Bernard smiled. 'I find it hard to love her any more.' He was amazed that he had spoken so openly to his mother-in-law. Amazed too, that he had never spoken such a thought aloud. But it was true. He didn't love her. He didn't even pity her. She was just a monumental unfair nuisance in his life, and he wanted to be rid of her. He wondered whether people ever died of fantasy. Sometimes he had fantasies himself of waking up one morning and finding her spread-eagled, dead and deflated on the bed, like some vast parachute that, post-flight, had come to rest. Often he dreamed that he had murdered her, by pricking her belly with a carving-knife.

'We've simply got to do *something*,' his mother-in-law was saying.

'I'll go back and see the doctor,' Bernard said. 'Perhaps he'll actually come to her and persuade her to some treatment. After all, it is his job.'

'But not to be put away,' Mrs Joseph said quickly.

'If that's what treatment means, they'll put her away. It won't be for ever,' he said. 'She's bound to get better in time.'

'Can't we force her to have an X-ray?' Mrs Joseph said. 'Then she'll come to her senses.'

'No one can force anyone to do anything. Unless she were committed.'

'Oh no.' Mrs Joseph pleaded.

'In any case,' Bernard went on, 'she's mad enough to refuse to believe the X-rays. She'd say they'd doctored them.'

They finished their lunch in silence.

'I'd better be going now,' Mrs Joseph said. 'I won't disturb Sheila. She's probably sleeping.' She wouldn't have minded disturbing her at all – her life's role had been one of disturbance – but she was afraid to confront Sheila so soon after their last bloody battle. 'It's not an easy life,' she said, as she put on her coat. And indeed, there was little joy in it.

As she sat on the bus, she totted the tally of her distress. Her husband was dead, her son was in prison, and her daughter had gone round the bend. And as if that weren't enough, she was on her way to see her mother. Perhaps she would feel better after that, she thought, though she knew that it was improbable. After each visit she returned, her guilts multiplied. Is it possible that it's all my fault, she wondered. She stopped herself at this thought. There was no truth in it, so it was pointless to pursue. But none the less, she *had* thought it. But no one must ever know, and even she must erase it from her mind, else history would give it a small credence.

When she had gone, Bernard cleared the table and poured himself a drink. He noticed that nowadays he seemed to be drinking heavily. What's more, he had acquired a taste for it. Ever since that night, when his seed had finally curdled, he'd regularly tasted the solace that alcohol induced. A small drink at lunchtime kept him going in the office for the rest of the day. Often he would dine and wine himself alone in a restaurant, for he dreaded every homecoming and the monumental vision that barely greeted him. He had to do something, and do it quickly, for he feared his own violence.

He dialled the psychiatrist's number. He was surprised that the doctor himself answered the phone. It was lunch hour, but yes, he would give a little of his time. They went over the same dreary story, and Bernard's plea that something had to be done, the doctor's repetition that Sheila was obstructive, and that he himself was doing the best he could. He was trying to think of other methods though, and he did have a contact with a colleague in another hospital, he said, who was beginning to take a special interest in patients in Sheila's condition.

'D'you mean to say that there are others?' Bernard grasped at the hope that he was not alone.

'The fantasy syndrome is a very common one,' the doctor said. 'It manifests itself in different ways. That of your wife, Mr Rosen, is fairly exaggerated, I must admit,' he added, 'though basically, she shares the condition with many others. They are experimenting with a new kind of treatment. I intend to investigate it on your wife's behalf.'

'Is there any hope?' Bernard said.

'Only if she submits to some kind of treatment.'

'And if not?'

'You see your wife, Mr Rosen. Her personal fantasy symbol happens to be physically dangerous. Yes, I would say, and it must come as no surprise to you, Mr Rosen, that if your wife doesn't accept help pretty soon, her life will be in danger. I'll be in touch, Mr Rosen,' he said, and he replaced the receiver.

Bernard took another drink. He could not deny a sense of relief. If she insisted on her pregnancy, she would die, die quite naturally, of unnatural causes. The thought crossed his mind that he would no longer encourage her to treatment, and let nature take its unnatural course.

Note from Dr Brown. I have never had much time for psychiatrists myself, and it always gives me great pleasure to see one of them proved wrong. The cosy prognosis of Sheila's psychiatrist was well off the mark. Sheila refused treatment, yet Sheila survived. Daily she grew more gross, as was natural for one in her condition, and when Buster was three years old, his mother was declared non-ambulent. Her faith in her baby was never shaken, and her patience was unassailable. Occasionally over this period, she was persuaded to try a number of so-called cures, and she allowed herself to be taken to various consulting-rooms, because she didn't want to spend any energy in argument. Such strength as she had, she devoted to nurturing her child. With her total indifference, she was shunted from one therapist to another, each with his own foolproof methods. Bernard even tried a faith-healer, but all to no avail. Sheila's baby grew stubborn and sturdy inside her. During this period, as I have said elsewhere, the entries in Buster's journal were spasmodic. He was spending most of his time in silent practice, and when he did write, it was not so much as to record events, but to reflect philosophically on his condition. It occurs to me that an exact copy of one of Buster's entries from this period might not be out of place here. I quote one passage in full.

'Poor old Mum. She is dragged from psychiatrist couch to couch. In the time-lapse between my minor and major sixth, she has laid herself down on rexine, dralon, uncut moquette,

141

and her declaration does not vary with the upholstery. "I have a baby inside me," she always says. "It is not ready to be born." Today we went to something quite different. It's called "image therapy". I gather it's the very latest. My mother said she had a blockage to her heart. The man asked her to describe it, and she said it was a rat, that, sentry-like, was blocking the way to her soul. My mother went on and on about her rat. I think she was playing the man along. Then this man said, believe it or not, "My name's Peter, and I'd like to talk to you, Mr Rat. D'you like your work, Mr Rat?"

'Now I ask you, which one of us is crazy? But at least this therapist isn't interpretative, which is what most psychiatrists are about. And they're only human after all and their interpretation can't help but be based on projection, and is thus judgemental. At least this Peter fellow respects a separate neurosis and allows it to speak for itself.

'I'm rather pleased with this entry, because I've used lots of long words. Sometimes, I long to come out and have it published. I want to show off. But I realise that such a desire is a mark of immaturity. The true pursuit of self-fulfilment has no need of audience, of praise or rebuke, and here in my little cell, with my music and my journal, I need nothing more. I fear that there will come a moment when I must, for others' sake, declare myself. I long for that moment to be postponed. Poor mother.'

Do you understand now, dear reader, my deep affection for this little boy? In the course of perusing his journal, he became my mentor. He had come to his small cell, already richly endowed with such wisdom, and I knew that, like all sages, he must finally acknowledge that the end of wisdom is silence. But I was not prepared for the devasting blow that finally tied his tongue.

142

Chapter 9

'Well, we've tried just about everything, Mr Rosen,' the psychiatrist said. 'Your wife's case defies all the rules of medicine. It's a wonder to me that she's still alive. The strain on you must be overwhelming.'

The strain certainly showed. Bernard seemed to have shrunk. As his wife's bulk grew larger, so his shrivelled, as if part of her fantasy was to consume him as well.

'I hate her, Dr Peabody,' he said 'I wish she *would* die.'

'Don't be ashamed of such feelings,' the doctor said. 'They're natural, and it's good that you can acknowledge them. She must be very trying to live with.'

'What am I to do?' Bernard said.

'There's one method we haven't tried as yet, and I've seen some very good results with it. Perhaps your wife will agree to give it a try, since it involves other people as well as herself.'

Bernard looked at him questioningly.

'It's family therapy,' Dr Peabody said. 'We know that environment plays a large part in creating and feeding neuroses and the family is certainly a known breeding-ground. In family therapy, we examine the disturbances that prevail in all its members. We try to discover whether one member of the family is being used as a scapegoat for the others' sicknesses. This may well be so in your wife's case. I think it's worth a try.'

Bernard didn't know what he was talking about, but he nodded his assent. Anything was better than nothing. 'What do I have to do?' he said.

'You must gather the family together. Brothers, sisters, mothers, fathers, grandparents – they're very good, especially grandmothers, they hold a lot of keys – and we all meet together on a regular basis, and try to thrash out the core of the problem. How many participants can you muster?'

Silently Bernard picked at the branches of Sheila's family tree. There was the root itself, or one of them at least, in the old-age home outside the town. Though how anyone could explain to Mrs Singer how and why her services were needed he could not imagine. Perhaps they need tell her nothing, and she could look upon it as a family outing. Then there was Mrs Joseph herself, and Robert, who would take some persuasion. And Sheila and himself. That made five. He offered his list to Dr Peabody.

'That's fine,' he said. 'I'll make arrangements at the Family Therapy Clinic, and I'll be in touch.'

He saw Bernard to the door. He wanted to offer him some words of hope, but he had little reason for optimism. He, like Bernard, shared a wish that Mrs Rosen would be decent enough to die, and remove once and for all the irritation she was causing him. 'It can't go on much longer' was all he could offer Bernard, with the inference that death was always at hand, yet at the same time leaving the door open for some possibility of cure. Then he realised that he'd had exactly the same thought, and had probably said exactly the same words, when Mrs Rosen had first come to him almost three years ago. Phantom pregnancies were not uncommon amongst highly charged women who'd been trying for so long to conceive, but he'd never known one more stubborn and persistent. He was not at ease with the likes of Mrs Rosen. She threw all his deductions out of gear. While her condition was without doubt an object of deep medical fascination, her reluctance to present herself for their experimentation hindered any exciting discovery. He looked forward to her death. Hers was a post-mortem he would attend with smug curiosity. Her belly would be inflated with phantom wind. It would only be a pity that

144

she wouldn't be around to hear his 'I told you so'.

Bernard went home and drew up a plan for the in-gathering of the clan. His mother-in-law would be a willing participant, obstreperous no doubt, but she would not miss out on any opportunity to have her angry self-righteous say. Robert would require a little persuasion. Since his release from prison he had seen nothing of his family. His was a deliberate withdrawal, and probably for the sake of his own sanity. His only contact was a telephone one with Bernard, of whom he used to enquire about Sheila's welfare. He didn't trust himself to come and see her, lest her pitiable state should lure him back into the family web. Bernard decided to write to him. The biggest stumbling-block, without doubt, would be Mrs Singer. What words could he use to her to explain the notion of family therapy, when he hardly understood it himself. And even if she managed to understand it, would she then be willing to play her part? His task was made more difficult by the lie that Mrs Joseph had told her. He had overheard his mother-in-law's telephone conversation fobbing the old lady off by pronouncing their child still-born. Now he would have to undo that lie. He would have to resurrect a child that in fact had never been, and explain to her that it was up to the whole family to bury it once and for all. The whole sorry business was so confusing he hardly understood it himself. What could he expect an old woman of eighty-six to make of it all. He could plan no speech, no preamble of explanation. He would have to go and see her and play it by ear. He did not tell his mother-in-law he was going, or she might have taken advantage of his protective company to pay a duty visit. He had never been to the home before and he had some difficulty in finding the way. As he drove he tried to stop himself rehearsing what he would say to her. He vaguely hoped that she might give him some lead, though since she had no idea of the premise, it was unlikely that he could depend on her. He'd say for openers that he happened to be passing and had dropped in to say hello. He would take it from there.

He was directed to Mrs Singer's room. 'I just happened to be passing,' he said, wondering what she was doing sitting outside the door. Or was it she? He'd only met her once, years ago at his wedding, and old women tended to look very alike to him.

'They took away Daddy's shop,' Mrs Spengler informed him, glad of a new face, and a possible new response.

'Who took it away?' Bernard said, hoping for some clue that would confirm that this woman was indeed Sheila's grandmother.

It was the first time that anybody had taken Mrs Spengler up on the identity of her father's dispossessors. She was bewildered. She had never concerned herself with the answer to that question. It had always seemed so irrelevant.

'*They* did,' she said.

'Who's they?'

Mrs Spengler was rattled. That wasn't what she wanted to talk about at all.

'They took away Daddy's shop,' she said again.

Bernard looked at the number on the door she was sentry to. Number 27. Mrs Singer's address, according to reception downstairs. If this woman were indeed Sheila's grandmother, she would, in her present state of mind, which was not likely to improve with age, be of little use in a family therapy session, and would probably use up most of the time in bemoaning the loss of her father's holding. He had it in mind to go away. Then suddenly Mrs Spengler shifted her chair away from the door.

'She's inside,' she said.

Bernard was a little disappointed. He would have to go through with it after all.

Mrs Singer recognised him immediately. She even remembered his name.

146

'Bernard? It's Bernard, isn't it? Sheila's husband.' Saying it aloud brought to her the full realisation of his identity. He was an in-law, a non-kin, of the category that was always delegated as the carrier of bad family news. She quickly recapped on her family. Her daughter? Her granddaughter? Her grandson? The pain would not be so much in their deaths but in the rude illegal fact that she had outlived them. She blushed with the shame. 'What's happened?' she said.

'Nothing,' Bernard took her hands. 'I was just passing. I had a business call in the area. I thought I'd drop in and say hello.'

'Oh, so nice,' she said, offering him a chair. 'So nice to take the trouble. My own daughter should take the trouble sometimes. Children, Bernard,' she confided, 'only aggravation.' Then she remembered his bereavement. 'I'm sorry for the still-born,' she said. 'I know from still-borns. I also had. So you try again.'

Bernard took a deep breath. 'Grandma,' he said, hoping that the fond appellation would put him on a surer footing. 'It wasn't still-born.'

'You mean it lived and then it died?'

'No Grandma, it never lived.'

'Such riddles you're talking,' the old woman said.

'I have to do a lot of explaining to you, Grandma,' he said, 'and it'll be difficult to understand.'

'An idiot I'm not yet. So tell.'

'Well you see, Sheila never was pregnant. Oh she looked pregnant all right. She had all the symptoms, and when the nine months were gone, she even went into labour. But there wasn't any baby. Never was. It's what they call a phantom pregnancy.' He paused.

'Phantom pregnancy?' Mrs Singer reminisced reeling the diagnosis off her tongue with an uncanny familiarity. 'Do I know about phantom pregnancies. I also had.'

Bernard could have hugged her. This woman had had

everything. 'Tell me about yours,' Bernard urged her, hoping that he might learn something for Sheila's benefit. This old lady had survived into a ripe old age, phantom pregnancy notwithstanding. 'How did you get over it?' he said. 'Tell me about it. All of it, as much as you can remember.'

Mrs Singer took momentary offence. 'Everything I remember,' she said. 'I was married,' she said, stressing the point, as if such a condition were inconceivable outside wedlock. 'Already I had Phoebe. In those days, everybody had big families – nine, ten children. I tried. Nothing happened. And then, thank God, again I was carrying. Isaac was so excited. I had it at home. In those days, no hospital. Only when you were very poor. But, God rest his soul, the baby was what you call, still-born. I tell you Bernard,' she leaned forward confidentially, 'you get over it. You have another one. So why not? We try again. And before I look around, again I'm carrying. Bigger and bigger I'm getting, with that business in the morning of being sick, with all the – well you know from what I'm talking. Then the time comes. I get into the bed. Isaac walks up and down, downstairs. The doctor comes, he shakes his head, he says to me, "Missus, there's nothing there." '

'That's right,' Bernard said, excited. 'That's what it was with Sheila. But what did you do then?'

'The doctor said to me, "Get up," he said, "Pull yourself together." That's all.'

There was a silence. Bernard looked to her for further information. She couldn't withhold it now. 'What happened then?' he said.

'That's all,' she repeated. 'I got up and I pulled myself together. The baby was not in my belly. In my head it was. So I pulled myself together.' She began to cackle with the recollection of her former silliness. 'In those days,' she added, 'there was a lot of it about.'

'But what happened to your stomach?' Bernard insisted.

'Gradual, it disappeared,' she said. 'I pulled myself together. Like the doctor told me.'

Bernard didn't know what to make of it all. She could hardly have made it all up. She knew the symptoms much too well. But her cure had been too easy. 'What did you do after that?' he said.

'Well, I said to my Isaac, God has blessed us with one, I said. We must be satisfied. Believe me, after what he'd been through, he was grateful. So. We had a nice marriage. A saint he was, my Isaac.' She took Bernard's hand. 'So nice it is to have a little talk with you.'

He smiled at her. He wondered why she didn't ask about Sheila, why she did not seem curious as to the outcome of Sheila's phantom. He realised that it was so rare that she had the opportunity to speak about the past with anybody, that, once given the chance, it blunted any interest or curiosity in anybody else.

'Grandma,' he said, 'my Sheila's still pregnant.'

'You mean from the phantom?' she said, jerking herself suddenly into the present.

Bernard nodded. 'Three years,' he said.

'Oi, veh is mir,' she keened. 'She's so fat?'

'She's in a wheel-chair.'

'Oi, oi,' Mrs Singer said, over and over again, rocking herself to and fro. Then suddenly she was angry. 'She should pull herself together,' she shouted.

'Perhaps you could help her,' Bernard said.

'To me she'd listen?' Mrs Singer said with scorn. 'Who listens to an old woman?'

Then Bernard told her about the possibility of family therapy, and he explained to her the rudiments. He no longer had any fears that she wouldn't understand them. She was pretty clued up on everything, except the terminology, and that, Bernard simplified.

'Natural, I'll come,' she said when he had finished.

'You'll bring me in the car. I shall stay by you for the night,' she said, organising her own outing. 'I should stay perhaps longer by you,' she said, on second thoughts. 'I should talk with your wife a little.'

It seemed to Bernard that it was suddenly Sheila who'd become the non-kin, and he himself of the old lady's own blood. He really rather liked her, he thought, and he couldn't understand how she had produced for him such an unpalatable mother-in-law. He took his leave, promising to give her good notice of their first therapy appointment.

On his way out, Mrs Spengler put her hand on his arm.

'I know,' Bernard said. 'They took away your father's shop.'

She was furious. He had up-staged her, robbing her of her only line. 'It wasn't my fault,' she shouted after him. She watched him go down the corridor, and heard in the echo of her amazing words, a volcanic eruption. And it was her own mouth that had ignited them, those terrible, beautiful and remedial words, and she clapped her hand over her lips, in fear that the sudden truth they had unbridled would tear them asunder. 'They took away Daddy's shop,' she whispered to herself, 'and it wasn't my fault.' She said the words to herself, over and over again, each time in a deeper and more rueful whisper, with a small breath of regret that whenever she would say those words again, it would be more out of habit than pain.

A few days later, Bernard received a reply to his letter to Robert. It was short and to the point. 'Dear Bernard. I think family therapy will be a fine piece of entertainment for us all. If anything helps to dethrone my mother, I will gladly be a party to it. Please let me know of your arrangements. My best to Sheila.'

Well, Bernard thought, each one of us will have his own axe to grind. He was well pleased with his tribal in-gathering and he began to look forward to the first session. Then he remembered that he'd forgotten about Sheila, she who

150

was the very centre and the purpose of the treatment. Recently she had been docile enough. She had not exactly co-operated, but she had refrained from resistance. Still, even her patience could be tried. He hoped she would not make a final stand on this last desperate manoeuvre, for that is how Bernard regarded it, and he dared not think of the consequences of its failure.

She was in the drawing-room with Clarissa. He marvelled at her repose, how she sat there, evening after evening, her chair at growing distance from the piano, and finding her bulk and its meaning so undisturbing. And Clarissa too, with her gentle collusion, feigned or real, it didn't matter, accompanying her fantasy, and both of them, in melody and tone, so moving, that for a moment pity overwhelmed him, and he too was in danger of collusion. He opened the drawing-room door just to look at her, the ugly swelling land-mass of her, in order to dispel the pity that threatened him. He gave himself a generous eyeful, and it was enough. He closed the door, wholly repelled. Even the music, melodious as it was, could not in his mind be dissociated from the players, and he ran to his study to black out all sound of it.

But Buster was listening in ecstasy. His fiddle was tucked under his chin, and he drew the bow across the strings, but a centimetre above them, so as to make no sound. In this way, he played the Mozart E minor Sonata along with Clarissa, though he was of the opinion that his phrasing was more subtle. He heard how his mother's playing had improved, and he took a little credit for it himself. His presence in her body, the very musicianship of it, was bound to affect her playing. During the course of the sonata, he was never tempted to play out loud. It was the last thought that would have occurred to him. To play aloud would have been an act to evoke response, praise or criticism. It would have been an act which spelled out the craving for audience, and he had freed himself of that hunger long ago. Nothing would induce him to sing his songs aloud. Sometimes, his mother's patience and her simple faith so moved him that he feared he might be tempted to declare himself, simply for her sake, but if he did that, it would start that unending crippling cycle, the avoidance of which had been his sole reason for refusing sortie. A self-declaration at this point would annul all his former debate, all the sweat and toil he had donated to his final decision. It would be counter-productive in the extreme. So he played a centimetre above the strings. But he heard it; in his inner ear he heard it, and it filled him with joy.

'That was beautiful,' his mother said, as they came to the end of the first movement.

'I think we're getting better,' Clarissa giggled.

'We're so ready for a concert,' Sheila said. 'What a pity that we can't take any engagements.'

It was the first time that Clarissa had heard any regret from Sheila of her condition. And it worried her. For such a feeling could only intensify. 'It won't be for much longer,' she said.

'D'you know, Clarissa,' Sheila said, wheeling her chair away from the piano, 'sometimes I wonder whether what they say about me is true. That I'm just indulging in a crazy fantasy, and that the whole thing is an illusion.'

'Don't be silly,' Clarissa said, wondering whether she was altogether saying the right thing, but she felt herself catching something of Sheila's sudden uncertainty. 'But it's got to be a baby. What else could it be?' she said lamely.

'I don't know,' Sheila said. 'That's what keeps me going. That it's got to be a baby. It can't be anything else. In any case I feel it inside me. I feel its growth, and I feel its love, I feel its tenderness, and I feel its peace. It's on my side, I know.'

Buster turned his ear from the listening-wall. Such talk shook him, it threatened his firm resolve, it flooded him with ruinous sentimentality. It was dangerously luring, and he couldn't afford to avail himself of its seduction. Don't make me play aloud, he begged her. Please. Let me survive within my own true self, not as any part of you, a being that has grown into a self that is none of your doing. Do not feed me with *your* hunger to sing my song into your ear. Let me dwell in my own chosen silence.

For the first time since his withdrawal, Buster was engulfed by an overwhelming sadness, induced by the realisation that finally, despite all resolution, man cannot live alone. He cannot live for himself. Not even in a sheltered womb. That the act of conception itself is a forfeiture, and that whatever he is, however he survives, he *owes*. That at some time, and in some place, he must sing for his supper. Or else he must inflict pain. Oh, what shall I do, he cried to himself, to safeguard the silence of my song?

Note from Dr Brown. At this point of Buster's journal there is a peculiar entry. I had some difficulty in decoding it. Not that it was illegible. The writing was distinct enough, but the characters of the letters were of the Hebrew script. My research led me to the discovery that the entry was a simple saying of the famous Rabbi Hillel, taken from his collection, 'The Ethics of the Fathers'. Here it is, exactly as I found it, and its translation follows.

אִם אֵין אֲנִי לִי מִי לִי׃
וּכְשֶׁאֲנִי לְעַצְמִי מָה אֲנִי׃
וְאִם לֹא עַכְשָׁו אֵימָתַי׃

'If I am not for myself, who is for me? But if I am only for myself, what am I? And if not now, when?'

153

Chapter 10

Word had got around the Family Therapy Clinic that a case of historic interest was about to go into production. Drs Worcester and Lessor, who were directing proceedings, were besieged with requests from psychiatry students, social workers, anthropologists, and even the odd priest, to attend as part of the unseen audience, and on the morning of 29th June, the day of Buster's third unbirthday, the auditorium was crowded with eager students. They were of all ages, and from sundry fields, but one thing they had in common: a firm belief in the fantasy diagnosis, and a profound scepticism in any alternative. The priests from various orders were fully cloaked in their trappings, their crosses and their bibles, as safeguards against the evil eye. For there was nothing like fantasy to lure the devil into one's soul. Unlike the others, they carried no note-books. They would retain in their minds only that which confirmed their faith.

Before the family session began, Dr Worcester addressed the gathering which was the normal form of procedure before therapy began. Dr Lessor sat at his side, occasionally confirming with a nod of his head the wise deductions that his colleague was offering.

'The Rosen family,' Dr Worcester was saying, 'have come here as a last resort. Mrs Rosen, around whom the case is centred, has been in a condition of phantom pregnancy for over three years.'

There was a stifled gasp throughout the auditorium. 'Indeed, ladies and gentlemen,' the doctor went on, 'this is a case that causes us to wonder. In my knowledge and in so far as I can ascertain, in the whole history of psychiatry, it is the longest phantom pregnancy on record. The case itself is complicated enough, but it is aggravated by certain factors. Not the least of these is Mrs Rosen's aversion to treatment of any kind. Over the last three years she has been persuaded to a small number of treatment centres. She started an orthodox Freudian analysis soon after her abortive delivery, but she withdrew after two sessions. She flirted for a while with bio-energetic therapy, but after a short while became disillusioned with that too. Recently she had one session with an image-therapist, and likewise with a faith-healer. In all these sessions she has been a reluctant participant. Only to one form of therapy, if one may call it that, has she volunteered with any willingness, and if I may say so, even desire. She has regularly visited a clairvoyant, not on her own behalf, she assures me, but for the benefit of her child, of whose future she is completely assured. Mr Rosen is quite obviously under great stress. Quite naturally, the abortive delivery has sown grave doubts in his own mind as to the nature of his own virility. Living with a woman like Mrs Rosen would try anybody's patience, and Mr Rosen's attitude varies from one of solicitous caring, to one of downright indifference. He has been responsible for persuading the family to gather here today, and he regards family therapy as a last resort.

'Before we begin, I will give you some basic information about the participants. The oldest member of the family is Mrs Singer. She is eighty-six years old, and is the mother of Mrs Joseph, who herself is the mother of the patient. Mrs Singer is widowed, and is a reluctant resident of an old-age home, where she was placed some years ago by her only child, Mrs Joseph. Mrs Joseph herself is sixty-six years old, also widowed, living alone in the old family house. She has two children, Sheila, our patient, who, at thirty-four, is the elder. The younger is Robert at thirty-one. Robert is of no fixed abode, and of no fixed occupation. He has recently served a term of two years' imprisonment in Strangeways Jail, Manchester, on a charge of drug trafficking. The last member of our group is Mr Rosen himself, our patient's husband, to whom she has been married for ten years.

'So you see, ladies and gentlemen, here we have a very interesting spectrum. We will be able to view a family through three generations, or, as our patient would insist, through four.'

The audience tittered slightly, making quite clear which side they were on.

'It is a most fertile area of family therapy investigation, and I hope that we, at least, will profit by it. We will use the same procedure as is customary, but for those in the audience who may be new to this type of therapy, I will elucidate the form. This window across the wall behind my back gives on to the family room, and as you see, although it is now empty of people, the room itself is distinctly visible. This pane of glass is a one-way mirror, and those who are in the family room will view the glass as a window looking out on a blank wall. Although they will not be able to see you, they are aware that you will be looking in on them. It is the policy of this clinic to be as open as possible with its patients, and we regard it as unethical to keep them in the dark about their exposure. In the corner here, as you see,' Dr Worcester pointed to a contraption standing on a table, 'we have a video-camera which will record all the proceedings and dialogue from the family room. We find such a record invaluable for our research studies.

'Now a word about the session itself. I myself shall remain in this room as an observer. My colleague, Dr Lessor, will go into the therapy room to meet the family. He will be accompanied by Mr Wyndham, one of the social workers attached to the clinic. He and the family will be in discussion for about half an hour, after which time he and Mr Wyndham will leave the room, ostensibly for a coffee-break. For a quarter of an hour the family will be left to themselves. We have always found this interval period most valuable to our assessment, for although they know that they are being overhead and overlooked, the family by that time will normally have lost most of their inhibitions, and their revelations are most useful. After his break, Dr Lessor will continue therapy for another thirty minutes. The family will then go home, and we shall remain here, re-view the video-tape, and start our discussions. Any questions which worry you may be asked at that session. Ah,' he said, looking at the door, 'here is Mr Wyndham.'

The social worker entered, his head full of worry and his arms full of books. 'They are ready,' he said.

Dr Lessor rose and went to join Mr Wyndham. 'We'll be on our way then,' he said. They left the room. The students shuffled their note-books, the priests offered up a prayer, and Dr Worcester took up his observer's post at the table.

There was silence as the rank and file of the Singer/ Joseph/Rosen pedigree entered the lion's den.

First to present himself was Robert, in all his Earls Court Hare Krishna tourist splendour. He faced the window, and knowing his audience, he acknowledged their presence with a small bow. Nobody was fooling him, he let them know. He was obviously here to enjoy himself, and taking a chair at random, he planted it against the screen and, with his back to the audience, he settled himself down.

Mrs Singer came next, on Bernard's arm, followed by Mrs Joseph with an air both of a rejected escort and an unwanted escortee. Bernard helped Mrs Singer to a chair, then settled his mother-in-law, before sitting down himself. There was a pause, which was right and proper before the star's entrance. Then Sheila wheeled herself in, her face a mask of bland indifference. The audience gasped at her girth, which, in profile was titanic. She looked around for a space between the chairs, one large enough to preclude neighbourliness, and she found it in a corner of the room,

157

next to a table. Then Dr Lessor and Mr Wyndham entered. Mr Wyndham took his appointed place near the table, and Dr Lessor proceeded with a rearrangement of seating. The placing of participants in a family therapy session is of prime importance, in that it can define a hierarchy. The shifting of places during a session is encouraged by the therapist, and those moves tend to reflect a shifting of power. But the primary seating must be arranged according to the natural order. To this end, Dr Lessor placed Mrs Singer stage centre, where, from her ruling manner, he had no doubt she would remain. Next to her he placed Mrs Joseph on the principle that it was better to sit next to your enemy than opposite him, thus avoiding visual confrontation. Opposite her, in his green ignorance, Dr Lessor placed Robert, and next to him, Bernard. He then wheeled Sheila into the centre of the circle, like a poor Jenny with whom no one wanted to play.

'Are we all settled then?' he said, taking his seat. 'If at any point you wish to change seats, please do so. We are all free to do as we wish.'

There was no response from the players, except for Bernard, who shifted in his chair, and loosened his tie. He gave the air of one who was going to do his damnedest to co-operate, and he hoped the others would follow his example.

'Now,' Dr Lessor said, 'the first thing to remember is that no one is on trial here. It will help us to help Sheila if we can get to know her family, and how you all feel about each other.'

This remark was greeted by a loud guffaw from Robert. 'D'you really want to know that?' he said.

'Yes.' Dr Lessor leaned forward greedily, sensing that he was going to get a fruitful earful. But then Robert got cold feet. He didn't want to be the first to set the ball rolling. It might create an avalanche. 'Ask the others,' he said.

Mrs Joseph offered her opinion. 'I want to get this clear,'

she said, and her remarks were addressed to the non-kin. 'There's never been anything like this on our side of the family.'

Bernard shifted again in his chair, and loosened a tie that was already almost unknotted.

'Anything like what?' Dr Lessor said.

'This psychology business.' She was being as polite as she knew how.

'Sheila's condition isn't hereditary, Mrs Joseph, and no one is to blame for it,' Dr Lessor said firmly.

This was undoubtedly Mrs Singer's cue. 'Of course it's hereditary,' she said, as if with a lifetime knowledge of genetic legacy. 'I also had.'

It was clear that, apart from Bernard, this was news to the rest of the family, and the audience were quick to make a note of their spontaneous reactions.

The first came from Mrs Joseph. 'She had one like I'm a grandmother,' she said with scorn, managing in one short statement to encapsulate her feelings towards each side of her genealogy.

'Is it true, Grandma?' Robert said.

'I should live,' the old lady insisted.

'She's doing it for sympathy,' Mrs Joseph said. 'And my daughter doesn't need sympathy. She needs a jolly good hiding.'

'You want I should speak from my phantom?' Mrs Singer said in a you-can-take-it-or-leave-it tone.

'Please, Mrs Singer,' Dr Lessor said. He would have preferred to pursue the Mrs Joseph tirade, but he did not want to antagonise the old lady, who, out of pique, might then shut up altogether.

'I had everything,' she said. 'Like Sheila here. Same reasons. I wanted so bad a baby. So I imagine. I invent. The big belly I invent, the pains, I invent. Even the labour. But a baby,' she began to laugh, 'that, I couldn't invent. I tell you Mister,' she said, leaning in Dr Lessor's direction, 'when I could invent a baby, then I'd be the Almighty.'

'Why do you think Sheila is in the same condition?' Mr Wyndham opened his account with his first question.

'She wants a baby,' Mrs Singer said, as if it were all so simple. 'What young woman doesn't want a baby, I ask you? So she makes like she's pregnant.'

Now it was Sheila's turn to smile, and the sudden change in her expression was not lost on Dr Lessor. 'D'you want to say something, Sheila?' he said hopefully.

'No. I'm just listening,' she said.

'Take that smirk off your face,' Mrs Joseph was beside herself. 'You think it's all one big joke, don't you.'

'How d'you feel about Sheila?' Dr Lessor said, cashing in on her anger.

'What do you mean, how do I feel. What should a mother feel? I've always done my best for her. It's breaking my heart.'

Laughter from down-stage right. Robert was back on set. In the auditorium, almost all the observers wrote the identical note in Robert's column. 'Hostile.'

'Why are you laughing?' Mr Wyndham asked.

'My mother's heart has been breaking ever since I had ears to hear. Why doesn't it break and be done with it.'

More frenzied note-taking in the auditorium.

'Nice talk from my son,' Mrs Joseph announced to the assembly. Then she ignored him and focused her attention on her stubborn daughter. 'Didn't we always do what was best for you? You wanted piano lessons. You had them. The best teachers. Special classes for accompanying. Whatever you wanted, we gave.' She paused, not for effect's sake, but for a desperate need to draw breath. 'Did you ever want for anything?' she shouted.

'A baby,' Sheila said.

Dr Worcester made a note in Sheila's column. 'Does she expect her mother to give her a baby too?' But he'd misread Sheila's remark. She was talking to nobody. The statement of her needs was for no one's ears, but as a simple self-confirmation. Whatever the others may have thought of Sheila's contribution, they each reacted in worried silence.

Dr Lessor looked to Mrs Joseph to start the ball rolling again.

'What did I do Doctor?' she pleaded with him. 'What did I do to deserve all this?'

Then Robert blew. 'Why in God's name don't you stop thinking about yourself for just one minute,' he shouted. 'There are other people in the world. We're fucking well here to help Sheila.'

Everybody noticed the tears in his voice, and the note-taking in the hall was fast and furious. And probably identical.

Mrs Singer shivered. She'd heard of such language, but she'd never actually been audience to it. And though she highly approved of what Robert had said, she refrained from agreement because it might have signalled that she was concurring with his language as well.

'Sorry Grandma,' Robert said, noting her reaction.

'*You*,' Mrs Joseph spat in her son's direction. 'I've got nothing to say to you.' Then she turned to Dr Lessor, who had somehow assumed for her the role of her defence lawyer. 'That one's been a great disappointment to me, Doctor,' she confided.

My, my, Doctor Worcester thought, turning to look at the audience. This was indeed a field day.

'Can't you leave me out of this?' Robert said quietly. 'We're here for Sheila.'

Dr Lessor thought that this was a moment when Robert might be forthcoming. 'Robert,' he said, 'do you have any ideas about your sister's condition?'

'Sure,' he said, as if he was only waiting to be asked. 'I think she wants a baby, but at the same time, she's afraid to have one.'

161

Mrs Joseph was not going to sit by and be party to such nonsense. 'What does he know,' she said to anyone who cared to listen, unmindful of the fact that there were a couple of hundred ears waiting on her every syllable. 'What does he know about having babies? Afraid?' she said with scorn. 'Nowadays they give you drugs. You don't feel anything. Not like in my day.' She shot Robert a murderous glance. Then once more turning to her advocate, she said, 'I almost died with him, Doctor.'

Now without doubt, they were getting somewhere. The half hour was up, but now was no time for a break. Dr Lessor quietly signalled to Dr Worcester that he was carrying on. He turned to Robert. 'I don't think you were referring to the physical pain,' he said, 'when you said that Sheila was afraid of having a baby. What did you mean exactly?'

'With her history, and mine too, for that matter,' Robert said, 'she's afraid the baby will disappoint her. That he won't live up to her expectations. That's all we've heard about, all our lives. And our parents' disappointment. Sheila feels guilty about it, so she wants a child to make it up to them. One that will fulfil everybody's expectations. But she's afraid it won't. That's what she's afraid of. My God,' he said, 'anybody with a modicum of insight could see that. I don't know why we need a shoal of psychiatrists to tell us.'

'What do you think, Sheila?' Dr Lessor ventured to the heart.

'Robert knows everything,' Sheila said, and nobody could tell whether or not she was serious.

The silence that followed was uncharged. Dr Lessor considered it a good time for a break. He stood up. 'Mr Wyndham and I will give you a break for a few minutes,' he said. 'Someone will bring you some coffee. We'll be back shortly.'

When they had gone the silence continued, out of shame,

pride or sheer boredom. Each member avoided the others'
gaze, and it was a sigh of relief that greeted the girl who
came in with a tray of coffee. She went first to Mrs Singer in
acknowledgement of her chieftainship. Mrs Singer was
thoroughly enjoying herself. Just to be out of that dreary
sitting-room of hers was treat enough, and the prospect of a
night's truancy was sheer bliss. She sipped her coffee with
relish.

The tray moved to Mrs Joseph. 'I couldn't touch a
thing,' she said. 'I'm too upset.'

'You know they're listening, don't you,' Robert said. 'Is
this still for their benefit?'

'I don't care any more,' she shouted at him. 'Already
I've been put to shame by my clever son. What more can
you tell them about me?'

'About when you came to see me in prison?' Robert
offered.

Mrs Joseph, who had never been totally unaware of an
audience, now sensed the need for a filter. 'Sh,' she pleaded
with him. 'They can hear everything you say.'

'That's all you care about,' Robert shouted at her. 'What
other people think. That's why Sheila's here. She's the poor
bloody scapegoat for the lot of us.'

'Huh, my clever son,' his mother said. 'There's nothing
wrong with your sister. She wants her head read, that's all.'

'That's what they're doing.' Robert said patiently.

'So she thought she was carrying,' Mrs Joseph ignored his
interruption. 'Anyone can make a mistake. But it's gone on
too long already. She should get out of that chair and walk.
Do some excercise. Go on a diet. Fat, that's all she is. She
should pull herself together.'

'If anyone needs treatment here, it's you,' Robert said.

Back in the auditorium, they salivated at each revelation.
And then Sheila went and spoiled the party. 'I want to go
home,' she said.

'You sit there, my girl,' Mrs Joseph thundered, 'until the

163

doctor cures you. That's what we're paying him for.'

'I want to go home,' Sheila said again.

Bernard rose from his seat. He suddenly realised that during the whole course of the session he hadn't opened his mouth. Then he considered that in fact he really had nothing to say. He had to live with the problem, and the living drained him of all coherent vocabulary. 'We'd better go,' he managed to say.

At that point, having overheard Sheila's wishes, and sensing a deep deprivation to medical research, Dr Worcester, in his full-blown directorship authority, entered the room. 'It would be such a pity,' he said, 'if you were to go now. We think we are discovering some very important factors in Sheila's case, which may be helpful in the future.' He wasn't specific about the recipient of such help, and it was left open whether it was Sheila in particular, or medical science in general.

But Sheila was insistent. 'I want to go home,' she said again.

'We can't stop you,' Dr Worcester said. 'Here one is free to come and go. But I do beg you to reconsider.' He refrained from asking Mrs Joseph to intervene on behalf of scholarship, but she did so, notwithstanding.

'It's for the sake of medicine,' she said. 'They've never had a case like it before, Sheila,' she begged. 'You're special.'

'Special?' Sheila said. 'Why have you never said that to me before?'

Mrs Joseph crumbled. 'Oh my God,' she said. 'Whatever you say is wrong.'

'Take me home, Bernard,' Sheila said. 'This is a waste of everybody's time.'

Bernard wheeled her out of the room, and the others followed. Mrs Joseph attempted to take her mother's arm, but she suffered rejection even from that frail quarter.

'Helpless I'm not yet,' the old lady said, tottering on her

164

eighty-six years. 'I'm sorry,' she said, turning to Dr Worcester. 'I was enjoying it. I had so much more I could say. Especially Robert I enjoy. Such a clever boy that one.'

Dr Worcester gave her his arm and took her to join the others.

Buster had heard every word, and he was sorely distressed. It was not the therapy in itself that depressed him. In his opinion, family therapy was very much on the right track, and given a chance, could well get to the root of any neurosis. It was his mother's silence that moved him, the sad overall sense of others' manipulation, and also a fear that she was losing her will to resist them. All the doctors had for her pregnancy was her word, her lunatic fantastical word. No X-ray photographs, and no sign, after three years, of an impending arrival. She deserved some small reward at least for her abiding patience. He had to give her a slight but unmistakable proof of his presence. Yet, if he gave her that, however small, it would be a sign to others too, and they would open her up again, and pull him out, struggle as he may; they would wrench him from his hermitage, punishing him for hoodwinking them for so long. He had to think of something that would prove his presence to her, and to her alone. Some aspect of himself that she could not share with others. Then he realised what it had to be. He had to lower his bow onto the string, and sing his songs aloud. It was only his playing he would give her. And he would choose his audience. He would play only for her. And perhaps, for his weakness, for his poor father. He would eavesdrop for any other witnesses, and their presence would raise his bow again. He would play for Robert, if he could sniff out his presence, but his grandmother would never hear him. Nor any of those doctors who viewed imagination as a disease, who scorned fantasy, who would take the magic and the glory out of a sunset, and measure Mozart in cold decibels. Not for them, his songs. They were solely for his mother's gentleness, her

165

love, and her total and abiding faith. He would give her proof of her trust in him.

Sheila was hoisted into Bernard's car, and Mrs Singer and Mrs Joseph sat in the back. Robert chose to make his own way home. He kissed Sheila goodbye. 'Whatever you think,' he said smiling, 'I agree with you absolutely.' He turned to go, then coming back, he whispered, 'But we may be wrong.' Then he put his arm around her. 'I don't want anything bad ever to happen to you,' he said.

'I wish you'd come and live with me,' she said.

He turned and left quickly. Sheila knew that he was crying, but she dare not wonder why.

They were all to go back to Sheila's house. Mrs Joseph had calmed down. She had said nothing since they'd left the clinic, but it was not a silence of reproach, but sheer weariness and depression.

'Cheer up,' Mrs Singer said. 'We should all have a nice cup of tea.'

'I'll make it as soon as we get home,' Bernard said. He was glad he was not alone with Sheila, that others were around to share the burden, but Sheila was happier without any company, except for the child inside her. She wanted to go home and to be alone, and sit at the piano and play. It was a means of achieving some kind of peace. She wished they would all go back to their own homes, including Bernard whose presence became more and more overbearing.

'I know,' Bernard said suddenly, 'I'll take you all out to tea.' It was a way of disposing of Sheila, whom everybody knew was not fit to be seen in public.

'That'll be nice for Grandma,' Sheila said. 'But take me home first. I want to practise a little.'

When they reached home, the two older women stayed in the car, and Bernard helped Sheila into the house.

'You'll be all right, won't you?' he said.

She found his occasional solicitousness even harder to

166

bear than his irritation. 'Perhaps your mother's right,' he dared to say, wheeling her into the drawing-room. 'You should try and get up and walk. Go on a diet,' he laboured on. 'Your mother may have all the wrong reasons, but she may be right all the same. How about trying to walk?'

'Could *you* walk,' Sheila said angrily, 'with a three-year-old growing child inside you?'

He held her firmly by the shoulders. 'There's nothing inside you,' he said as gently as he could. He left her at the piano and went quickly out of the house. Perhaps he hoped, as he hoped so often nowadays, that he was seeing her for the last time.

Sheila had never felt so unhappy. Bernard's parting shot had not made her angry. Not any more. But it had frightened her. And so had Robert's when he'd left her. 'I don't want anything bad ever to happen to you,' he had said. She began for the first time to have fears for herself, for her own life as well as that of her baby. She felt so deeply and helplessly sad. She wheeled herself away from the piano. It no longer held out for her any hope of solace.

There are what are known as propitious moments. And now was surely one of them. It was at this moment that Buster, having eavesdropped on no one's presence, chose to make his playing début. He tucked the fiddle under his chin, and held the bow at the ready. He realised that this was the first time in his present life that he had played in public, distant and small as that public might be. He was suddenly nervous. He wanted to play at his very best, not so much at this moment for his own sake, but for the joy and the confirmation of his mother's, whose sadness throbbed in the very walls of his cell. He took a deep breath and launched into the Bach Chaconne for solo violin, the very piece which Clarissa had played with such love and such hope for his sortie. Even as he was playing it, he knew that he had never played better. He played his little heart out, and outside his cell, it sang with the voice of an angel.

Sheila listened and wept. She wept for her own now-proven madness. Not only was she feeling things in her stomach, she was now hearing them too. Perhaps the others were right after all. She was mad. Totally. When Bernard came home, she would ask him kindly to put her away.

At the end of the movement, Buster heard her weeping, and they were clearly not tears of joy. He had not bargained with this reaction. How could he prove to her that he was real, that the music was not in her own tortured mind, but true, concrete, and real inside her. He started on the next movement of the Partita. Sheila let her head fall, and the tears flowed as she listened. She was now convinced, as her mother never tired of saying, it was all in her head. The music was so beautiful that no human hand could have had any part of it. She listened, mad as she might be, lulled by its beauty. There was a pause before the last movement, and in that pause, she heard something other than music, that caused her to rethink her surrender into madness. She actually heard a violin tuning. And then the last movement was in full swing. She felt it coming from inside her. She had no doubts about that. She tried desperately to bend her ear to her stomach wall, to ascertain the source of the music. But with her vast girth, it was anatomically impossible. Yet she was sure now that whoever was making such divine music dwelt inside her. And what's more, he was making it on Clarissa's missing violin. She waited till the end of the movement. 'Bravo,' she shouted through her tears, clapping her hands until they hurt.

Buster heard the acclaim, and he bowed, smiling from ear to ear. Although Sheila was now almost totally convinced that it was her child who was playing, she needed a final proof to set her sanity at rest. She would invite her unseen partner to play the Spring Sonata. That would mutually seal their trust, their faith, and their unspeakable loving.

168

She wheeled herself to the piano, opened the lid, and gave her partner an 'A'. To her delight, but no longer her surprise, Buster picked it up and retuned his fiddle accordingly.

'Let's play the Spring Sonata,' she said. It seemed to her a simple matter of courtesy to let him know what they were going to play, especially since it was a work in which both players began together, and there was no opportunity for the one to take the cue from the other. 'Are you ready?' She gave him the beat. 'One, two, three, four.'

She started to play. His was the melody and she listened to it sing. She wept again, but this time for sheer joy. She would happily have died at that very moment, with such music in her ears, and of her own patient waiting. She needed no more proof that it was her little one who played, and when the movement was finished, she patted her stomach, and whispered, 'Yascha, my darling, you and I will make music for ever.' Then she began to test him, by playing the openings of each sonata, and waiting for his entry. And each time he obliged. Then she did the same with the Mozart cycle, and his response was equally faithful. 'My God,' she said, after listening to his heavenly response to a Schubert sonata, 'he knows the whole repertoire.' She leaned back in her chair, exhausted. 'Play something on your own, Yascha,' she whispered.

And out of the depths of his soul and hers, she heard again the Bach Chaconne, and she thought she had entered heaven.

The spell was broken by the sound of Bernard's key in the lock. Buster must have heard it too. For the music cut out, quite suddenly. This worried her a little, for she feared that her child would not give proof to others of her sanity. She patted her stomach. 'Yascha,' she said. 'When I ask you, will you play for Daddy. Just for Daddy. No one else. For my sake.'

He plucked a wide-spread chord, and she took it for his giving answer.

Bernard came in with his allies. 'We had a lovely tea,' he said. 'Did you eat something?'

'No,' she said. 'I've been playing.'

'I'll make you some,' he said. He was relieved to get himself away into the kitchen, and leave the uneasy air to the women. They both sat themselves down on armchairs, and looked as if they had come to stay. Sheila desperately wanted to get Bernard on his own, and she needed the piano as an accompaniment to her grand revelation. She had no wish to say to him, 'I told you so.' Her joy was so full that it held no room for malice. She looked at the two worn-out old soldiers and wondered how she could decently get them to go away. She wanted them out of sight, but especially out of earshot.

'You're looking very flushed,' her mother said. 'You seem excited.'

'I've had an exciting day,' Sheila said.

Mrs Joseph couldn't quite see, herself, what was exciting about their therapy session. She looked at her daughter with abject despair. 'What in God's name will become of you?'

'I'm going to be a mother,' Sheila said, with utter calm.

'Like a stubborn mule she is.' She turned to her own mother for her support.

Mrs Singer decided to try her own brand of therapy. 'A mule she isn't,' she shouted at her daughter, making quite clear where her support lay. 'But I'm asking you Sheila,' she said quietly. 'Whoever heard from a baby being born already three years old? Is against nature.'

'Perhaps it will just grow inside me,' Sheila said, 'and never be born at all. It's still my child.'

'Why not?' Mrs Singer said. 'That also is a solution. But how much bigger will it grow? Soon, and time flies, believe me, like Robert it'll be, and when your baby's like Robert, tell me please, how big are *you*? A giant you'll be.'

'That's right,' Sheila said. She seemed quite happy with the prospect.

'So you'll be a giant,' Mrs Singer said. 'My grand-daughter, the giant,' and she dissolved into laughter.

'Two lunatics we've got in this house.' Mrs Joseph was beside herself again. 'I can't stand it any longer.' She got up and prepared to leave. One down, Sheila thought. One to go. Grandma was staying with them, and after her tiring day, she was bound to make an early night. She would have to wait till evening before she could share Yascha's secret with Bernard.

When Mrs Joseph was gone, things were calmer and almost jovial. Mrs Singer showed no signs of fatigue, but regaled them endlessly with stories of her childhood, interspersed with gruesome details of her present mode of existence. It seemed that all of them had suddenly forgotten the seriousness and heartbreak of Sheila's condition.

At length, Mrs Singer wished to be shown to her room. Bernard took her upstairs, and Sheila waited for his return. She wheeled herself towards the piano. 'Yascha,' she whispered, tapping her stomach, 'soon I want you to play for Daddy. Just for me and for Daddy.' She held her hand on her stomach, caressing the shape of him. And she waited.

'Aren't you going to bed?' Bernard shouted down from the stairway.

'Could you come down a minute?' she said. 'I want to talk to you.'

He was puzzled. He and Sheila had so very little verbal communication, or any other for that matter. He had a sudden hope that she might have come to her senses, and was going to volunteer for an X-ray to settle matters once and for all. 'I'm coming,' he said, and she heard the gaiety in his voice. I'll give him cause for joy at last, she thought.

Note from Dr Brown. When Buster made his critical decision to declare himself, I doubt whether he was aware of the dire consequences of such an action. From his entry in his journal at this time it is clear that his motives were innocent enough. He

171

simply wanted to reward his mother for her faith in him. He gives no hint in his entry of any fear that his confidence would be abused. He meant it simply as a contract between his mother and himself, and marginally, for his mother's sake, with his father. I find his naïveté hard to understand. He was a child of such great wisdom, he was bound to have seen the pitfalls of such a contract. So I presume it was not naïveté at all. He was simply overwhelmed by a deep and passionate love, in the name of which all folly is committable. At this stage of his journal, I feared his downfall. My fears were justified, though the subsequent manner of Buster's undoing was beyond my poor imagination.

Chapter 11

On Sheila's instructions, Bernard drew a chair up to the piano, and sat alongside her. What new madness had entered her head, he wondered. But he would play along with her. After the fiasco of the family therapy, he knew he had no alternative now but to commit her. And that he had in mind to do. He would set the wheels in motion on the following day. 'What am I to do?' he said, feigning some interest in the game.

'Just sit still and listen.'

'To what?' he said.

She smiled at him. 'To my phantom baby.' She patted her stomach. 'Yascha,' she said, 'Daddy's with me. Only Daddy. And we're going to play the Spring Sonata.'

Poor woman, Bernard thought. She's well and truly gone.

'One, two, three, four,' Sheila counted, and she began. And so did Buster. Bernard listened to the first few bars. Full of suspicion. He felt it was a trap, some machination of her twisted mind to lure him, his sane, solid practical self, into her madness. He thought it must be a recording and he went over to the record-player. The turntable was still and recordless. He began to tremble. The very last thing he would entertain as a possibility was the child's being, and likewise any evidence to that effect. Yet the playing continued. He had never heard the like of its tone before. It was magical. He was tempted to put his ear to his wife's monstrous growth, but in doing so he would be showing himself available to belief, and he didn't want to give her trickery any encouragement. He took up his stand in various parts of the room, and listened. He checked the ceiling for microphones. His eyes darted around the room into every corner, desperate to find some clue as to how the trick was done. But there was nothing. 'Tell him to stop,' he shouted at her, then regretted it, for if she could do that, then the trick would be compounded, and it was already puzzling enough.

'Not in the middle of a movement,' Sheila said, and she continued playing.

Bernard tiptoed to the piano and stood alongside her. At such proximity he had to acknowledge the possible source of the sound, and then, unable to restrain himself, he laid his ear flat against her stomach. He paled. There was now no doubt in his mind at all. The child was playing inside her.

He listened and he wept. He wept not only for the music's beauty, but for his own lack of faith, his terrible disloyalty. He kissed the woollen cloth of Sheila's dress, and whispered, 'Forgive me.'

Buster heard it through his playing, and his bowing swelled with joy. I'll play for you, Dad, he thought, any time.

At the end of the movement, Sheila stopped, and stroked the head that lay on what passed for her lap. 'I wasn't mad, was I?' she said.

'It's unbelievable,' he said. 'What are we going to do?'

'Do?' she said, suddenly nervous. 'Why should we do anything?'

'But—' He was astonished at her naïveté. 'How can we *not* do anything?'

'I don't understand you,' she said.

So he had to spell it out to her, loud and clear. 'We're sitting on a gold-mine,' he said.

'*I'm* sitting on a gold-mine,' she said, wishing to get the priorities straight, before she dealt with the principle. 'Isn't it enough for you that you have a son who plays the violin like an angel?'

174

'And isn't it enough for you,' Bernard shouted, sensing her opposition, 'that after all your plans, all your hopes, all your expectations, yes, even all your certainties, you actually have a genius on your hands? Or in your stomach, if you want to be particular?'

'Of course it's enough,' she said. 'Just that. Exactly what you've said. It's enough. I don't want any more.'

'But a genius must be heard. We owe it to the world to put him on show. The Festival Hall, the Carnegie.'

She looked at him, dumbfounded.

'We owe it to society,' he said desperately. He, who all his life had rarely cast a glance in that direction. Perhaps if he framed his ambition in a moral context, she could be persuaded.

'Since when have you cared so much about society?' she said.

Now was not the time to argue with her, he realised. In any case, he must savour the miracle before formulating his plans to put it on a conveyor-belt. For that is exactly what he intended to do, whether his stubborn wife liked it or not. 'I'm sorry,' he said. 'You're right. Let's just listen to him play.'

She smiled, grateful for his understanding, and patting her stomach, she played the opening bars of the Kreutzer Sonata, to give him his cue. For the next hour she and Buster made music together. Occasionally she would apologise to him for her inadequate technique and their unequal partnership. In the second variation of the Andante, she was so stunned by the brilliance of his staccato bowing, that she lost all measure of her own part, until she gave it up, and listened to him, rapt in wonder. Then Buster repeated it, as if urging her to play her part. Once, in the difficult Presto, she needed a little practice in the precision of their ensemble. By stopping, and repeating phrases, she was able to indicate that she needed rehearsal. In the course of time, she was convinced that she and her

Yascha could develop lines of communication, non-verbal, but solely through notation. When the Kreutzer was finished, Bernard applauded, as much for his wife as for the little genius inside her. 'Bravo,' he shouted.

Buster heard the applause, and bowed in response.

Note from Dr Brown. Forgive my interference, dear reader, at this critical juncture, but the entry in Buster's journal after this short recital is worth passing on to you, exactly as I found it. It shows not only Buster's bookish learning but also his growing and fearful realisation that no man is an island. Buster himself gives its derivation.

Proverbs. Chapter 14. Verse 28.

'In the multitude of people is the king's glory; but in the want of people is the destruction of the prince.'

'So that's what happened to Clarissa's violin,' Bernard said, realising it for the first time. 'She won't be too happy when she hears. D'you think he'd play for her, and Grandma and Robert and your mother?' Bernard said. Once he'd persuaded Sheila to a family gathering in their drawing-room, it was only a few steps towards a great audience in the Carnegie Hall.

'I don't know,' Sheila said. 'I've got a feeling he's going to choose his audience. We can try. I'd like my mother especially to hear him,' she said. 'Then I'd have such pleasure in watching her eat all her old and angry words. It's late,' she said. 'I'm tired. Could you help me to my room?'

He wheeled her up the specially constructed ramp to her bedroom, and instead of leaving her by the bedside, as was his wont, he offered to help put her to bed. She was moved by his solicitousness, but also frightened by it, frightened of the marital requests that it might lead to. She still felt an affection for her husband, but over the past years she had grown so self-sufficient, so exclusively concerned with the child in her body, that she'd given very little thought, and certainly no credence, to him who had put it there. She had

come to look upon Yascha's conception as almost immaculate, and the events of this day had only served to
strengthen her belief in that regard.

'I can manage,' she said. She didn't want to hurt him,
but she had reasons for undressing alone. Although she had
never found her girth repulsive, knowing with certainty
what the spread was made of, she had to admit that, to a
dispassionate observer, her nakedness was ugly in the
extreme. Bernard had not seen her body since the day of
her child's non-birthday, and now she did not wish to risk
his repulsion. Besides, now that her body had been proved
to be largely that of her child, it would have been a double
exposure, and she guarded her child's privacy as closely as
her own.

'I'm a bit shy,' she said, watching him hover beside her.

'Of me? But I'm your husband,' Bernard said.

She hadn't heard that word for a long time. She knew it
meant other things, things that were attached to economy
or agriculture, but its marital connection seemed to her to
be the least familiar. 'I'd rather undress alone,' she said.

'Then I'll come back when you're in bed.' He said it as if
he were returning to collect his conjugal rights, and that
she would never hear of. Her body, both out- and now
certainly inside, was a shrine, and its worship did not lie in
penetration. She hoped he'd have the sense not to force her.
Her lack of mobility made her very vulnerable. She could
not overcome him physically. She would plead for her
baby's sake, for *their* baby's sake, she would allow. For the
sake of their genius, even. He might retreat on that plea.
She dreaded his return.

But when Bernard came back, he did not come into the
room. He stood in the doorway. 'I just wanted to say
goodnight,' he said.

In her relief and gratitude, she put her arms out towards
him, then withdrew them quickly, in case he misread her
innocent gesture. He came towards the bed and bent down

177

to kiss her. She allowed that, then she distanced him from her with her hands. He tried not to show his hurt, and went quickly from the room.

In bed, he wondered whether she had smelled the lust on him, and whether she had refused him out of shyness or lack of love. Either explanation angered him, for both ways spelt rejection. Once again he wanted to punish her for the unfairness of it all. He would use the child. In or out of the womb, children were always exploitable. And their little genius could undoubtedly make their fortune. He would try gentle persuasion with his wife, and if that failed – his thinking faltered. He didn't quite know what he would do, for at this stage the punishment of his wife would entail like punishment for his child. Tomorrow he would gather the clan together once again. They would have a mini-concert, and let both performers taste the sweets of audience. Who knows, they might volunteer, with little persuasion, to an international concert career. He envisaged his retirement from business, and his role as their travelling manager. He closed his eyes. It had been a wondrous day. He had witnessed a miracle, one that would reap his fortune.

In the morning, he set himself once more to the rounding-up of the tribe. Mrs Singer was already on site. Mrs Joseph took a little persuasion on the telephone. She was not happy in her daughter's company, she said. It only gave her heartache.

'Come over,' Bernard pleaded. 'We've got a surprise for you.'

'Surprise?' she said, trying to veil the excitement in her voice. 'Nothing any more surprises me.'

'This will. Come and see for yourself.'

Bernard expected the most difficulty with Robert, but he agreed straight away, since he was going to be in their neighbourhood to visit a friend. Bernard arranged the recital for early evening. He had brought in some champagne, to celebrate afterwards. In his mind, the evening's concert was a rehearsal for the great events of the future. He supposed that Sheila would have a word with Yascha beforehand, and together they would work out a programme. That was the artists' department, and he did not mind having no part in it. He would act solely in a managerial capacity.

He went to his office that day, but with little aptitude for the business. He did not imagine that he would be in it for very much longer, and he was tempted to drop hints to that effect all day. But he knew that, for the time being, their miracle must be kept a secret. In any case, no one would have believed his story, a story that was barely acceptable even on the premise of seeing is believing. For Yascha's recital would be the greatest non-appearance of the age.

He came home early that evening, and arranged the living-room as for a salon. He suggested to Sheila that she might dress up for the occasion, since, in this new partnership, it was her début. But Sheila did not want to make a grand production of it. She felt that Yascha would deplore too much fuss. He did not press the matter. It occurred to him that in their new threesome life together, Sheila would need a varied performing-wardrobe, and that he would have to employ a special designer, or more suitably, an architect, for her vast proportions.

At six o'clock, Bernard asked the small audience to take their seats.

'Is this now the surprise?' Mrs Singer said.

Mrs Joseph was glad it was to be a surprise for her mother too. She hated the idea that her mother should know more than she, especially if it concerned Sheila, who must surely be the matter of the surprise in hand. Robert drew his chair apart from the two women. He supposed that Sheila was about to confess her folly, and was willing to submit herself to hospitalisation and proper treatment. Whatever that meant. He just wondered why they were all required to sit themselves so formally to hear the news.

179

Then Bernard stood in front of them, beaming. 'We're ready with the surprise.' He said. 'I just want you to sit and listen. Come on, Sheila.'

Sheila wheeled herself to the piano. She tapped her stomach. 'You know the concert I was telling you about, Yascha darling, well, we're going to start it now.'

Nuts, Robert thought, she's stark raving bonkers.

'Tell him what you're going to play,' Bernard said excitedly.

My God, Mrs Joseph thought, he's caught it from her. The whole place is a madhouse.

'He knows what we're going to play, don't you darling. And it's for all the family. But for your information,' Sheila said, looking at her startled audience, 'we're going to play a Mozart sonata. Are you ready?' she said to her swelling. 'One, two, three.'

Sheila played the opening chords, and waited for Yascha's entry. So did they all. Bernard panicked, realising how Yascha's non-co-operation reflected on his own mental balance. 'Play,' he shouted.

'Don't shout at him,' Sheila said. 'I'll try again. Perhaps he doesn't feel like it. Yascha darling,' she called again. 'Are you ready? One, two, three.'

Again she gave him the opening chords, and again Yascha refrained. It was clear he was not coming out to play.

Bernard wanted to kill him. No less.

'I told you he won't play for an audience,' Sheila said. 'He'll only play for you and me.'

Bernard was beside himself. 'What's the point in having a genius on your hands, if you can't show him off?' he moaned.

Buster giggled inside his little cell. 'And that, ladies and gentlemen,' he said to his cell walls, 'is the nitty gritty.'

In his eavesdropping during the day, he had had notice of his audience. He would have gladly played for Robert,

180

and perhaps with a little persuasion, for the old Mrs Singer, but he was damned if he was going to lift his bow for the pleasure of his grandmother. Or indeed anybody who would only find his gift exploitable. And because he could not read his father's thoughts, he did not place him in this category.

There was a silence outside the wall, and he supposed the audience had left in disgust. He didn't mind. He would play later on, when they were alone. Especially that Mozart sonata they had programmed. It was one of his favourites.

Buster was right. The silence outside the wall was due to the empty room. The audience had withdrawn all right, but at Bernard's bidding. For he had conceived a plan. He motioned to Sheila that she should stay where she was, and with his wild gesticulations, he informed her that he would fix the audience, because he had an idea. Then he closed the sliding-doors between the rooms, and faced the frayed fray.

Mrs Joseph asserted that she'd been brought there to be made a fool of, and all it had done was to break her heart. Robert told her to give that bloody heart of hers a rest, and hinted at two lunatics in the family. Mrs Singer said nothing. She just looked bewildered, but nothing could spoil the pleasure she took in being anywhere at all, and under any circumstances, as long as it wasn't in the old-age home.

'Sheila's right,' Bernard said. 'He won't play for an audience. The only way you can hear him is to pretend you're not there.'

Madder and madder, Robert thought. 'Who's him?' he said. 'And what are we going to hear?'

'A miracle,' Bernard said, and left it at that. 'Now we'll tiptoe back into the room, and I'll say something to Sheila about your having gone away. You see,' he said, 'he can hear everything.' He realised how crazy he must sound to them. 'And then Sheila will ask him to play. For her and his Daddy.'

Then Mrs Joseph did a very strange thing, which revealed the extreme measure of her total desperation. She actually turned to her son, and used his name. 'Robert,' she said, 'what are we going to do with these two lunatics?'

'Please,' Bernard said. 'Listen to me. I promise you won't be sorry.' You'd better play, you little bugger, he said to himself, or I'll murder you.

He opened the dividing-doors and let the audience through, his fingers pressed to his lips, ordering them to silence. To cover their footsteps, he began his recitation to Sheila. 'They were pretty angry,' he said, and his voice was overloud. He couldn't risk Yascha missing a syllable. 'So now we're on our own,' he said. 'Ask Yascha to play for just you and me.'

You could have heard a pin drop in the audience. Not out of any belief in miracles, but that they were terrified of Bernard's wrath. Sheila was hesitant. She knew it was disloyal to Yascha, yet she desperately needed her mother to hear the proof of her sanity. Yascha would understand, she was sure. So she acquiesced to Bernard's plan. She patted her stomach. 'We're alone now darling,' she said. 'Just you and me and Daddy. So now we can get back to the Mozart. Are you ready? One, two, three.'

She played the opening bars, and hovered for his entry. And in he came, in all his innocent melodic glory. Bernard looked at his audience, and saw their total astonishment, which threatened verbal expression, and he put his fingers to his lips to remind them of their oath of silence. He saw Robert scanning the skirtings of the room, the ceilings and corners for microphones. He saw him peer at the record-player. He saw him go through every identical movement that he himself had made in his former disbelief. He caught his eye, and shook his head. Then he pointed to his stomach, and then to Sheila. That's where the sound is coming from, he was telling him, and from nowhere else.

At the end of the movement he again put his fingers to his lips, but Sheila did not go on playing. Instead, she said, 'Mummy's a bit tired, Yascha. Why don't you play something on your own?' She smiled at Bernard. He was delighted with her. She was entering the scheme with full abandon, and even with plans of her own.

But Sheila's motive was not as Bernard thought. She anticipated her mother's disbelief, her possible insistence that it was an electronic trick, and she wanted to prove to her that her son was real and talkable to, and was willing to please.

'What will he play d'you think?' Bernard said, reinforcing the fact that he had no hand in the programme.

'How should I know?' Sheila said. Then Yascha started to play. 'It's a Bach sonata,' she said.

They sat back and listened. Bernard looked them over. There was not a shadow of doubt amongst them. When it was finished, Bernard gave his usual applause and bravos, and Buster, his automatic bow.

Sheila was anxious that Yascha should not know of her betrayal, and said that she was tired and was going to lie down. Bernard approved. It was a good move on her part. It was certainly easier to get one person out of the room than three.

'I'll come up later,' he shouted. 'I've got some work to do.' He shut the dividing-doors after her, waited for a moment, until he heard her chair climbing the ramp, then he turned to his audience, triumphant. 'Well,' he said, mightily pleased, as if he'd done it all himself, 'what do you think?'

They were silent. None of them knew what to think, a state of mind which had never stopped Mrs Joseph's tongue, but even she was speechless. Robert broke the silence. 'Where on earth did he get the fiddle from?' He found it comparatively easy to accept the fact that Sheila was harbouring a violinist, but what bewildered him was how the instrument had got there in the first place. Did she grow a fiddle too?

Then Mrs Joseph found her tongue. 'You remember,' she said, 'the story Clarissa told about the birth? How her violin and bow just disappeared? So,' she said. 'Now we know where it is. It must have somehow got into Sheila's stomach, and they sewed her up without noticing it.'

'Rubbish,' Mrs Singer said, but neither she nor Robert could offer an alternative explanation.

'What's Clarissa going to say, I'd like to know,' Mrs Joseph went on.

'She's not likely to hear him, is she? Or anyone, for that matter. You can't go on pretending that no one's there,' Robert said.

Now it was Mrs Joseph's turn to declare such a suggestion rubbish. 'He'll get over it,' she said. 'He's got to play. People have to hear him. All over the world. He's a genius.' She was getting in on the act too, and Bernard didn't know whether or not it pleased him.

'So what are we going to do?' she directed the question at Bernard.

'Only a short while ago,' Robert said, 'you witnessed a miracle and already you want to market it. Oh my God, Mother,' he said, getting up. 'You've got no grace.' He kissed Mrs Singer goodbye, and left the house. Bernard was not sorry he was gone. In his plans for Yascha's future Robert would prove no ally.

'So what are we going to do?' Mrs Joseph said again, and with bravado this time, now that the enemy was gone. But she had not reckoned on her mother, who, silent up till now, had to ask the question which seemed to her the most obvious of all.

'What about Sheila?' she said.

'What about Sheila?' Mrs Joseph echoed. 'Sheila's the pianist. He can't play without her. Well, he can,' she said, remembering Yascha's solo, 'but she's got to be there. Everywhere. All over the world.'

'But what about Sheila?' Mrs Singer insisted. 'It's the life I'm talking about. What about Sheila's life?'

'What about Sheila's life?' Mrs Joseph echoed again. She just couldn't understand what all the fuss was about.

'She'll die,' Mrs Singer shouted. 'That's what's about her life.'

'Why should she die?' Bernard said. 'She hasn't died yet.'

'So how much bigger can she get?' Mrs Singer said. 'She should go to hospital. They should take the baby away.'

Bernard was not going to have any fortune of his frittering down a hospital drain. 'If she gets ill,' he said, 'of course she'll go to hospital. But she's well. She's as fit as a fiddle.'

Mrs Joseph laughed. 'Two fiddles,' she said. 'So what are we going to do?'

Bernard ignored her plural. 'I'll have to think about it. I'll have to get advice.'

'From whom?' she fired.

'From a concert management or something. I don't know yet. I'll have to think about it. In any case, don't forget,' he said, 'I've got to get Sheila to agree to it. And then, somehow or other, she's got to persuade him to play for an audience.'

'Of course he'll play,' Mrs Joseph said. 'He's got to. His mother will see to that. Oh, he should have *me* carrying him.'

Now it was Mrs Singer's turn to giggle, and Bernard made no comment. 'Just remember,' he said, 'just in case, don't ever mention tonight's playing in front of Sheila. He can hear everything.'

'What about all those psychiatrists and all those doctors?' Mrs Joseph said. 'All those people who said that it was all in her head?' She seemed so quickly to have forgotten that

185

she herself was the most vociferous of their number. 'They've got to hear him, d'you hear me?' she shouted at Bernard. 'They've got to be made to see what fools they were.'

'We shall invite them to our first concert,' Bernard said. Then he remembered the champagne. The artists were in the green room, and it was too dangerous to invite them down for celebration. He did not trust the women's tongues. He would have to keep Sheila firmly apart from both of them. Mrs Singer was due to return to her discard-home in the morning. He would drive her back while Sheila was still sleeping. And if, in the future, his mother-in-law wanted news of her daughter and grandchild, he would be the informant.

'Let's celebrate with champagne,' he said.

'What's there to celebrate?' Mrs Singer said.

Bernard scratched in his mind for something the old woman would find acceptable. 'That Sheila wasn't mad,' he said. 'Will you drink to that, Grandma?'

'I'll drink to my genius grandson,' Mrs Joseph said.

'He should have a long life,' Mrs Singer said. 'Also his mother.'

Bernard tried to ignore the damper the old lady had put on the proceedings. Despite her objections, she accepted a glass, and made her own private toast. She raised her glass to Bernard, and said, 'To your next child. He should be healthy, he should be strong, he should be outside.'

'That too,' Mrs Joseph said. Then she suddenly expressed a wish to be taken home. No doubt she wanted Bernard on his own, to discuss the child's future without any interference from her mother. But Bernard was wary of leaving the old lady in the house with Sheila. She might well blow the fuse on his entire future. 'Would you like a ride in the car?' he said to her, seeing that as the only solution.

Mrs Singer didn't really want a ride, but when she saw

the look of annoyance on her daughter's face at Bernard's suggestion, she got up straight away, and announced herself ready. He bundled them both into the car, one in the back and the other in the front. During the ride, he decided he could no longer risk going to the office. He had to be constantly at Sheila's side to guard her from possible tell-tale. Once again, he swore the two women to secrecy, and though both promised their silence, he feared he could trust neither.

Note from Dr Brown. When I reached this point in little Buster's journal, I fell sick. Although I only had his view of the proceedings, and his view was obviously a very one-sided one, I knew instinctively from my knowledge of his family that this event marked their first act of treachery, and by juxtaposition of later events, my fears were confirmed. So close did I feel towards Buster by this time, that I felt myself personally betrayed, and I took to my bed with a depression that hung over me for some time. Until that moment, I had been accustomed to using whatever spare time I had in going to concerts. Buster had inspired in me a deep love of music, and I went to as many concerts as my busy schedule allowed. A violin recital I rarely missed. But after reading that entry I found it difficult to tune my ear into Buster's world. I knew the treachery that lay within. The sound of a violin to this day curdles my heart with pain.

In time, I rose from my bed and continued with the journal's decoding. But I had changed. I no longer wished to intrude my own thoughts, as I have done hitherto. And I resolved that, henceforward, the journal would speak entirely for itself, without any further foot-noting from me. So I shall not trouble you again dear reader, even for elucidation.

Chapter 12

Note from Dr Brown. There is no mention of the following event in Buster's journal. And for obvious reasons. He simply wasn't there. Moreover, he had no means of eavesdropping on the information, since it was imparted to his mother in writing. In this event, the first betrayal was compounded, and marked the beginning of many acts of treachery with poor innocent Buster on the receiving end. I myself, quite naturally, had no access to the information either, so the following chapter is pure surmise. The conjectural nature of this episode accounts for its comparative brevity. I have not concerned myself with ornamentation, for such a style leads to exaggeration, and even downright dishonesty. I have outlined a sequence of events which fall well within the possible boundaries of truth. I think I may well have succeeded, for in the light of following events, for which there are more data, my small surmise proved more than feasible.

After a week of house-confinement and sentry duty, Bernard managed to persuade Sheila of the vital importance of forever concealing from Yascha the manner in which they had hoodwinked him. Sheila understood the importance of that, but it was Bernard's frenzied insistence that worried her. Yascha's ignorance was to be a cornerstone of their future success and fame. It spelt crass exploitation and deception. He urged her to talk to Yascha and persuade him to an audience. But Sheila was wary of even suggesting it to her child, lest he, out of pique, withdrew his offerings altogether. She had to admit it was a considerable stumbling-block to an international concert career. But she was prepared to forfeit that. She was happy enough to make music in the privacy of her own drawing-room. Inwardly she felt that Yascha, too, was more than content with his present situation, and did not look for any change.

Meanwhile Bernard went about his business, that is, the business of promoting his astonishing duo. He scanned the concert advertising columns in the newspapers, and researched the posters outside the Festival Hall. Amongst all the managements, one name was prominent, in that it appeared more frequently than the others, and promoted a wide variety of musical talent. The name was Richard Bootle, and Bernard phoned him to make an appointment. Mr Bootle was surprisingly accessible. Bernard fully expected to be fobbed off with a subordinate. The great man himself was willing to give him an audience that afternoon, before he left on a world promotional tour. Bernard considered this piece of news in the light of its propitious timing. There might just be time to include Yascha on Mr Bootle's international artistes list.

Bernard arrived promptly at three o'clock. The shabbiness of Bootle's waiting-room surprised him. He had anticipated a large suite of rooms with an ornate reception milling with potted plants and glamorous secretaries. Inside, a rather dowdy middle-aged woman sat behind a beat-up desk, and offered him a cup of tea from a plastic mug. He declined, wondering whether he had made a mistake in his choice of management. Perhaps the woman sensed his nervousness, for she offered him a current list of their artistes for his perusal. He took it eagerly. He read it through, and it was indeed impressive. He'd heard of almost every name on the list, some of them legendary, and all of them of international repute. He felt easier and said that he would have a cup of tea after all.

The woman explained that Mr Bootle was in conference with a client, and that it was not her policy to interrupt him, but no doubt he would not keep him waiting long.

He waited for an hour, and his hostility grew. He told himself that he had a property on his hands that any management in the world would get down on its knees for, and would never dream of letting him cool his heels in his hall. As the waiting-time dragged on he thought more and more often of leaving, and was almost on the point of it when Bootle's door opened and the client emerged. When Bernard recognised him as one of the world's greatest 'cellists, all his hard feelings melted and he knew he could be in no better hands.

'I'm sorry, Mr Rosen,' Bootle said, appearing in the doorway. 'I was delayed. Do come in, will you.' His manner was brusque, and not over-friendly. He was a coarse-looking man, ill-shaven and stained. His office matched his shabby appearance, but it had an air of chaotic activity. Bernard settled for that, and took a rickety chair on the visitor's side of Bootle's desk.

'Now what have you got for me?' Bootle said, getting straight down to business.

Bernard was a little taken back. He hadn't expected brass tacks so soon. Though what he had expected he didn't know either. He had rehearsed sundry introductions to his phenomenal discovery, the length and convolutions of which would have tried the patience of any listener, especially a busy and down-to-earth one like Bootle. He decided to forgo whatever preparations he had made and to play it by ear.

'Well it's a bit extraordinary, Mr Bootle,' he said, 'to say the least.'

'Well let's have it then.'

'I don't quite know where to begin.'

'Try at the beginning,' Mr Bootle said, his patience already wearing thin. 'Or do you want me to guess?' he said, with what sounded very much like a sneer.

'Oh you'd never guess,' Bernard said.

'Is it *that* extraordinary?'

'That's the very least of it,' Bernard baited.

'Well,' Bootle said, his interest patently awakened, 'Richard Bootle, even if I say so myself, has made his reputation on the *artiste extraordinaire*. You've seen my list, no doubt.'

'I must tell you, Mr Bootle,' Bernard said, leaning forward in confidence, 'it's almost unbelievable.'

Either this man is a nutter, Mr Bootle thought, or he indeed has something extraordinary up his sleeve. 'I like it better and better,' Bootle said, a remark that would do equally well for a lunatic or a high-class salesman.

'I hardly believe it myself,' Bernard said.

'Believe what?' Bootle said.

Bernard looked around him. The door to the adjoining waiting-room was ajar. He got up from his chair and closed it. A small fear stabbed Bootle's chest. What if this man was really crazy? He decided for safety's sake to humour him. 'Now no one can hear us Mr Rosen,' he said. 'We have absolute privacy, and what you say is totally confidential. So perhaps now you will tell me about this extraordinary property of yours.'

'It's a violin and piano duet,' Bernard whispered.

Bootle was suddenly angry. 'If I'm giving you my precious time, Mr Rosen, it had better be a lot better than that.'

'Oh it is, a lot better,' Bernard said, unphased by Bootle's anger. 'The pianist is my wife.'

Bootle was now thoroughly irritated. 'And the violinist is your son, I suppose,' he said with sour sarcasm.

'Yes, he's my son. My son, the violinist.'

Mr Bootle tried yet again. 'So what's so extraordinary about that?'

'My wife's in a wheel-chair,' Bernard offered.

Bootle was fast losing patience. 'Well you have my deepest sympathy, Mr Rosen, but I honestly don't think I can be of use to you.'

Bernard stared at Bootle's face. 'Mr Bootle,' he whispered. 'My son is inside her.'

They stared at each other for a long time, and in a grating silence. Bootle positively paled.

'Extraordinary?' Bernard said after a while.

Bootle wiped his forehead. 'Mr Rosen,' he said. 'Let's start all over again.'

Bernard leaned back in his chair. He was rather pleased with the manner of his divulgence. He certainly had old Bootle on the hook.

'Explain to me how it all happened,' Bootle was saying.

So Bernard told him, with little regard now as to the style of his telling, but just giving him the bare facts from the time of the abortive delivery to the present date. At the end of the résumé, Bootle gasped. He did not believe a word of it, of course, but he was too cornered to express disbelief. 'That's certainly extraordinary Mr Rosen,' he said. 'If what you tell me is true, it's the greatest and most sensational musical event since Balcinello farted the whole of Ravel's *Bolero* in Fanfare Hall, Missouri. And I ought to know. I was his manager at the time.'

Bernard was not too happy with the crude comparison, and it must have shown on his face, for Bootle was eager to make amends.

'Not in the same class, of course, as your little act,' he said. 'Yours is of a far finer calibre altogether. Now,' he said, feigning to get down to business, 'when can I hear this extraordinary little ensemble?'

During his recital of the hard facts of Yascha's début, Bernard had omitted mention of the one stumbling-block to a concert career. He had been testing Bootle for his credence. Now, thinking he had won it, he was prepared to offer the snags. 'There are one or two obstacles, Mr Bootle,' he said.

'With a property like that, if you're telling the truth, Mr Rosen, nothing is insurmountable.'

'Well it's like this,' Bernard began. 'My son has indicated on certain test runs that we've had that he will only play for my wife and myself. The other day, when my mother-in-law was there, and one or two others, and he knew other

192

people were there – he eavesdrops you see – well, he refused to play. Not a note. But when they'd gone, and he could hear there was no one else about, he played like an angel.'

'That is no small obstacle,' Bootle said, playing his pencil on his front false teeth as an indication of his concentration.

And then Bernard told him about the trick they had played. It seemed a pretty obvious one to Bootle, and its overtones of treachery did not concern him. 'That's all very well in a drawing-room, Mr Rosen,' he said, 'with a handful of people. Perhaps at a push, we might get away with it in a recording or broadcasting studio. But in a concert-hall? This extraordinary act has to be seen to be believed.'

Then Bernard put forward his plan. 'I'm doing my best to persuade my wife to persuade Yascha to an audience.'

'To persuade who?' Bootle asked.

'Yascha. That's what we call him.'

'That's a bit presumptuous, don't you think?'

'Wait till you hear him, Mr Bootle,' Bernard said. Then he went on. 'If Yascha can't be persuaded, I thought we might – well – sort of make it all part of the promotion campaign. A sort of conspiracy of silence. The audience have to be told beforehand of the conditions under which my son will play, and that no sound, not a single sound, should betray their presence. You could promote it rather like a game, and the audience would be assembled and quiet before my wife wheels herself on to the concert-platform.' Bernard leaned back. He was rather pleased with his plan of campaign. He rather thought that Bootle should invite him to become a partner in the firm. And Bootle was indeed impressed by Bernard's promotional flair, even though he might be pushing a myth. He quickly threw in his own expertise.

'We might promote him as the invisible violinist. Must be unseen to be believed.'

Bernard laughed politely. 'It's an idea,' he said, without much enthusiasm.

'I must hear him,' Bootle said. He was curious. Mr Rosen looked sane enough. You never knew. He might have something. 'As soon as I get back from Japan. In about two weeks. I think you should arrange something at your home. Invite a small gathering. Very small to start with. We'll have a sort of dummy run. See if it works. I tell you, Mr Rosen,' he said, 'if it *does* work, we will both make a fortune.'

Bernard had come to hear that. Exactly that. He was pleased with his choice of Bootle, and confident that his son could not be in better hands.

'I'll make all the arrangements,' he said.

Bootle looked in his diary and fixed a date.

'About six o'clock,' Bernard said. 'My wife is well rested by then after her midday sleep.'

'You've really quite whet my appetite, Mr Rosen,' Bootle said, glad to show him to the door. 'Of course, I shall want exclusive rights, and it would be unprofessional to ask any other management to attend.'

'I wouldn't dream of it,' Bernard said. 'I hope we shall have a happy partnership.'

Bootle let the implications pass. 'I hope so,' he said.

On his way home, Bernard wondered how he would inform Sheila of his plans. He decided that writing to her was the only way. He couldn't remember when he'd last written his wife a letter. He'd sent the odd postcard when he'd been away on business travel. But he had never seriously corresponded with her. His present excuse for letter-writing might now give him an opportunity to come close to her. He began to look forward to her first reply.

When he reached home he noticed that Sheila's face was aglow. She and Yascha had been practising all day, she told him. They had almost perfected the Spring Sonata, and what deficiencies there still were lay squarely in the pianist's court.

'What a pity you can't both give a concert,' he said.

She put a protective hand on her stomach. 'You know that Yascha doesn't want an audience,' she said.

'I still think it's a pity.'

She motioned to him to say no more, and he went to his study to begin their correspondence. Downstairs in the living-room, Sheila manoeuvred herself out of the chair and lay on the settee. She had rarely felt so content. She closed her eyes from a gentle fatigue that was in no way weary. And softly out of her womb, she heard the strains of the Brahms lullaby. She marvelled at how accurately her little boy had caught her mood, for the lullaby was not a song to induce sleep, but rather to invoke the joys and glories of waking. She listened as he played it to the end.

'Thank you,' she whispered. She wondered whether anyone had loved in this way before, and whether it was indeed possible under circumstances other than her own. For as much as she loved Yascha, she loved herself, and the joy of such loving was its promise of permanence. She gave a fleeting thought to the stranger who had just left for the study, and, once again, she wondered what he was doing in her house.

Chapter 13

Dear Sheila,

     I have to write to you for it is impossible to say what I have to say in front of Yascha. It's funny, but even in the days when Yascha wasn't listening, I found it hard to talk to you. Really talk. I never tried writing, but now that I have to, perhaps I can put down in words what I feel. I know that when we got married, you were not in love with me. I knew it at the time. I knew that you were marrying me mainly to get away from home, and now that I have come to know your family, I can understand that perfectly. But I hoped that you would grow to love me in the course of time. We have not had an easy marriage. I thought that almost all the time you were angry with me. Now I believe you were only angry with yourself, because you were so unhappy. I hoped that when we could have a baby you would feel more fulfilled, but during your pregnancy you seemed more angry than before. I think of our future together and I don't know what to make of it. Would you let me know your thoughts on my letter?

          My love to you,

               Bernard

Dear Bernard,

     I'm sorry, but I have no thoughts on your letter. You wrote that you have things to say to me that Yascha must not hear. I don't like keeping secrets from Yascha, but if they are important, please write them to me.

               Sheila

Dear Sheila,

Now you just listen to me. Yascha's my son as much as he is yours. And the fact that you are carrying him does not in any way mean that I have no rights on him, and no say in his future. And it is his future that I want to write about. You may not have any thoughts on my feelings towards you, but you'd better start having some thoughts about Yascha if he means as much to you as you say. I have found a concert manager for him. His name is Richard Bootle. I had an appointment with him on Wednesday and I told him the whole story. He is as excited about it as I am, and he says that Yascha will make our fortune. I told him the snags in the story, Yascha not wanting an audience and so on, and he agrees with me that you should persuade him that an audience is good for him. Any audience. I think you can persuade him. I think it's your fault he's being so choosy. I think you talked him into it in the first place. Well, you'd better start talking him out of it, because our future will be all the rosier for his co-operation. Now, in case you can't persuade him in the next week or so, I must tell you in any case about our plans. I have arranged a recital here for a small audience, that we will organise exactly as we did the other evening when your family was present. A conspiracy of silence. I will leave it to you to arrange the programme. If you have any ideas for the guest-list, please let me have them in writing. Will you please let me have your thoughts on this letter.

Bernard

Dear Bernard,

I have no thoughts on your preposterous letter. Except to say that I think you are out of your mind.

Sheila

Dear Sheila,

   This is my last warning. Either I get your co-operation, or you will be sorry. Time is running short.

                                                  Bernard

Dear Bernard,

   I have all the time in the world. Can't we stop this silly letter-writing?

                                                  Sheila

Dear Sheila,

   I have arranged for the piano removers to come tomorrow. Steinways are anxious to buy back the instrument, and they have offered a good price.

                                                  Bernard

Dear Bernard,

   I am thinking about the guest-list. I will write again when I have it ready.

                                                  Sheila

Dear Sheila,

   While you are thinking about your guest-list, here is mine enclosed. You might also append Yascha's programme. I shall have it printed.

                         Yours faithfully,

                                                  Bernard

Dear Bernard,

   Clarissa, my mother, my grandmother, Robert. The Spring Sonata, Beethoven. Sonata in E minor, Mozart. Two Bach Partitas for solo violin.

                                                  Sheila

Dear Sheila,

This is a professional gathering. Must we have your family, who have in any case heard it all before? Can't Yascha play something that is absolutely brilliant? Like Paganini did.

Yours truly,

Bernard

Dear Bernard,

It's me and my family, or nothing. Must all those doctors be invited? Yascha is no Paganini.

Sheila

Dear Sheila,

I have invited the doctors mainly on your behalf, for your vindication. I would have thought you would have been grateful. I now have all I need. I shall send out the invitations tomorrow. I have arranged with outside caterers to make a buffet supper. This correspondence must now cease.

Yours faithfully,

Bernard Rosen

The first letter-less day between them marked the beginning of a long silence that feared to be broken. The letters had finally sealed their mutual incommunicability. They ate their meals in silence. Bernard checked every day that his wife and son were practising, and he prayed that they wouldn't let him down. He knew his relationship with Sheila was at an end, but it did not bother him. He had no time to give it any thought. He was too involved in the structuring of his son's future and the fortune and pride it would entail. It was simply a pity that Sheila had to be part of the package.

He looked at the invitations that the printers had just delivered. He had spent much time on their wording and layout and he was pleased with the results. The card was bordered with a gold frame, and it read: Mr Bernard Rosen – his first draft had been Sheila and Bernard Rosen, but since their bitter falling-out his sense of proprietary rights had grown to egomaniacal proportions. So it was Mr Bernard Rosen who invited so and so, to a buffet supper on Thursday, 18th January, at 6 p.m. to witness an extraordinary event. RSVP. He had decided not to be specific as to the nature of the event lest the guests suspect it as a hoax and refrain from attending. He would clue them in, in a short explanation before the recital. Apart from the playing time, Sheila would keep to her room for the whole evening. She would wheel herself in for the concert, or perhaps, for politeness' sake, he would wheel her himself, seat her by the piano and leave her to do her stuff. And when it was over, he'd promptly wheel her out again, out of the way. Out of sight and out of earshot. Then he alone would reap the harvest of his prodigious son. He alone would swell with the pride of their applause, their wonder. He alone could generously forgive the folly of the doctors, those experts who knew the answer to everything. He was looking forward to the evening immensely. It would mark the beginning of a new life for him, and when all the details of the concert-tour were settled between Bootle and himself, he would find himself a mistress. To hell with Sheila, he thought. Her involvement with Yascha was so exclusive and so acute, it was as if she had a lover. He *was* her lover, he realised, and one that was permanently inside her. The thought of being cuckold by his own son appalled him. He did not think he could bear to look at her again.

Buster found the continual silence outside the wall very unnerving. He hadn't heard his father's voice for some time, but he knew he was there by the sudden tightenings of his cell wall. His father's presence seemed to give his mother little pleasure. He knew that his playing made her happy, as much as it did himself. He felt her joy within him, especially when he volunteered a piece all on his own. He would have been happy enough to play for her for ever.

Things had changed on the outside, he knew. Clarissa hadn't been around for quite a while. He hoped he hadn't replaced her. They could have played duets together. There was the beautiful Bach concerto for two violins, he remembered. What music they could make together, the three of them. But it was the continued silence that disturbed him most of all. In it, his mother would talk to him in a way she had never done before. She whispered words of love and comfort, but they were not maternal words. They were the words of a young girl in the throes of a sad, bewildered passion. He had the impression that the words she uttered were more for herself than for him; it was as if it were she who needed the love and the comfort with which she wooed him. He felt she was trying to tell him something, and that if he listened long and arduously enough, she would confide in him the source of her sorrow. Sometimes he was tempted to talk back, but his voice he reserved for himself. He had to keep to himself something that was only his, something that he would share with no other. He had chosen to donate to her his song without words, but the grammar of his soul was his own.

He picked up his little note-book, and he wrote his day's entry. 'Still the silence outside. You know, God, that I personally am not sure that I believe in you. But there are plenty of people who do. I think my mother is one of them. Please look after her.'

Chapter 14

Note from Brown, your simple straightforward doctor. We are nearing the end of Buster's journal, dear reader. When I myself came across the penultimate entry, I was deeply disturbed. Buster's survival in itself had been against nature. As a medical man I could not fathom it, and could only call on the forces of the supernatural for explanation. But the gods, even of that domain, maintain a natural order of things, and the concept of life-span is part of that order. Buster had no reason at the time to believe his days were numbered. He was physically fit and emotionally secure. Yet this entry shows clearly that he had a premonition of his own death, and I can only surmise that, within his wordless melodic voices, there were other voices too. Well, whatsoever it was that prompted his prophecy, I give it to you here in full.

'Today, after tea, we're going to play the whole of the Spring. So she says. For Daddy, she says, when he comes home from work. Oh the joy of that sonata. Yet I feel a strange unease, a murmur of disquiet, a nudging in my limbs. Soon I must leave for limbo once more, and take to my wanderings. I am not afraid, but in so far as I chose my birth, I wish to choose my death too. I wish to time it. I conceived myself in Atonement and on that same altar will I consume my course. Dear God, or Whoever, lead this man-child into limbo out of the Adagio of the redeeming Spring. Let that be my psalm across Lethe.'

The guests started to arrive just before six o'clock. Sheila was safely ensconced in her bedroom. Bernard had actually locked her in. He would release her only for the recital, and would promptly return her to her room while the audience's silence still held.

Mr Bootle was first to arrive, rubbing his hands. He'd just returned from a highly profitable tour of the Far East and he was conscious of being on a winning streak. He had come to satisfy his curiosity. He was not afraid, because he knew that he would not be alone.

The doctors arrived in a posse, as if for protection. They had no idea what to expect. The invitation had simply asked them to witness an extraordinary event, a miracle, rumour had it. Of all the professions, psychiatry, for its very survival, will balk at miracle, and its practitioners are quicker than most to clip an angel's wing. But curiosity had driven them there, together with the chance to keep the door open on Sheila's treatment. For they each regretted her lack of co-operation. A group of Bernard's business associates had been invited, and they too huddled together, feeling themselves outsiders at the gathering, and were grateful even for the sight of Mrs Joseph who arrived with her mother, as a face that was at least familiar. Robert had declined the invitation. Since his release from prison, his two meetings with his family already constituted for him a bellyful of kin, and he'd had enough. Clarissa was one of the last to arrive, and when Bernard saw her, standing alone in the hallway, hovering for some introduction, or some elucidation of the extraordinary event she had been invited to witness, he regretted that she had been asked. He didn't know why, but around her small shabby person he saw disaster. For no reason whatsoever, he saw her as an innocent spanner in the works. He realised that, apart from the shock of Yascha himself, Clarissa would also reel at the discovery of the whereabouts of her precious violin. It might all be too much for her. He gave her a drink to ease her.

'What's all this about?' she said.

'I'm going to tell everybody very shortly,' Bernard said.

He was nervous, not only on account of the audience's obedience to the rule of silence, but on his own account, his own performance. He regarded the whole operation as his *mise en scène*. In return for Bootle's international contacts, he would offer him some pickings. But the lion's share was his. It was his responsibility to keep the partnership in trim, to

203

insist on long and daily practice, and to see that Sheila presented herself for each performance, properly attired, and on time. He had rehearsed a little speech to give to his present audience, but in his nervousness he had lost the thread. He decided that once all the guests had arrived, he would play it informally, while they were standing and still at their drinks.

He saw Mrs Singer detach herself from the group of his business associates. Glass in hand, she threaded her frail steps across the room, and found a chair in a corner. She looked distinctly worried. He went over to her. 'What's the matter, Grandma?' he said.

'I don't like it.'

'You don't like what?'

'Your mother-in-law told me,' she said.

'Everybody will be told very soon.'

'I don't like it,' she said again. 'Is not natural.'

'But it's true,' he said, as if authenticity implied nature. 'You'll hear for yourself.'

'But natural it isn't. I'm sorry for Sheila. Your wife,' she added, driving the point home.

'But why?' he said. 'She has everything. Everything she wants. And a great future.'

'No,' Mrs Singer sadly shook her head. 'A future she hasn't, Bernard,' she said.

Bernard turned away. He wished he'd never invited her. Or Clarissa, for that matter. They were both dampers on his high spirits. He was now anxious to get the proceedings under way. He made a sign to Bootle, that he'd like to get started. Bootle came over, and together they arranged the seating. The cushioned straight-backed chairs were placed carefully in rows, with decent distance between them so that contact with clothes or people would be kept at a minimum and the rule of silence easily obeyed.

'I think perhaps I'll start priming them,' Bernard said, 'while they're still standing.'

Bootle nodded and took up his position somewhere alongside Bernard, apart from the others, as one who had foreknowledge, and therefore power.

'Could I interrupt for a moment?' Bernard said, above the whisper of the cocktail chatter. There was an immediate silence, which Bernard allowed for a few seconds, testing them as it were, for their endurance. But Mrs Joseph was quick to break it.

'Sh,' she said, as if the silence were not acute enough. 'He's going to tell you about the miracle,' and, with the inference that she knew all about it already, she stepped aside and took up her position next to Bootle. Bernard could have done without her interruption, and he made this clear with a withering look in her direction. But it did not disturb her.

'Go on Bernard,' she said. 'You can tell them now. Or I'll tell them, if you like.'

'Will *somebody* tell us?' Dr Peabody said.

Bernard turned to face his guests. 'My wife, as you know,' he said, 'has been pregnant for much longer than is usual. Almost four years, in fact. My wife, as the doctors present will know, has always insisted that there is a baby inside her. The doctors have thought otherwise. They have diagnosed a phantom pregnancy. I must admit that I was of their opinion until a few weeks ago when I was given concrete evidence that a child actually does exist in my wife's body.'

Dr Worcester let out a polite laugh, which his colleagues took up fraternally.

'Have you seen it?' Dr Lessor said. 'Can we see it too?'

'No,' Bernard said. 'I haven't seen it, but I have heard it.' He allowed a pause for their disbelief, but they respected the silence. Encouraged, he went on. 'The child plays the violin,' he said. At this point, he avoided Clarissa's gaze. 'The child plays the violin with my wife. They play sonatas together. As you will soon hear.'

205

The doctors went into quick conference, and Bernard allowed a break, while he went to refill his glass.

'It all tallies.' Dr Peabody was saying. 'The strength and tenacity of Mrs Rosen is astonishing. She has actually inveigled her husband into her fantasy.'

'I hope he'll make a less reluctant patient,' Dr Lessor said.

'Unlikely,' said Dr Worcester. 'The stubbornness is as catching as the fantasy.'

'How ever is he going to do it?' Dr Worcester said.

'Simple enough,' Peabody said. 'Hidden microphones. These people will go to extraordinary lengths to prove us wrong.'

'Supposing we ask to inspect the room thoroughly beforehand?' Dr Worcester suggested.

'I think not,' Peabody said. 'It would signify a small participation in his game. I think we should keep well out of it.'

Bernard called for silence again, and continued with his story. He told them the bare facts of it, and in their logical order. He told them too, of his child's proved aversion to an audience, and he pleaded with them for their total silence. Not until Sheila had left the room after the recital could they speak or make any noise. He insisted on this ruling to the point of boredom, over and over again. The sea of faces around him was creased with disbelief or benign tolerance. But all, prompted by pity, avoided each other's glance. His business associates looked very worried indeed. When he had finished his factual recital, he paused. The silence in the room was now embarrassing, punctuated by a shuffling foot, or an uneasy cough. They were all guests in the house of a lunatic, and in a short while their embarrassment would give way to fear. Their host looked so self-confident. It was all very unnerving.

'I know that you are all sceptical,' Bernard said.

'I'm not,' his mother-in-law offered. 'I've heard it with

my own ears.'

'That makes three patients,' Dr Peabody whispered. 'We shall shortly set up a Rosen clinic.'

'I know what you're thinking,' Bernard went on, 'that this is a trick done with microphones perhaps. When I first heard my child play, I thought the same, and I tooth-combed the room for electronic devices. I shall now give you all that privilege before we begin. Please search the room as you will.'

The guests made no move. It would have seemed impolite, to say the least, to be seen to doubt their host's honesty. Perhaps, the doctors thought, this was what Bernard was counting on. Nevertheless, tempted as they were, they kept their stand.

'Please.' Bernard said. 'I want you to see for yourself. I really do. You'll be doing me a favour. Mr Bootle,' he said, 'would you make the first move?' And because Bootle was eager to uncover any trickery, he obliged and the others followed suit. The doctors tried to appear casual, but their eyes were skinned. Bernard poured himself another drink, and offered one to his mother-in-law. In this way he publicly included her in their foreknowledge, and she was grateful.

'What about a drink for Grandma?' she said.

But Grandma didn't want a drink, she said, neither was she interested in examining the room. 'It will all come to no good, I'm telling you,' she said. Mrs Singer's presence was a source of acute discomfort to Bernard, and he tried to pretend that she wasn't there. He turned his back on her, but her words echoed in his ears with terrible foreboding.

He saw Bootle leave the search and settle comfortably in his seat. He took out a note-book with pencil at the ready. He was smiling, anticipating his treat. The sight of his enthusiasm renewed Bernard's spirit, and he was anxious to get on with the performance. 'Are you satisfied?' he said to the room, 'or do you want a little longer?' There was a general murmur of satisfaction. The guests turned themselves to the upright chairs, and settled down.

When they were all settled, Bernard spoke again. 'I'm going to make another offer to you,' he said, 'which will prove to you beyond any doubt that what you will hear is no hoax. When I first heard my child, I gave myself the same proof. I put my ear to my wife's stomach, and I verified, beyond question, the source of the sound. I suggest that one of the doctors, who have every right to be sceptical — they have many words to eat, after all — I suggest that one of them should accept this offer, so that his word may be taken on greater trust than mine.'

Everyone turned around to look at the medical delegation, who were conferring amongst themselves as to who should represent them. The choice fell on Dr Peabody, possibly because he was the most senior.

'I would be most interested,' Dr Peabody said.

'Then you shall do it when my child is tuning up,' Bernard said. 'My wife will tell him it's me. I shall signal to you when we are ready.'

The doctors were now totally flummoxed. Supposing the sound did come from inside. What electronic device could account for that? But none of them believed that it was possible. It was simply that Mr Rosen's fantasy had gone to even further limits than that of his wife.

Clarissa, too, was totally bewildered. Bernard's account certainly unravelled the mystery of the disappearance of her violin, but if she accepted that, she would have to buy Bernard's whole story. In accepting the real, she would have to accommodate the surreal too. She folded her arms around her body and wondered who was driving whom mad.

'Now are we all ready?' Bernard said. 'Will you do all your coughing and your shifting now.'

And they did. They all shifted for little reason, and coughed for less. But Bernard gave them time, insisting all

208

the while on their obligation to silence. 'Now I shall fetch the artists,' he said, 'and your silence, I repeat, must be maintained until they leave the room.' He walked towards the door, and he found himself tiptoeing. He didn't quite know why. He heard the deafening silence behind him, and he was suddenly very nervous.

He unlocked Sheila's door. 'Are you ready?' he said. He tried a smile, but Sheila's face was ungiving. She was doing what she had to do, for without a piano, that threat that he daily held over her, by signs and mouthings, she could no longer live. She knew that the day would come when the price to play her music would be too high. Until then, she would allow his blackmail.

'Yes,' she said, and, patting her stomach. 'Yascha darling,' she said. 'I'm going to the piano now, and we're going to play. Daddy's just come home.'

'And I'm going to put my ear to your tuning,' he said, reminding her of their former arrangement.

She nodded, disgusted. He took the handles of her chair, and wheeled her down the ramp. The silence in the living-room was obedient still, uncanny almost, and Bernard would have wished to break it with his heavy footsteps and the creak of the wheel-chair. But both were soft-pedalled by the thick-piled carpet. So he threw words into the silent air.

'It's so nice to come back from the office and to listen to some music. I've been looking forward to it all day.'

Sheila wondered whether it sounded to the others as hypocritical as it did to her. She hoped that Yascha would not catch the undertones of his fraud.

As he neared the piano, Bernard beckoned Dr Peabody to join him. Peabody tiptoed across the floor, and the others held their breath as he negotiated each silent step towards the evidence. He stood at Bernard's side.

'Are you ready, darling?' Sheila said, tapping her stomach.

At a sign from Bernard, Dr Peabody laid his ear against what he had so confidently confirmed as Sheila's fantasy. There was something so unmedical about his posture that it embarrassed him, and he was seen to blush a little. Sheila gave an 'A', and out of the bowels of her, unmistakably, Yascha confirmed his pitch. He even played an arpeggio for unwitting good measure. The rosy hue that had lately flushed Peabody's face now gave way to a very pale grey, and the audience knew that this 'extraordinary event' was no understatement. Sheila played the 'A' again, together with the lower 'D'. Yascha went on tuning till he was satisfied. Dr Peabody raised his ashen face. He was thoroughly shaken, and Bernard had to support him back to his chair to cover any possible disturbance. Then Bernard spoke. 'Let me just settle down first, Yascha,' he said. He saw Peabody to his shaky seat, then took his own, facing the audience to watch their reaction. Then, with a nod in Sheila's direction, he gave her the go-ahead.

'One, two, three, four,' she said. And they started in unison. As the sound soared, Bernard watched the audience's movement. Each slowly turned his head in wonderment to his neighbour, except Mrs Joseph, who darted her head at all of them in turn with such pride and gratification, as if she were totally responsible. Bootle was writing furiously in his pad. He was obviously engrossed in promotion preliminaries. Bernard relaxed. He felt he could now just listen to the music, for its sheer beauty. And gradually during the course of the movement, the others did likewise, putting aside all their doubts and fears of consequences. If it were a hoax, they were gladly prepared for collusion. Occasionally the doctors would shake their heads, dumbfounded, and look at each other for some gesture of explanation that they knew would not be forthcoming. Bernard looked over at Mrs Singer and saw that she was weeping. He was angry and frightened that she might betray her presence. He didn't care about her

210

sorrow, as long as she kept it silently to herself. Then he saw Clarissa, burying her head in her lap, and that gesture unnerved him too.

When the first movement came to an end, he said. 'That was beautiful Yascha. You give me such joy.'

Sheila looked at him with contempt, a look that was not lost on the doctors, and their interpretation of it confused them even more. They ascribed it to her irritation at his disturbance between movements. It was feasible that way.

They started on the Adagio. Sheila was first with its haunting theme, that, like a song of a dying swan, pleaded for echo. And when it came from the child inside her, Clarissa raised her head from her lap. Bernard noticed her movement and saw that she had been crying. She listened to the melody, drinking every note, but there was little joy on her face, and as Bernard looked at her he knew, with a heart-stopping instinct, that the chips would soon be down. He knew it, and he didn't know why.

Poor Clarissa didn't know why either, but if asked, in a calmer moment, she might have ascribed her outburst to a sadness that had slowly become unbearable. When she had first heard her violin, she was too astonished by its very discovery to give much ear to its tone and splendour. Towards the end of the first movement she had begun to listen, and in its beauty she felt a sense of overwhelming loss. Not just for the instrument itself, but for the unique song it had stolen from her. Had she gone further in her self-probing, she would have admitted to her inability, whatever the instrument, to sing with such an angelic voice. All in all, it spelt for her redundancy, and it simply wasn't fair. Throughout Sheila's pregnancy she had been her friend. Over the last three years no one could have been more loyal, and the thought of now being put out to grass was finally too much for her. It was the plaintive song of the Adagio, that same melody on which Buster's heart would break, that unlocked the flood-gates of her sorrow.

211

And mid-phrase, so unlike the musician she was, but so deep was her anguish, she gave forth a terrible cry.

'It's not fair,' she moaned. 'It's *my* violin and it's not fair.'

Yascha cut out immediately. Sheila went on playing.

'Come on Yascha,' she said, but with little encouragement. She was somehow relieved that their fraud had been uncovered.

'Now look what you've done,' Mrs Joseph shouted, in her anger forgetting her vow of silence.

'Sh, sh,' the others whispered.

Dr Lessor made to go over to Clarissa to calm her, and in his haste, knocked over his stool.

'Now you've blown everything,' Bootle shouted.

Buster listened. Over the din of the crowd voices, each urging the other to renewed silence, he heard his father's voice.

'Play,' he shouted. 'D'you hear me?'

Buster put down his violin, and softly began to hum to himself the adagio melody that was so cruelly cut off mid-phrase. Sheila heard, and softly she hummed with him, as if in begging reminder that they were one. He wept for her. She had no part in the treachery, he was sure. But she housed him, and that house had now become his prison, and Samson-like, he must destroy her too. He listened to the clamouring outside, pleading for his voice, and it sickened him. He picked up his journal, and made his last entry.

'God, or Whoever,' he wrote, 'forgive me.'

Then he took up his bow in one hand, and in the other, the umbilical cord. He used the movement of détaché bowing, mourning that such a diligently acquired skill was obliged to perform such an act of destruction, and he sawed the cord, backwards and for-, flexing his wrist on each down and up-bow, donating to his lethal movements the dignity of his innate artistry. At last, he sawed it through.

Then he lay back, like a loose underwater swimmer, cut off from his life-line. With his last breath, he hummed the Adagio of the Spring, his shibboleth into limbo.

Sheila's head dropped gently onto her chest, in a movement quieter than death itself. The murmuring in the room ceased. Bernard caught sight of Mrs Singer's face, and by its look of rude and shameful survival, he knew that the fruit of her fruit had fallen.

Epilogue

When all the various post-mortem investigations were over, the official cause of death was registered as heart-failure, due to excessive overweight. For myself, I was convinced that Sheila Rosen died quite simply of a broken heart, which woefully lost its beat when her love-object withdrew. But the medical establishment does not recognise a broken heart as a cause of death. They scoff at it. They regard it as an amateur's diagnosis that does not look good in the records.

As to the contents of the uterus itself, they remained unrecorded, on the principle that if you pretend something is not there, it will oblige you by going away. The pencil that Buster had used for his autobiographical outpourings was worn down practically to a stub. This was discarded, despite my plea for its keeping. The fiddle was laying by Buster's side, and the bow on his lap. Buster had been right. It was indeed a Guarnierius, of the del Gesu vintage. The very best. I managed to persuade the doctors to turn a blinder eye to the fiddle than they did to the pencil. The instrument was returned to a penitent and tearful Clarissa, who swore that it had lost none of its tonal beauty, despite its long amniotic rinse. The bow too was returned, but Clarissa was loath to use it ever again, considering what gross act it had finally perpetrated, so she sheathed it in a leather scabbard, as if it were a sword.

Buster himself, apart from his self-severed life-line, was splendidly intact. He was rather a beautiful boy, who bore an uncanny resemblance to his mother. He had a mane of white hair, which I suspect had lost its colour in the shock of the gross treachery. His skin was rather pale, though

214

that was possibly attributable to his long period of confinement. His eyes were blue and wide-awake, with a pained look of apology for the manner of his quietus. It is a look I shall carry with me to my grave.

I miss him. I miss him terribly. Ever since this work of mine was completed, and the autopsy findings over once and for all, I find myself rereading the journal, though, like a lover with old letters, I know it practically by heart. The other day, while rereading it yet again, my eye fell upon an entry that somehow I had missed in my thorough first reading. Perhaps it was because it was written in a corner of a page, a page that Buster had, at some time or another, turned down to keep his place. I have no idea when or where in his story this entry was made, but it seems to me that it would have fallen logically into place almost anywhere. In my leave-taking of you, dear reader, I give it you, as it was found.

'Central on the upper lip of every human being, is a small mark of indentation, a birthmark as obligatory as the navel. It is said, that when we struggle into birth, an angel presses his finger on our lips, and seals them from our retelling of our pasts. That indentation is his fingerprint, and it condemns us to repeat our former follies, and to live out once again our human frailty. We must, for if we dodge that finger, we would, all of us, be gods.'

The Rattlesnake Stradivarius

TERESA KENNEDY

Louisiana 1830 or thereabouts: Mary Faith Beaudine, rich slave-owning mute, is jilted by her gypsy music teacher and switches his Stradivarius violin for her own inferior instrument.

Later that century: Icy Fee Moulder, sorceress, adds a rattle to it.

Atlantis County, Texas, the present: Boo Strait, enchanted fool, grabs the fiddle and runs like hell.

It is when the Strait family comes together for the reading of a will that the Stradivarius and its passionate power ties the past with the present—the lives and loves of those who have gone before with those who come after. The object of love, lust and intrigue, the violin makes its way through a wonderful tale of thieves and preachers, cowboys and conjure-women, and cranky old ladies with more secrets than they can shake their Bibles at.

0 349 101027   FICTION   £4.99

THE WAR AGAINST CHAOS

Anita Mason

THE SOCIETY OPERATED WITH A NIGHTMARE LOGIC. CURIOSITY HAD NO PLACE. NOR DID READING, STROLLING, JUNK-COLLECTING – ALL THE THINGS JOHN HARE RELISHED

He had been upwardly mobile on the ladder of Universal Goods when his wife left him and his career in jeopardy. He seemed the ideal, expendable scapegoat in a powerful company official's much-needed cover-up. And with a trumped-up charge worthy of Kafka, Hare found himself cast into the netherworld of a dreaded population known as the 'marginals'.

What the authorities never reckoned on was the reawakened cunning and imagination of these outcasts. Or the greater threat to them that Hare was to discover – based on self-respect and humour – steeling itself in the bowels of the city.

0 349 10031 4   FICTION   £4.50

Also available in ABACUS paperback: